Seeing green

I glanced across the room at the wide-eyed beauty, her eyes clamped to Tom as tight as her fingers had wrapped around his arm. "Is that what she is? A new *client*?" My fake smile iced up.

Tom's eyes registered a sudden perplexity. "Why would I say it if it weren't true?"

"I don't know." I waited for him to spill out The Secret History of Tom and Stewart.

He opened his mouth to say something, thought better of it, and replied, "This young woman has a very serious problem. I met with her and her father last night in Washington until very late, and ran out of the office without my cell phone or I would have called. I'm going to go back to her table now and I cannot invite you to join us." He leaned down and whispered in my ear, "Jealousy doesn't become you, Flip."

As he started to walk away, I glared, a green-eyed monkey, at the lady in distress.

"Yeah," I muttered, "I'm sure her problems are serious. Real life and death stuff."

Tom didn't skip a beat. "It is life or death," he said over one shoulder, so low nobody else heard him. "It certainly is life or death."

Berkley Prime Crime mysteries by Susan S. James

THE BELLES OF SOLACE GLEN
THE SIREN OF SOLACE GLEN

THE SIREN OF
SOLACE GLEN

Susan S. James

BERKLEY PRIME CRIME, NEW YORK

THE BERKLEY PUBLISHING GROUP
Published by the Penguin Group
Penguin Group (USA) Inc.
375 Hudson Street, New York, New York 10014, USA
Penguin Group (Canada), 10 Alcorn Avenue, Toronto, Ontario M4V 3B2, Canada
(a division of Pearson Penguin Canada Inc.)
Penguin Books Ltd., 80 Strand, London WC2R 0RL, England
Penguin Group Ireland, 25 St. Stephen's Green, Dublin 2, Ireland (a division of Penguin Books Ltd.)
Penguin Group (Australia), 250 Camberwell Road, Camberwell, Victoria 3124, Australia
(a division of Pearson Australia Group Pty. Ltd.)
Penguin Books India Pvt. Ltd., 11 Community Centre, Panchsheel Park, New Delhi—110 017, India
Penguin Group (NZ), Cnr. Airborne and Rosedale Roads, Albany, Auckland 1310, New Zealand
(a division of Pearson New Zealand Ltd.)
Penguin Books (South Africa) (Pty.) Ltd., 24 Sturdee Avenue, Rosebank, Johannesburg 2196, South
Africa

Penguin Books Ltd., Registered Offices: 80 Strand, London WC2R 0RL, England

This is a work of fiction. Names, characters, places, and incidents either are the product of the author's imagination or are used fictitiously, and any resemblance to actual persons, living or dead, business establishments, events, or locales is entirely coincidental.

THE SIREN OF SOLACE GLEN

A Berkley Prime Crime Book / published by arrangement with the author

PRINTING HISTORY
Berkley Prime Crime edition / April 2005

Copyright © 2005 by Susan S. James.
Cover design by Erica Tricarico.
Cover art by Joe Burleson.
Interior text design by Kristin del Rosario.

ISBN: 0-425-20200-3

BERKLEY PRIME CRIME®
Berkley Prime Crime Books are published by The Berkley Publishing Group,
a division of Penguin Group (USA) Inc.,
375 Hudson Street, New York, New York 10014.
BERKLEY PRIME CRIME is a registered trademark of Penguin Group (USA) Inc.
The Berkley Prime Crime design is a trademark belonging to Penguin Group (USA) Inc.

PRINTED IN THE UNITED STATES OF AMERICA

10 9 8 7 6 5 4 3 2 1

To Tramp, Grayman I and II, B.B., Chicora,
Theodosia, Frippy, Floozy, Rebel,
and especially Sammie and Yanni—

Loyal companions, royal pains,
Kings and Queens of carpet stains,
Protectors, guards, the sounds of alarm,
Whimpering babes in thunderstorms.
For all you have been, your hearts so true,
Good dogs, rest now,
And thank you.

ACKNOWLEDGMENTS

Thanks to Christine who makes what is bad, good, and what is good, better. To Mary and Jena, thanks for sticking with me. Humble gratitude to the faceless, unseen copy editors who never seem to run out of red ink. Thank you, Jim, for giving in and allowing me to adopt Schatzi. And thanks to all my dog-loving friends and family, whose tales keep Schatzi and I highly entertained. Obsessed and fanatic we stand; without our Schatzis, Drifters, Stars, Prissys, and Billy Bobs, we are at the mercy of cats, who have no mercy.

PART ONE

⁜

Fireflies and Fortunes

Chapter 1

❊

THE FIREFLIES COME back every June, just when the days start to simmer. One evening the twilight is soft and hazy, the next evening a pack of lightning bugs ignites all across your backyard, as if an angel suddenly yelled, "Gentlemen, start your engines!"

It can snow in Maryland in April, freakish, right on top of the cherry blossoms, but it does happen. In May, you almost hand over your trust to the sunny, fragrant afternoons, trees waxed in green, when suddenly you find yourself at the Preakness or a lacrosse game, hugging a windbreaker to your chest and cussing, dipping your face away from the bone-chilling rain. Finally, it's June, and the warm nights are no illusion.

You can trust a firefly, the twinkling light on the delicate wings. The fireflies wouldn't have it any other way. They know their business.

I guess I know mine, too. Nobody else in Solace Glen has ever been fool enough to own a cleaning service but me, Flip Paxton, and I've taken full advantage of other people's good sense for the past twenty-four years. At the start, word of mouth proved the only advertising I could afford, but small talk turned into a slow-moving blab-fest because I finally had more customers than I could handle after a few years. I kept slugging and plugging all on my own, though, too proud and too cheap to ask for help. But when Tom went crazy and asked me to marry him—in a wildly impetuous April Fool's Day moment while he fed his old dog Eli some table scraps—I figured it was time. Time for Flip Paxton to start thinking about herself for once, time for a forty-two-year-old woman to let somebody else scrub a toilet or two. It took a couple of months for the idea to really sink in, but near the end of May, after Sam and my best friend Lee walked down the aisle, Flip Paxton's Cleaning Service posted a Help Wanted ad on the bulletin boards of the four churches, and tacked another one up at the Placement Office of the local high school. The ad read:

FLIP PAXTON'S CLEANING SERVICE
Help Wanted! Have Come to My Senses at Last!
Anybody! Any Age! Introvert or Extrovert!
Need a Hard Worker Who Enjoys Toxic Fumes
and Rubber Gloves.
Hours and Wage Negotiable,
But Everybody Knows I Am Cheap.
Tear Off Tag Below with My Phone Number.
Serious Inquiries Only. This Is No Joke.
I Need Two Extra Hands.

Naturally, Tom volunteered a legal opinion. "You could have left off the 'toxic fumes' part." He removed his reading glasses and huffed on a lens. "You won't get any Methodists that way."

"Fine with me. You're all such a lazy lot." I finished dusting his conference room table with something that smelled like lemons but would probably cause me to pass out if I breathed in too hard. "I don't mind killing off a fellow Presbyterian, though. Or a teenager."

The trace of a smile crossed his lips. "That's why I asked you to marry me, Flip. You are a woman without scruples."

"All I know is, I'm a woman without any help and I can't take it anymore." I placed the back of my hand across one temple and wobbled as if I might faint, collapsing into his lap. "Would you still love me if I had a scruple or two?"

Tom grunted as if a Toyota had landed on his legs (though I weigh no more than a glass slipper) and tenderly drew my rubber glove to his lips.

O you whom I often and silently come
    where you are that I may be with you,
As I walk by your side or sit near,
    or remain in the same room with you,
Little you know the subtle electric fire
    that for your sake is playing within me.

A familiar warmth swooshed through my veins. "That's not fair." I melted against his chest. "It's too early in the day to turn me into jelly."

He started to peel off the glove and nuzzle my neck but I shot up. "No time for that, Mr. Scott. You Methodists are all alike—lazy and sex, sex, sex. Anyway, you told me you have a new client in ten minutes."

"Much can be accomplished in ten minutes, my Frozen Chosen." He bent over to pet Eli, the noble black Labrador, whose head turned to accept high praise for merely existing. "But you're right. Don't want to shock the new client."

Ever curious, I pressed for information. "Why? Is it an old lady with a heart condition?"

He kept petting Eli, silent.

"Is it an old man on his last legs eager to leave me his fortune?"

Tom took his fingers and stretched Eli's black lips back so that he appeared to bare his teeth at me. "You're upsetting Eli. Talk about something else. When was the last minute you went out to look at the house?"

"About sixty-three minutes ago." He knew me too well. The dream house rising from the charred ruins on the O'Connell property looked more like home every day, only no home I had ever dreamed could be mine. "Abner says it'll be in move-in condition by the end of summer. So," I batted my eyes attractively, "maybe we could nail down a wedding date?"

He usually replied with a vague, "When the house is ready, dear," but this time ignored the issue entirely. "It's not like Abner Diggs to sound optimistic, but I must admit he and his crew are ahead of schedule after only three weeks. The weather's been good."

I pouted at the way he slipped past The Big Question. In the course of an average workday, convincing Tom Scott, legal workaholic, to set an actual wedding date proved far more difficult than accepting his marriage proposal made while temporarily insane. But with Tom,

I'd learned to bite my tongue and bide my time, just one of the many lessons of life and love he'd passed down over the past several months after he'd gently, surprisingly, lulled me into his world.

"Yeah, I can't believe it's the second day of June already." I stuffed dust rags into the carryall. "OK. Enough small talk. Why won't you tell me who your new client is? Privileged information?"

Eli shook Tom's hand away with a big flap of his head. "When are the new and improved Mr. and Mrs. Sam Gibbon due back? I keep forgetting."

He obviously wouldn't tell me what I wanted to know. My suspicious nature carved a frown, but I answered his question for the hundredth time. "Sam and Lee get back a week from today. That'll make *two* weeks. *They* get to go on a two-week honeymoon."

"Don't rub it in. A week is all you get for marrying the only lawyer in town."

"I'm not complaining." Although I was. Pocket atlas ever at the ready, worn and creased, many a time I'd flipped through the mapped pages and imagined a long getaway in Europe. French wine for breakfast and lounging around in a gondola before flying off to the Alps in a hot-air balloon. Violins, lutes, and medieval minstrels peopled my dream honeymoon. Remembering that honey catches the fly—and the town lawyer—I crooned, "I'll be happy with whatever you come up with, sweetheart."

Sam and Lee patriotically chose the New York Finger Lakes for a wedding trip, content with drinking good old American wine for breakfast and lounging around in a wooden canoe. Of all people, Screamin' Larry, our criminally insane disk jockey at WFIB in Frederick, gave

Sam the idea. He held the mistaken notion the honey-mooners would rent a house on one of the lakes, Cayuga or Skaneateles, and let him stay for free when he went up to Syracuse for a lacrosse tournament. When they opted to hop around at bed and breakfasts, Larry played "I'm Shadowing You" about fifty times on his jazz program and dedicated it to them, making everybody in Solace Glen nervous as sin. Fortunately, all it amounted to was his distasteful idea of a joke, and he remained safely in town and on the air following the ceremony.

"I'll let you know our honeymoon plans in due course so you can pack accordingly." *Would this be before or after a real wedding*, I wondered. "Speaking of Lee, how do you like the house-sitting arrangement? Lee's Historical Society suit you until we make the big move?"

"Perfectly." I'd listed my house with a realtor the first of May, and it sold so fast, with settlement scheduled in another week, that I'd been forced to cull through everything I owned like lightning. Half of my beat-up furniture went to charity or friends and the other half lay in storage, waiting to mix with Tom's things in our new house. I suppose I could have thrown propriety to the wind and moved in with Tom, but Lee saved the day (and my reputation as the town harlot) by suggesting I house-sit for her. She and Sam wanted to start their married life in the house she'd inherited from her Aunt Leona, the big Bell family home. My family. My skin fairly tingled whenever I thought of how Lee and I made the connection, how we'd discovered my secret heritage from the Bell family Bible I inherited from Leona, and from the mysterious letters the Bell women kept hidden for decades. So I couldn't be anything but happy in Lee's 1794 red brick Historical Society filled with books, artifacts, two life-size dolls (Plain Jane and Dear John), and the beautiful Civil War letters that changed my life and gave me the gift of family.

"Jane, John, and Jeb are lively companions, even though only one of them is actually alive. I swear, Tom, Jeb has come to hate me now that I smell like Eli most of the time. He yowls in the middle of the night and bites my toes through the bedspread if I don't get up to let him out."

"Cats." Tom wrinkled his perfect nose, so used to smelling old ladies' lavender water, now putting up with my Eau d'Lysol. "What we need around here are more dogs. Isn't that right, Eli?"

Eli looked bored but in total agreement, like a government undersecretary.

"Maybe your new client has a nice, big dog. Does he?"

"Nice try. How are Garland and Hilda? I've been meaning to stop by the Bistro this week, but bag lunches have been my mainstay lately."

"They're fine," I said impatiently. Why so secretive? "In fact, just the other day, Hilda announced she'd done so well in school this year, she can graduate at the end of the summer. Looks like college at Hood is a real possibility. And the Bistro is doing so well, Garland wants to start paying a little rent on Louise's house, but I told her not to even think about it. The mortgage is paid and the trust can easily maintain the property. She and Hilda deserve a stress-free life for a change."

"Agreed. Roland really put them through the ringer. I'm sure Garland can't wait for the divorce to be done, but you know Roland."

Did I ever. Wife-beating, cheap son-of-a-bitch. There

were no nice words for him in my book. "Yeah, Garland told me he's dragging things out and making her miserable, especially since she 'stole' most of his kitchen staff and clientele. I hear C.C. and Marlene still frequent his establishment, though, whenever C.C. comes to town."

Tom's dark eyes rose heavenward and a corner of his mouth twitched. "Did I tell you Leonard and C.C. are moving back to our happy little paradise?"

You could have toppled me over with a pencil point. "You know you didn't!" I had hoped that snooty pair would discover the material joys of Montgomery County, closer to D.C. where Leonard defended rich corporate scoundrels. "When? Where are they going to live now that we've bought their property?"

"I'll fill you in later. So where are you off to now? Margaret's?"

"Nope, Lindbergh Kohl's, then Miss Fizzi's."

Tom's dark eyes softened a notch. "How *is* Lindbergh? I haven't had much of a chance to talk to him since he settled back in. He's something of an enigma to most people around here. What do you make of him?"

"Me?" I shrugged. "I've only been out there twice, and he's not exactly the talkative type. All I know is what the Circle Ladies tell me, which is (a) he's a seventy-year-old lifelong bachelor, so according to them, he's either gay or a complete nerd; (b) he's some sort of superwhiz government scientist; and (c) he's retired and has come back home. Margaret studied a year behind him in high school and remembers him as 'reticent and reclusive,' and 'very attractive, except for the genius IQ.' She's so brilliant herself, you'd think there'd be an attraction. Personally, I find it sweet and sort of flattering that he's always kept a house here, though up till now he's come and gone like a leaf in the wind."

Tom wryly remarked, "*Lindbergh* may not be the 'talkative type,' but . . ."

"OK, OK. So none of the women in this town have taken a vow of silence." The Circle Ladies represented the four churches of Solace Glen, banding together to tend the sick, oversee new births, cook, clean, and spread the word. Spreading the word, an especially cherished tradition. "Why ask me about Lindbergh, anyway? Think he's divulging nuclear secrets to his new cleaning lady?"

Maybe no one else could tell, but Tom's black eyes always betrayed him. I could see he knew far more about Lindbergh Kohl than any of us, even Margaret, and whatever he knew, he admired.

"Yes, and I'm handing you over to the FBI along with your recipe for tofu burgers, which is highly suspect."

The tofu burger attempt remained a sore subject.

"So—Miss Fizzi's house." He gracefully veered away from the subject of Lindbergh. "I'm sure one or more of the Circle Ladies will be there, tossing casseroles and gossip at her. And, as we know, Miss Fizzi appreciates the latter more than the former." He stood up, straightening his tie, all business at once. "You best be off then."

I looked my handsome fiancé hard in the eye. "You trying to get rid of me? Why won't you tell me who the new client is? Who you represent is no secret. Unless . . . the client doesn't want anybody to know he or she is seeing a lawyer. Is that it? Is that the big secret? Somebody getting a divorce besides Garland?"

"Flip," he pushed me out the door of the conference room into the hallway, nudging my backside along with every word, "you're getting to be more like a lawyer by the minute. Maybe you should ditch the cleaning business and go to law school."

"I'd miss the smell of Clorox in my hair. So would you. Good . . . bye." I kissed the tip of his aristocratic nose and headed down the stairs to the street, slightly annoyed I couldn't coax out more information. Just as I set the carryall down to turn the brass knob, the door flew open. The most stunning, beautiful woman stepped abruptly in and jumped in surprise when she saw me.

"Excuse me!" she gasped. "I didn't know anyone was here. You . . . you scared me."

"A hazard of my profession. That's OK." Appreciating the good manners that matched the good looks, I eyed her up and down, quickly making an appraisal as if I might want to buy her or have a copy made. If she weren't shaking so nervously, I'd have sworn she was made of gold. Her age probably matched Lee's, mid-thirties, with honey-blonde hair like a young Grace Kelly. In fact, she could have passed as Grace Kelly's twin, her good looks the definition of classic. She wore a tailored, raw silk suit the color of butter that melted under the highlights in her hair. Her lips glistened in a deep, crimson red—1950s movie star lips. Even in flat bone shoes, she had at least three inches on me, which put her in the five-foot-nine category. I suddenly felt very plain, insecure, and wallflowerish in my apron and sneakers with my drab brown hair always in dire need of another haircut, but I brightly directed her upstairs. "Go right on up. I believe Mr. Scott's expecting you."

She glanced up the stairway as if there lay her

salvation, but still remembered to stick an introductory hand out for me to shake. Somehow, touching her seemed a sacrilege.

"Oh, no, my hands smell awful."

She smiled brilliantly. "That's OK. I can at least introduce myself. I'm Stewart Larkin."

I drew in a little breath. "*You're* Stewart Larkin? You're the 'man' who bought my house?" Now I felt both ugly and stupid. "I'm Flip Paxton."

"Uh-huh. Flip Paxton." She said my name, no spark of recognition. Then suddenly, "Oh! My new house! *That* Flip Paxton! I thought you were a man, too, like Flip Wilson. Isn't that funny?"

I had to admit it was. "And you're here to see Mr. Scott?" I couldn't imagine why, since the settlement wouldn't occur for another week. No papers had to be signed before then.

She again glanced up the stairs where my fiancé waited in his office, sighed prettily, and combed trembling fingers through shimmering gold hair. She completely forgot I stood there. "Oh, Tom"—her tone of voice restrained desperation—"it's been too many years. Too many years. God, I hope you can help."

As she gracefully whisked up the stairs and disappeared around the corner, my heart almost beat out of my chest. *It's been too many years. Too many years*.

It was all I could do to walk out that door and not fly back to Tom.

CHAPTER 2

❋

IN THE FIVE minutes it took to drive to Lindbergh Kohl's house, I fought butterflies in my stomach and disasters in my head. A blank calendar with no wedding date, a framed house with no foundation, a spliced family tree with no roots. In place of those hopes and dreams crept doubt, fear, and worry. And an impossibly beautiful blonde from Tom's past.

I sat slumped in the car, face ashen, breathing deeply. One breath—trust Tom. Two breaths—erase worry. Three breaths—refocus. Focus on something fun or entertaining or curious. To me, that usually meant somebody from Solace Glen. Since I sat in his driveway, huffing like a yoga master, I focused on Lindbergh Kohl.

Tom wasn't the only one who knew more about old Lindbergh than he let on. Cleaning ladies pick up more than dirty laundry, if you get my drift. I'd come across more skeletons in more closets than I'd care mention. Not that I would. And not that Lindbergh Kohl presented me with either dirty laundry or skeletons. Like Tom, you could eat off the man's kitchen floor.

No, what I'd been able to glean from those first two trips to Lindbergh's house came from the skilled, observant eyes of a seasoned domestic. Book titles speak volumes. Home furniture and accessories tell many a tale. Art works and framed photographs release untold secrets. And medicine cabinets—well, we don't need to go there.

Lindbergh's walls of books could give Lee's Historical Society some serious competition. To my surprise, science texts didn't make up the main event, biographies did. Scientific fact took a back seat to personal history. Everyone from Coco Chanel to Alexander the Great claimed residence in Lindbergh's house. Other people's lives simply fascinated him. Presidents, artists, actors, aviators. Also, nothing on his walls or tables signified ego. No diplomas, no pictures of himself with government officials or politicians, no trophies or awards or framed letters of achievement. The furniture in his modest, yet historic brick home looked as if it hadn't been moved in more than one hundred years. Ruby-red, hand-knit Afghans covered the worn spots on the burgundy velvet sofa in the small parlor. Behind the sofa, a picture window framed a pretty view of the fire pond in the distance, edged on either side by two massive fir trees that served as a privacy screen for the house. The plain, white dishes in the cabinets never filled the sink. The greens in the refrigerator always looked fresh, as if, just in case, company showed up for dinner. Upstairs, the wood floors creaked and the sheets on the mahogany sleigh bed appeared clean and white every time. Lemon oil permeated the air.

Each time I arrived, including this morning, Lindbergh greeted me courteously wearing a beige sweater vest, then he'd slip away to a small study off the kitchen to read and nod his head to Mozart until I poked in to clean that one last room. He would offer a quick, polite smile, rise with book in hand, and continue reading upstairs. I would slide the check he placed on the Hepplewhite table into an apron pocket, and listen for the soft pad of his deerskin moccasins as he crossed the bedroom floor to the reading chair beside the bed. The footwear suited him to a T—quiet, soft, gentle, like Mr. Rogers come back to life, only not as tall or as eager to make a friend.

All this I knew about Lindbergh Kohl. Such an incomplete biography.

WILMA FIZZI PERCHED on a white, wrought-iron patio chair in the backyard, pouring iced tea for her three guests. She wore her trademark pink lipstick and a floral cotton dress of gloppy peonies that appeared to bloom right off her tiny body. One hand poured the tea while the other held a paper fan with a picture of Jesus on one side and a host of Bible verses on the other.

Margaret Henshaw spied me first. "Oh, Miss Fizzi, there's Flip. Hey, Flip! Come have some tea with us before you start cleaning."

If Miss Fizzi played the role of my grandmother, Margaret filled the part of mother, shoes she slipped into when I thought all the mother figures in my life had left me—my own who died in a car crash along with my father when I was eighteen, then Marie, Leona, and Louise. Margaret no doubt surprised even herself by taking me under her wing the way she did. Her lifelong detachment from others seemed to melt away when Louise died that cold first day of December and Margaret reached out to me, taking my hand after the funeral and saying four little words of rescue, "You're not alone, Flip."

I thought of that moment as I approached her. In the same instant, a picture of Stewart Larkin desperately clinging to Tom popped into my head. *It's been too many years. Too many years. God, I hope you can help.* I flew straight for Margaret and hugged her. In the old days, Margaret would have stiffened her perfect posture and reprimanded me in her strictest teacher's voice, but now she beamed and patted my arm affectionately.

"What's all this about?" she asked tenderly, quickly checking her gray bun for stray pieces.

"Nothing. I'll tell you later." I drew up a spare plastic chair and wedged myself between Margaret and Tina Graham. Tina tried to scoot over in the heavy iron chair, but her own bulk prevented the slightest budge.

Melody Connolly crossed her arms and watched the struggle. "Give it up, Tina. I swear, you've gained ten pounds on that new diet."

I placed a hand on Tina's shoulder to signal she could quit fidgeting. "What is it this time, Tina? The goat's-milk-and-cigarette diet or the tequila-and-jelly-bean diet?"

Miss Fizzi pursed her pink lips. "Those don't sound very healthy, dear. You're going to do yourself in." She added sweetly, "Fasting at Lent always works for me."

Tina huffed in Melody's direction. "For everyone's

information, since everyone is always so interested in my weight problems, I'm starving to death. Starving! I'm on a fruit-and-rice diet, and I hate it so much I end up eating a box of Snickers every night to console myself."

"Well, no wonder." Melody shuddered and readjusted the new, lovely piece of jewelry she invariably wore from the Connolly's store. Eye candy advertising, she liked to say. "What do you expect? Fructose, carbs, and a nightly box of calories, now really. How old are you and I now? Fifty-six or something? Maybe I'm different from most women our age, but *I* can go on any kind of diet, shed the pounds in a week, and not feel the least bit hungry."

Tina eyed Melody's trim figure. "Yeah, maybe you are different, you lucky, skinny little dog."

"If you came to work for me," I fished, knowing Tina had recently suffered a layoff from her secretarial job with Frederick County, "you'd lose ten pounds in a week. Guaranteed."

"That's an attractive offer, Flip," she sniffed, "but I think I'll pass."

This was my problem getting good help. Everybody loved what I did for them, but nobody wanted to do it with me.

"She values her fingernails too much," Margaret explained, drawing attention to Tina's beautifully manicured hands and my own unfortunate paws. "Tina, why don't you apply as Tom's secretary? I hear he can't keep anybody more than two weeks at a time since Ferrell T. went off to jail."

"That's true," I agreed. "His last secretary stormed off the job claiming he actually wanted her to use a computer. She outdated Miss Fizzi by twenty years, and couldn't see past the wart on the end of her nose."

Miss Fizzi slowly fanned her eighty-year-old face and clucked, "People more than a century old have no business working. She should try turpentine. That took care of my warts."

Margaret rolled her eyes at me and Tina blinked at Miss Fizzi, intrigued at the idea of working for Tom. "Now that's an idea, and I could still help Sally out at the salon on Saturdays."

Sally Polk's name usually elicited spicy conversation—the raciest forty-one-year-old mother of two sets of twins you ever saw. The first set of boys she bore at age nineteen with husband number one; the second set popped out on New Year's Day with husband number five. She still ranted and raved about how she might cut him loose, too, considering Wilbur Polk's unwillingness to abandon a barroom stool while she dropped the litter in the back of the Eggheads' ambulance. So named due to their closely shaved, bristly blonde heads, our paramedic Eggheads, Jesse and Jules Munford (besides Sally's brood, the only other twosomes born in Solace Glen), got the thrill of their lives birthing twins like themselves out of a real beauty queen. How those two dummies managed to accomplish such a sterling feat remained a mystery. We figured the only answer lay in the fact they grew up on a Frederick County farm overrun with pigs and cows, and couldn't have missed the natural cycle of life if they'd tried. Sally said the whole time she labored, the Eggheads bugged her about naming the boys after them. In the meanwhile, as if she didn't have anything better to do, Sally grunted and screamed at her husband over a cell phone.

"Hell, wouldn't ya know the Longhorns would be playing in my hour of need," she'd grumble, two fingers pointing skyward in a Longhorn cheer while she snipped hair. "Damn fool's never even been to Texas, not to mention college. Wilbur barely crawled out of high school."

After mentioning Sally's name, Tina picked up a strand of my hair and examined the split ends, a not so subtle hint, time to visit the salon. Stewart Larkin, I conjectured, probably got her hair professionally shellacked once a day.

"I'm overdue to see Sally," fussed Miss Fizzi, gazing at my dull ponytail. "My hair looks like something a squirrel could call home."

"It sure does," said Tina, impolite but ever vigilant in drawing customers to Sally, especially now that she had a baby hanging off each hipbone. "Speaking of home, how's the new house going, Flip?"

The one subject I never tired of, my face lit up. "Great! I tell you, it's going to be as beautiful as C.C. and Leonard's house before Larry blew it up."

We all accepted as true the theory that Screamin' Larry exercised his criminal inclinations against his archenemy, C.C. The insurance company simply found that a gas line exploded, but everybody in Solace Glen knew Larry's calling card when they saw it. If he'd tinkered around with anybody else's gas line, we might be attending a trial right now, but people openly cheered the departure of C.C. and Leonard Crosswell, making Larry something of a local folk hero.

"Oooo," I remembered the bomb Tom dropped on me, "heard the latest on C.C. and Leonard?"

The ladies automatically leaned closer.

"Don't tell me they're moving back here," Melody moaned. "Oh, please God, not the fox and the hen."

"I know a better word than hen," said Tina.

"Whatever you call them," I said, "they're blowing our way again."

"Ugh," Margaret grunted pointedly.

"Where will they live?" asked Miss Fizzi, eyes ping-ponging around like she was trying to remember who we were talking about in the first place. "Did they buy your old house, Flip?"

"Lord, no." That would be the Mystery Woman of the Century who, for all I knew, was at that moment re-minding Tom of their hot, storied past as she peeled his clothes off with perfectly manicured crimson nails. "Tom said he'd tell me later where they're going to live." I added under my breath, "A woman named Stewart Larkin bought my house."

"Stewart Larkin?" Both Miss Fizzi and Margaret spoke in unison, Miss Fizzi commenting, "I thought you said a man bought it."

My spine straightened. "She's got a man's name. You two know her?" Great. It was probably all over town by now. *Suave Town Lawyer Dumps Maid for Grace Kelly Look-Alike; Who Can Blame Him, Locals Ask.*

"She went to Hood," Margaret recalled. "A gorgeous girl with a fortune to boot. Lee brought her home from college for Leona and Jake to meet several times. Those two girls were good friends for awhile."

"I don't remember." I tried to sound uninterested. "Never met her. Lee never mentioned her name." Truth be told, Lee and I didn't become serious bosom buddies until after she'd graduated from Hood.

"Probably no need to mention her to you," said Miss Fizzi. "You know how a lot of college friendships are, people part and go their separate ways. There was some-thing about her father, too. He's a big industrialist. Oh, what's his name? Con . . . Conway . . . Conrad Larkin! I remember, something scandalous happened, and Stewart was very upset." She twisted her pink mouth, forehead creased, and stared into space a moment. Her shoulders rose and fell and she released the flickering memory into the air as a child lets loose a lightning bug. "I forget. But I do remember that girl. What a bell ringer!"

Margaret tapped a finger against her cheek. "You know, I seem to recall Tom knew her, too. He taught a class at Hood for a semester, just to see if he liked professorial work, and I believe Stewart was his star pupil."

"How would you remember that?" I beat my teaspoon around the glass so hard, the tea almost frothed. *And why didn't Tom tell me his "new client" was a woman from his past?*

Margaret's brow wrinkled at my tea glass. "He used to ask my advice about teaching and would rave about the work this one student did for him. 'Gorgeous girl, unforgettable name, brilliant.' Gosh, does *he* know Stewart's moving to Solace Glen?"

I stared at her, my whole future suddenly charred black.

Fortunately, Melody couldn't sit still any longer about C.C. and Leonard's depressing reappearance. "How long have we got? I can't stand the thought of having to serve Leonard in the store again. He makes you drag out everything and never buys a thing. Not a ring, not a bracelet, not a cufflink—Nothing."

"Make Michael do it, then," Tina offered. "Or . . . ," her green eyes flashed, "send Leonard over to Marlene's store. They're *compatico*, right?"

Marlene Worthington, only daughter of my favorite

"mother," Louise, did employ Leonard briefly after Louise died, in an attempt to gain more of her mother's fortune. Unfortunately for Marlene, Louise employed equal legal talent in setting up a trust her daughter could not touch, leaving Marlene a monthly sum to help with expenses, but nothing you could retire on. As a result, Marlene hated everybody in town even more than she did before her mother died, especially me and Tom, the trustees of Louise's estate.

"I never see Marlene, anymore," I commented. "She sort of avoids me."

"She avoids everyone," Margaret said, graciously topping off our iced teas and quietly removing the spoon from my glass. "You have to actually venture into the Gift and Flower Shoppe to see her. Lives like a bear in a cave, sort of like old Lindbergh Kohl. He won't even answer the doorbell for a casserole, for goodness' sake, and believe me, many a Circle Lady has tried."

Despite Margaret's indignation, I defended my new customer, the very civilized image of neatly hung guest towels popping into my head along with the strains of Mozart. "Oh, he's no bear in a cave. He simply enjoys a quiet, private life surrounded by good books and music, not gossipy women bearing broccoli casseroles. You all are just steamed because there's finally a 'mature,' attractive man to flirt with around here, and he won't play into your web. And really, you shouldn't mention his name and Marlene's in the same breath."

"Maybe not," Margaret conceded. "Still, it's strange what a homebody he's become given the way he used to blow in and out of town."

"Like Charlie Scott," Tina trilled. "Wonder when he'll blow into town next?"

They all set eyes on me expectantly, as if my engagement to Tom guaranteed the whereabouts of his brother, an extremely handsome, but elusive photojournalist. I raised both shoulders. "Got me. He and Tom barely communicate. Let's get back to Marlene. What's up with Our Lady of Vicks VapoRub?"

"Garland and Hilda still see her," Melody chimed in. "She drives by Louise's house at least twice a week, Garland says, making fish eyes at the house like it should be hers, and Garland and Hilda have no right to live there."

"Maybe *Mr. Worthington* will show up some day and help Marlene reclaim her property!" Tina's body jiggled with laughter. The greatest joke in the world to the ladies of Solace Glen was that Marlene's ex-husband, whom many doubted even existed, would ride into town one day and cause some havoc. We made up every kind of scenario, more comical with each performance, as to what he'd do and how Marlene would react. "I can see it now. Mr. Worthington is a performance artist who specializes in . . ."

"Gas stations," Melody interrupted. "And he will convince Marlene to buy Pal Sykes's Crown station and live above the garage. . . ."

"With Monsieur Worthington performing nightly, juggling oil cans, and co-starring Suggs Magill as their house boy." As one who appreciated fine literature, Margaret relished the game, always painting our characters with the most creative brush.

Miss Fizzi twittered at the idea of her awful, unsociable nephew Suggs leaving his job as Pal's mechanic to don a crisp, white housecoat to bow and scrape to people who came to the door. We joined her in the twittering until who should emerge from Miss Fizzi's basement door but the nasty creature himself. The giggling immediately ceased.

Miss Fizzi screwed up her nose. "Oh, Suggs. I thought you went to work hours ago."

Suggs scowled as if she'd called him a contributing member of society, hiked his work pants up in a revolting, suggestive manner, and stalked off.

Margaret visibly shook. "Oh, that man." I knew she wanted to say more, but would never offend Miss Fizzi.

Miss Fizzi waved her Bible fan, contemplating the somewhat feminine picture of Jesus as if doing so would magically give her the right words. "None of us is perfect," she said at last, the magic having worked, "least of all Suggs, but I'm sure God has some part for Suggs to play."

"Yes," I said, deadpan. "As Marlene's houseboy."

The festive mood returned and we added a few more outrageous scenes to our Mr. and Mrs. Worthington play before I excused myself to clean Miss Fizzi's house. As the dust rag swept over her massive Victorian tables and chairs, a different scenario played through my mind than the one starring Marlene, her ex, and Suggs.

Over and over again, the shapely legs of a beautiful blonde stranger ran up a staircase toward Tom leaving me at the bottom of the stairs with my heart in my mouth, all alone. Exactly the place I'd been most of my life—all alone.

CHAPTER 3

✳

LATER THAT NIGHT, I picked up a cheap bottle of gin on my way home to replace the cheap bottle I'd finally emptied after three months. Tom's tastes ran the way of fine Pinot Noirs and smooth Merlots, and he'd spent the past few months trying to steer me toward more impressive labels than Budweiser and Burnett, but he knew he'd found a hopeless cause.

Now, with a chorus line of rich, gorgeous blondes dancing in my head, the glaring differences between Tom and me suddenly began to jut all out of proportion. I shook my head hard to clear it, and strode into Lee's Historical Society, unbagging the new bottle of booze on the kitchen counter. "You can lead a horse to water," I called out to Plain Jane and Dear John, "but not if she wants gin and tonic."

The two artsy life-size dolls Lee placed around her

kitchen table like visiting neighbors stared at each other's dyed condom and neon IUD eyes, the same wicked tilt to their lips. Jeb, annoyed at the daylong absence, mewed as he encircled my ankles. All in all, it beat coming home to an empty house the way I had for so long.

I flicked on the radio, WFIB 102.7, to catch Screamin' Larry's evening program. He never deviated from the way he introduced the show. "The DEFIANT jazz station that DEFIES country. DEFIES classical. DEFIES rap. DEFIES, most especially, bluck! The oldies."

Nobody could understand what Larry had against the oldies, but if you even started to hum something around him like "Take the Last Train to Clarksville" or "Mrs. Brown, You've Got a Lovely Daughter," he'd about rip your tongue out.

His choices for the evening focused on Billie Holiday, Cleo Lane, and Susannah McCorkle. Larry loved women, he just didn't associate with any personally.

I stuck a few carrot and celery sticks around a store-bought dill dip to snack on until Tom called to tell me where we'd go for dinner. That made up our usual routine: Sunday nights we'd eat in, taking turns at the stove; Monday, Friday, and Saturday we'd eat out; Tuesday through Thursday, I'd cook. When we first got together in December, I stepped far out on a culinary limb and purchased a serious assembly of new cookbooks, sure that the way to Tom's heart lay across his impeccable taste buds. The poor man got experimented on in the worst way—a pot roast that shriveled into a Vienna sausage, tortillas that tasted like burned bricks, a Cajun steak you could have lit a forest fire with, the infamous tofu burger that could melt in your mouth, or anywhere else for that matter. The list grew long. Finally, I achieved success with a certain number of dishes (a number too small to mention) so I kept repeating them, using different sauces and vegetables to throw Tom off the scent of a revolving trail of disappointing entrées.

I poured myself a gin and tonic and took the plate of rabbit food out to Lee's back patio. Her herb garden flourished, and the smell of lavender, rosemary, and sage punctuated the early evening air. Jeb came out to keep me company and hunt the first fireflies of the season.

I took a long sip from my glass and listened to Billie Holiday sing "Comes Love." The mood felt just right until a replay of that ravishing, brilliant creature floating up the stairs to my fiancé burst the bubble. *What did she need Tom's help for, and why did she act so nervous and desperate?* I checked my wristwatch and placed one hand on a jittery stomach. Nearly 6:30; Tom should have called.

"Oh, well," I started a conversation with the inattentive cat to calm my nerves. "He probably had to work late. Court clerks call all the time, you know. And clients." I bit hard into a carrot. "Clients can ask lawyers to do the stupidest things. For instance, say you have a domestic case and the husband and wife can't stand the sight of each other. Good point, Jeb. Just like Garland and Roland. And one calls up the lawyer, we'll say Roland for argument's sake, and Roland says, 'That damn woman took my best spatula! And I want you—cuss, cuss, cuss— to git it back!' Now, Jeb, wouldn't you hate to be a lawyer and have to hear that sort of foolishness day in, and day out?" I glanced at my watch again. "Sometimes even into the dinner hour?"

Jeb gave a noncommittal twitch of the tail and

headed into the house to his own supper. I kept talking to fill the time.

"Why would anybody, I wonder, choose a profession where you have to be at somebody's beck and call at all hours of the day and night? I don't know how Tom does it. Or the Eggheads, for that matter. I mean, there's nothing wrong with working long hours, but at the end of the day, you ought to be able to kick back and not have the phone ring off the hook." My ears strained toward the kitchen in case my babbling interfered with the sound of a bell.

Nothing. Nothing at 6:45. Nothing at 7:00. Nothing at 7:15, 7:30, or 7:45, when I finally poured a can of generic soup into a pan to the strains of Cleo Lane singing "I Want to Be Happy." I sank into a chair between Plain Jane and Dear John. Plain Jane's red yarn hair matched the color of the tomato soup. She looked upon me with pitying eyes. At that moment, my only comfort lay in the Eggheads' ready availability twenty-four–seven for my depression-instilled heart attack.

"Oh, hell," I snapped at Dear John, picturing Tom's perfect features across the doll's rubber-worm mouth, bottle-glass nose, and neon-green IUD eyes. "Why am I acting like a seventh grader? All I have to do is pick up that phone like a grown woman and call him! We're getting married, for God's sake!"

I marched over to the phone and maturely snatched up the receiver, punching out the familiar numbers connecting me to Tom's office. After four rings, his voice answered.

"Tom? I've been . . ."

The answering machine. I hung up. No message.

"Maybe he's at home. Maybe he just this second

walked through the door to feed Eli and slip into something more comfortable, like the Terps T-shirt I gave him, before he takes me out for a late, romantic supper."

Plain Jane appeared hopeful. I dialed Tom's home number. Wary of technology overtaking our lives, he kept no answering machine within the walls of his very private, very British-looking stone house outside of town. The phone rang and rang and rang. I must have hung up at the twentieth ring. Even with a permanent smirk on her bent-spoon lips, Plain Jane resumed the pitying expression.

I tried to imagine all kinds of possibilities, like the unpredictable Charlie Scott suddenly showing up after a long trip to Borneo. Or Miss Fizzi suddenly deciding to change her will again because this time she was sure that the aches in her joints meant bone cancer. Or Eli tragically mistaking an electric wire for a snake and at that very instant, as I stood there playing guessing games, Tom's sweet stone house burned to the ground.

What was it Louise used to say to me? "You don't give yourself enough credit. No self-confidence. But you possess the heart and the stamina to sustain us all."

To hell with the heart and stamina. Where the blazes did I leave the self-confidence? I knew I had it. For a while, I had it. When Tom first took my face in his hands and reset the world on its axis, I had a future's worth of confidence. Now doubt and fear and the familiar chill of loneliness seeped back in.

When the phone rang, I must have jumped three feet before grabbing the receiver. "Tom? Where are you?"

"Tom?" answered a bright voice, a voice I almost recognized. "Who you callin' Tom, you puny little lovesick maid. This is Ivory Williams, and I'm calling about that job you're dying t'gimme."

I shook myself out of fantasyland and became all business. "Ivory? Aren't you still the church sexton?"

"That's me, honey, a ton o'sex, but you know Reverend McKnight's leavin' and I just don't have the energy to break in a new minister."

McKnight had served as our Presbyterian minister for at least twelve years, and Ivory worked right along beside him, loyal to the core. I never saw her without a smile on her face and a song on her lips. "Shoot. I keep forgetting he's leaving. He's been such a fixture. Where's he going again?"

"Hotlanta. Gone with the wind. He's leavin' on a jet plane, baby, and don't know when he'll be back again."

For a thirty-something, modern African-American woman, Ivory held a peculiar reverence for old, white-bread music.

"Does he have another job?"

"Job? He don't need a job. His momma won the Lotto and she's making him her CEO. Christian Entertainment Officer. They're already planning their trip around the world with the grandchildren." She broke into a strange version of "What the World Needs Now," punctuated by a giggle. "The new interim starts in two weeks, and that's when I'll be church history, same as McKnight."

My mouth drooped. Reverend McKnight, a towering redhead with a Scottish temper, held a special place in my heart. He'd rescued me from a flipped-out Ferrell T. and saved the precious family Bible along with the letters that Leona bequeathed, which gave me what I longed for most—family.

"Oh, Ivory. It's so sad and upsetting. People are really going to miss him. I hope the new interim is half as good."

"That's my worry, too, darlin'. You know, Ivory don't take to everybody. I've been in my own Ivory tower for twelve years. Then, just as this mess hits the fan, I see your ad on the bulletin board. 'Anybody! Any age!' That's me. 'Introvert or extrovert!' That's both of me. 'Hard worker.' Child, you know how hard Ivory works and how hard it is to find good, honest help. 'Enjoys toxic fumes and rubber gloves.' I live for 'em. And I know you are the cheapest woman in town and Ivory's got respect about you. R-E-S-P-E-C-T. Whatcha say, Flip?"

I didn't have to think twice. "You start two weeks from today. I'll drop by the church next week and we'll go over a schedule and figure out your wage."

Ivory squealed. "Ooooo! You won't be sorry, honey! Ivory's gonna do good by you! We'll get your cleaning done twice as fast and you can start putting time in a bottle and more time into that wedding you're planning. God bless ya, Flip."

I hung up and slowly mixed a second gin and tonic. This felt good, hiring Ivory, a known entity. My clients would welcome a former sexton into their homes and I could start to put my feet up. Now I could enjoy my engagement and put more thought into planning the wedding and setting the date. Now I could spend more time with my fiancé.

If only I knew where he was. And who he was with.

CHAPTER 4

✻

THE NEW HOUSE going up on the O'Connell property, now our property, appeared to grow straight out of the ground—a huge, captivating tree amid the orchards of more familiar peach, pear, and dogwoods. Freshly planted cherry trees, handpicked by Tom, lined the driveway leading up to the house.

I parked my hideous old Volkswagen sedan at the top of the drive and waved at Abner Diggs. Abner calmly barked out something to two men at the center of the chaos and ambled down to meet me. A hard, gnarled countenance, rough hands shaped by countless hours of using heavy tools of iron and steel, Abner could have posed for a poster of Carl Sandburg's Chicago, his rumored birthplace. Rumor made up most of what anyone actually knew about Abner. Unlike Lindbergh, who merely lived a reclusive life, Abner's whole background remained shrouded. Where he had come from, things he'd done, where he had traveled to for days or weeks at a time, the places he'd lived before settling into a small rancher outside of Solace Glen five years before—these questions dangled in the air. If he'd ever employed me as his cleaning lady, half of all the questions would have been answered pronto, but Abner never asked for help in anything, even in picking up his dirty socks. All we knew about him was that he lived alone. We also knew he maintained an unrivaled ability to build a house. No one had ever complained of shoddy work or cheap practices.

"Flip, don't you ever get tired of coming out here? It's hardly grown an inch since you saw it yesterday. Three times, was it?"

Abner never smiled or got excited. His mouth would twitch or an eye would crinkle if anything struck him as either funny or horrific. He'd reached the approximate age of my father at the time of his death—sixty-five, give or take a year—but the two struck me as different as trout and Salisbury steak. My father, short and compact compared to Abner's sinewy height, loved to talk, and dramatized everything he said with exuberant hand gestures and hysterical facial expressions. He gave me and my mother something to laugh about every day.

I blushed. "Can't help myself, Abner. Coming out here makes the dream real."

"Dreams can be real," Abner replied. He added gruffly, "Sometimes, they can be nightmares."

In those stoic, slate-colored eyes, I saw both a realist and a visionary, a man who had built too many dreams for other people to deny that imagination could become as touchable as stone, and could just as easily crumble.

My puffy eyes rested on the concrete foundation rising out of the ground. I hadn't slept much the night before, convinced the phone would ring but it never did. So much of me, the deepest part of me, lay in the beams of wood that Abner's workmen bound together with nails.

"Don't let me keep you, Abner. I just had to take a peek at it this morning."

He nodded, slapping dirt off a pair of rough work gloves. "Take a good stroll around. Looks like you could use a pick-me-up."

I let the obvious reference to my puffy eyes and droopy mouth pass and took his advice. Sure enough, the sound of hammers striking iron and the high-pitched whir of electric saws soothed a troubled spirit and restored hope. No need to worry; Tom would explain everything.

MARGARET'S HOME STOOD in the heart of Solace Glen on the opposite corner from Lee's Historical Society on Center Street, the key to the front door hidden under one of the boxes of red geraniums that lined each side of the unsheltered stone porch. Not very original, but crime rarely poked its ugly head into our affairs. We weren't big enough to have our own police department, but the Frederick County Police had an off-duty deputy program where a cop could earn a few extra bucks for helping us with special occasions like school vandalism and Fourth of July traffic control. The job previously belonged to an officious, lazy, do-nothing type called Officer Lukzay (known to most of us as Officer Look-away).

But fortunately, after his transgressions lay exposed to the light (his aid and succor to the town felon, Ferrell T.) the department forced him into early retirement in exchange for his testimony at Ferrell T.'s trial. After that, we experienced a short series of blue uniforms, but lately the same young cop kept signing up for off-duty patrol in Solace Glen, Officer Sidney Garrett. Both times I'd seen him (chomping down tuna sandwiches at Garland's Bistro, oblivious to Hilda's puppy dog looks) all he seemed able to talk about was how expensive property had gotten in Deep Creek where he'd grown up. Even Hilda, who possessed a special knack for talking about nothing for grotesque periods of time, would get bored with that conversation, no matter how good-looking the young officer.

The dark-green door of Margaret's home creaked open, and I slid the key back under the geranium box before walking into the German clapboard house that suited her so well. Painted a tranquil green with Charleston green shutters and bearing a regal air, the home had sheltered Henshaws for five generations. The lot the house stood on made up one of the largest on Center Street, outlined partially by a six-foot-tall privacy fence around the back patio and completed by a double rail fence that wrapped around ornamental grasses, orange daylillies, and tall shade trees. Margaret confided to me once that she dreaded turning over the stately place to any of her nieces or nephews. They owned sterile condos and newly built townhomes in planned communities. She feared they'd sell her beloved home to some unscrupulous, money-grubbing developer who'd turn every nook and cranny into studio condominiums. Not one of the nieces or nephews would want to maintain a large, older home or move to a dip in the road like Solace Glen, she'd moan.

I got busy dusting and, as usual, spent too much time lingering over her new book titles. Like so many of the homes I cleaned in Solace Glen, the walls of Margaret's house needed no wallpaper owing to the shelves and shelves of books. Margaret belonged to about thirty mail-order book clubs, including a canine literature club and one that sold only cookbooks. She rarely cooked, but liked to imagine she could whip up a ten-tier Lady Baltimore cake on a dare. The canine book club granted her equal inspiration. Something of an Anglophile, she liked to imagine herself trotting around the countryside with a devoted dog companion the same way the Queen is always seen with a Welsh corgi nipping at her sensible walking shoes. Lacking the Queen's income, however, she settled on decor that featured King Charles spaniels and royal pugs with disdainful, needlepoint expressions.

Organized to the point of no return, Margaret kept her massive library arranged according to subject, then sorted alphabetically by the authors' names. Fiction, poetry, history, travel, religion, on and on. She could talk to you about anything but music, both ears made of tin.

As I vacuumed her dining room with its graceful Queen Anne furniture and deep teal oriental carpet, I thought about my clients and their houses, the familiar rooms I'd tended for twenty-four years. Living rooms, dining rooms, bedrooms, nurseries, and kitchens paraded through my memory. I imagined my own fine house, finished, furnished, and filled with an admirable mix of my things and Tom's. His masculine British antiques, my country cottage mishmash. And somebody else polishing the dining-room table and scrubbing the shower stall. The little house my parents left behind lacked almost everything in comparison to the new home going up, but it didn't lack charm. Stewart Larkin would find all the charm in the world in the humble Paxton cottage. She'd no doubt make all kinds of eye-catching alterations and tasteful additions. In no time at all, people would be jibing me with questions. Why didn't *you* think of that, Flip? Why don't you let *Stewart* help you decorate your new house, Flip? Come to think of it, Flip, why don't you just step aside and let the beautiful, kind, and perfect Stewart Larkin take over your whole life? *It's been too many years. Too many years.*

When I'd made myself good and mad, I attacked Margaret's kitchen, almost wishing she lived like a slob so I'd have something to scour to death. Her house offered no such relief, however, and I quickly finished and moved on to the McKnight house, which never failed to represent a challenge. The four McKnight kids, all red-headed boys aged six to sixteen, saw to it that boredom didn't become an issue for me. On top of the usual muddy floors and bathtub rings, I had to negotiate my way past moving boxes and stacks of clothes. I left poor Mrs. McKnight arguing with the phone company and scrambling to get a hamster back in its cage.

My stomach signaled the lunch hour, so I drove over to Garland's Bistro, grateful I no longer had to frequent Roland's Café and Grill. As hateful as ever, he pinned the blame for his present misfortune on Lee, who "stole" his inheritance, and Garland, who "stole" his livelihood. He'd lost so much business since his soon-to-be ex-wife opened her own place that he'd pretty much stopped serving dinner except on weekends and had taken to serving breakfast as a way to offset the financial drain from the competition.

"If he wants to serve waffles to I-70 truckers at five A.M., that's fine with me," Garland crowed. "Just proves how powerful I am."

Compared to the scared mouse she resembled while living with Roland, no one could disagree. Nothing gave me greater satisfaction than watching Garland pull up her bootstraps last March and open her own business. Tom and I co-signed the loan from Louise's trust, knowing how thrilled she would have been to help a downtrodden friend triumph over evil.

The Bistro proved a thriving success, with Garland overseeing the kitchen and her daughter Hilda, among others, waiting tables. With her high school days almost at an end, and more than ready to take on college course work and a social life, Hilda had shed pounds and the weight of the world over the past few months. She looked like a different girl since her parents' split. Wavy black hair bouncing as she moved, milky skin, strong cheekbones clearly defined, a tribute to her heritage, and reason enough for Officer Garrett's baby blues to go off duty and check her out. But he hadn't caught on yet that this was no kid waiting tables. She saw me walk in and hustled over, ready to drop off the latest gossip and pick up a new order.

"Hey, Flip, guess who just left here with a shrimp salad sandwich? That old Lindbergh Kohl! Wanna hear the specials?" She still fought a losing battle with Maybelline, however. She'd neglected to blot her mascara that morning and spindly, black spider legs crept across her eyelids. Hilda could use a good half-day with Sally and Tina showing her the ropes. I tried not to stare at the dark lip liner she'd crayoned on with a heavy hand.

"Sure. Shoot." Unlike Roland's Cafe, where the customer performed all the work, Garland's Bistro featured an easy-to-read chalkboard on the wall with the regular items written in pretty colored chalk. The staff greeted you politely, another deviation from Roland's establishment, and let you in on the specials. And nobody complained about the added attraction of a wine and beer list. With our proximity to New Market and Frederick, Solace Glen now saw more tourists gazing at our sampling of historic buildings and old churches once word spread of a nice, new restaurant.

Hilda shot through the specials—cold roast beef sandwich, triple pasta salad, a sophisticated grilled lemon chicken with roasted vegetables—and sprinted away with my order, too busy to chitchat. The Bistro brimmed with customers besides Officer Garrett, and I took a good look around, sorry I'd missed Lindbergh, but happy to hear he'd made a rare public appearance. Sooner or later, the widows and busybodies of Solace Glen might draw him out.

The large room with its refinished wood and rich redbrick walls held the usual suspects, I noticed, but for a stranger, probably a tourist, whose pale blonde features blended into his newspaper. The Eggheads sat at a corner table, flanking Pal on either side while all three argued over cereal brands. Pal stuck to Shredded Wheat as one Egghead yelled, "Cocoa Puffs!" and the other droned nonstop, "Trix, Trix, Trix." This is what they called conversation.

The Ladies Who Lunch gathered in full force: Miss

Fizzi, Tina, and Melody. Margaret would join them over the summer when school let out. Sally and Wilbur huddled at one table with an evening candle lit early. I heard Sally brag to Hilda they'd reached their third anniversary, doubtless a first for her, and that now a little lunch date was as good as it got.

I pictured my third anniversary with Tom, how we'd want to cozy up on a sofa at home in front of our stone fireplace with a bottle of Taittinger and a box of Godiva chocolates—a shared memory.

That's when he walked through the door with Stewart Larkin on his arm.

And I do mean *on* his arm. The woman had all ten fingers clamped so tight, she looked like a walking tourniquet. She wore the same nervous expression I'd observed the day before. Tom headed straight for a quiet table for two in the back, pulled out a chair for Grace Kelly, and slid in beside her, dark eyes serious, stapled to the lady. He didn't even glance up when Hilda stood over him for an order. He didn't even peep around the room to see if the woman he promised to marry happened to sit not twenty feet away with her mouth wide open and eyeballs bugging out of her pasty face. The room grew noticeably quiet, with mumbled voices and heads that bobbed in my direction.

Should I sit there as if fully aware of this little rendezvous, thank you very much? Should I continue to act floored until Tom finally noticed that the woman in the front seat of the audience was *me*? Should I march over and make a scene? *Take your perfect manicure off my man, you femme fatale! Go buy your own Taittinger and Godiva!* Or should I simply evacuate the building?

Fortunately, Garland saved the day. She recognized the shock in my eyes, the worry, the fear. She left her station behind the open kitchen window and headed straight to Tom, bent down, and whispered in his ear.

His head shot up, zeroed in on me, yet he appeared to freeze. Just for a moment, but enough that I picked up on it. He thanked Garland, excused himself to Stewart (who winced at his sudden departure), and hurried across the room to my table.

Come on home, honey. I forced my lips into a plastic smile.

Tom leaned down and kissed my forehead as he might a baby sister. "Sorry I didn't call last night. I have a new client with an urgent personal problem, plus several financial and contractual issues."

I glanced across the room at the wide-eyed beauty, her eyes clamped to Tom as tight as her fingers had wrapped around his arm. "Is that what she is? A new *client*?" My fake smile iced up.

Tom's eyes registered a sudden perplexity. "Why would I say it if it weren't true?"

"I don't know." I waited for him to spill out The Secret History of Tom and Stewart.

He opened his mouth to say something, thought better of it, and replied, "This young woman has a very serious problem. I met with her and her father last night in Washington until very late, and ran out of the office without my cell phone or I would have called. I'm going to go back to her table now and I cannot invite you to join us." He leaned down and whispered in my ear, "Jealousy doesn't become you, Flip."

As he started to walk away, I glared, a green-eyed monkey, at the lady in distress.

"Yeah," I muttered, "I'm sure her problems are serious. Real life and death stuff."

Tom didn't skip a beat. "It is life or death," he said over one shoulder, so low nobody else heard him. "It certainly is life or death."

CHAPTER 5

✻

SULKING OVER MY standard gin and tonic later that evening, it occurred to me that I never had mentioned to Tom the name of the person who bought my house, that "unforgettable name," Stewart Larkin. I'd simply told him, as I'd told everyone else, that some man signed on the dotted line and I had to hurry with the packing. A Frederick title company run by a friend of Tom's handled the paperwork and, as usual for the company's Solace Glen properties, the final settlement was scheduled to take place in Tom's office. So it wasn't until Stewart set up an appointment and walked through his door that Tom discovered his former student could claim Solace Glen, and my house, as home sweet home. For whatever reason—jealousy, fear, no self-confidence— her dramatic entrance onto our small town stage upended me as if, as a practical joke, the playwright inserted a second leading lady into a familiar scene, causing me to flub my lines.

At least Tom did call that night, complaining about his workload and the weekend conference he had to attend in Richmond. "This Larkin business has set me back. Can you spare me until Monday?"

"Monday! That's six days from now!" We'd seen each other every day since December. Now some strange woman swoops into town, captivates my fiancé, and picks up my house, to boot. "Oh, Tom."

"And don't expect a lot of calls or postcards, either. I'll be on the run or hitting the books morning till midnight. But I'll make it up to you. I'll add an extra day to the honeymoon."

That calmed the beast in me. Maybe by the end of the summer he'd have stacked up enough infractions to add an extra week to our trip.

"Well. OK." I had to ask. "Tom, I know you can't tell me what you and Miss Larkin talk about, but . . ."

"But what?" I detected a note of impatience in his voice, which made my mouth go dry.

"Can't you give me some reassurance?"

"Reassurance? That's a strange word to use. What do you mean?"

A direct question that deserved a direct answer. "I mean, you knew her before. Years ago."

"How do you know that, pray tell?" Now he was toying with me.

"Stewart said so herself." Certainly true, but I wasn't about to fill him in on how my circle of women friends gossiped on the subject.

"You had a right long conversation with the lady, did you?" The droll tone masked something else, but I couldn't put a finger on it, drowning in my own paranoia.

"Not exactly. She just happened to mention the long passage of time since she'd last attacked you before flying up the stairs to lay hold of you again and take up all your time for the next week so the saint you're *engaged to* can act the jealous fool."

Tom burst out laughing. "But you're not acting, are you?"

"Oh, I'm really chortling in my glee here, Tom. Stop laughing. I thought this Larkin business was so serious. So life and death."

The laughter quit at once. "It is. I can tell you this much, Stewart has been threatened. She's being stalked by someone with a particularly sick mind and has moved here from across the country. Her father is trying to help her, as am I."

"Oh." That put a slightly different spin on things. "She's lucky she has a father who'll go to such lengths. Are the police involved?"

"The L.A. police were involved, yes, but the stalking and threats started to escalate. Calls from phone booths, letters, 'gifts' left in her car. Whoever's doing this knows her every step and has, so far, eluded detection. She and her father are hoping that a temporary move across country to a small house in a small town will end the threat or draw the man out, so she can get on with her life without the police and investigators and bodyguards. For caution's sake, she will keep one bodyguard here, a man who's also a private investigator, but they don't want police involvement unless necessary."

"Jeepers, all that? I feel sorry for her, but she's not going to win Miss Congeniality toting around a bodyguard and bringing the threat of a stalker to town." The green-eyed monkey gripped less tightly, but didn't completely let go. "What is she going to do to make a living?" Maybe she could be the new church sexton.

"Stewart doesn't really need to make a living. Her father's a well-known industrialist with business interests everywhere, but it's my understanding she'll simply switch to working on his East Coast concerns. She has a law degree and an M.B.A."

That sort of beat out my high school diploma. Fortunately, the subject of Stewart Larkin ended. The talk turned to our magnificent new home, hiring Ivory, Reverend McKnight leaving us, the continual question mark of a wedding date, the usual small-town chitchat.

"It's just as well you'll be so busy and are going out of town," I said before we hung up. "Now I'll have time for my dual affair with the Eggheads."

"While I'm secretly making time with Tina and Marlene."

"Which reminds me!" Time to do something positive for a change besides wallow in jealousy and self-pity. "How would you like Tina as your secretary? She's experienced enough. And she's not a major felon like your last office manager."

"Ouch." He paused, pondering the suggestion. "I don't know. She's awfully sensitive. I might scare her."

"You are a tower of terror. Why not call and offer her a trial period? See how you fit each other."

He agreed and yawned, ready to crash. We said our good night's and sent our love both ways. I sailed off to bed, hoping the trust and security I felt wasn't a blip on the screen. My love for Tom floated again on an even keel, but all night long that irritating monkey whispered the million things that could rock the boat.

CHAPTER 6

❊

B Y WEDNESDAY AFTERNOON, there was nothing the whole town didn't know, in the usual skewed fashion, as evidenced by the high caliber of the Eggheads' conversation. I pulled up to the diesel pump at Pal's Crown station and fell under immediate fire.

"So that pretty blonde bought your place, huh, Flip? I thought you said a man bought your house."

"Yeah, you said a man. You must be blind as a bat wearing a blindfold."

The one Egghead slapped the other one in the chest. "Make sense, jackass. How's a bat gonna put on a blindfold?"

"That's my point." The inanity ballooned. "I heard her name is Stewart Larkin. Any relation to you and J.E.B. Stuart? I mean, you being basically illegitimate and all."

I pried open the gas cap. "Only you, Jesse/Jules,

whichever one you are, could magically equate a first name with a surname." He looked proud. "Let me explain this to you two brainless twits yet again. I am not illegitimate any more than you. Way back when, when J.E.B. Stuart's child was born, she was legally adopted. So technically, I have Bell and Stuart blood in my veins, but I can assure you, I am not illegitimate. Check it out with our town lawyer if you wish."

Egghead Number One guffawed and the other followed suit. "Seems to me that that particular lawyer might be a bit prejudiced, being engaged to you. He'd be motivated to slick up your legitimacy."

"Yeah," chimed in Egghead Number Two, "slick it up real good. The engagement's still on, isn't it, Flip? Nothing's come between you two, has *she*?"

They both found this horrifically funny. I sneered and pulled the trigger on the gas gun.

About this time, Pal stepped out of the office wiping his hands on a dirty rag. Suggs, the only help available now that Pal's little brother had returned to Georgia, lumbered around in the background against his usual trappings of greasy tools and patched-up tires.

"What's so funny?" Pal chirped. "You talking about that old Taco Bell commercial again, Jules? Don't you love that itty bitty dog?"

"No," I snapped, before either Egghead could spew forth any more drivel, "they were probing me for information on the newly arrived Miss Larkin and on the status of my engagement. For all ears to hear, her name is spelled with an *e-w* not a *u-a,* and just last night Tom and I were talking about a wedding date."

"But you couldn't get him to set anything in stone, could ya? Come on, now, could ya?"

My cheeks burned through the brave smirk I wore.

"What'd Miss Larkin move here for, anyhow?" Pal queried. "Smart, pretty woman like that oughta be in a big city."

"Yes," I agreed, real snippy, "she doesn't belong here in the State Center for Troll Women." It didn't seem out of bounds to reveal, "Some man's been stalking her in California so she moved here to get away from him."

"A stalker!" all three trilled in chorus.

"That happens a lot in California," offered a wise Egghead. "Everybody has their own stalker there."

Pal wagged his head. "I still don't get why she chose this place."

"She's here for safety's sake," I explained, "and because she knows some people here."

"*Some* people?" interjected an Egghead. "Or *one* in particular?"

"Yeah," sniggered his twin, "one in particular, like Tom Knight-in-Shining-Amore Scott?"

To add insult to injury, Marlene Worthington pulled up and wrestled herself out of an old Ford Mustang, a hefty turtle briefly shedding its shell. She had to throw in her measly two and a half cents. "You've been engaged two whole months now, Flip. Long engagement, quick divorce?"

"Oh, so nice to see you in the daylight, Marlene. You'd know about the quick divorce part, wouldn't you?" Marlene's personal life might prove a salve for my own sore subject. "By the way, I've been meaning to ask, does Mr. Marlene Worthington actually exist? Because nobody in this town has ever seen an eye or a tooth in support of the theory."

The Eggheads snickered at this new diversion while

Pal good-naturedly unscrewed the Mustang's gas cap.

Marlene, bug-eyed, huffed, "You mind your own p's and q's, Flip Paxton." The hatred and jealousy spilled out. "Don't fancy yourself traveling in a lofty social plane just because you somehow got engaged to Tom Scott and are vaguely connected to the Bells due to a historic one-afternoon stand, so to speak." Then she purred, "I'd keep a sharper eye on my fiancé, if I were you. People are already saying what an attractive couple he and Miss Larkin make. Much more attractive than the town maid on his arm."

Both Eggheads drew in a breath, prepared for the boxing match, but I didn't give them the satisfaction, and continued to spar with Marlene on my own terms.

"Exactly what sort of couple did you and Mr. Worthington make? Or was it Dr. Worthington? The Right Reverend Worthington? Cell block 27 Worthington?" Pal and the Eggheads particularly liked that one. "Maybe you could describe for us the circumstances of *your* engagement, Marlene. I might pick up some tips."

"The circumstances of my engagement, not to mention my marriage, are off-limits to you and everybody else in this stink hole. If my mother had had the decency to leave me anything at all, I'd be out of here in a flash."

I wasn't about to hear Marlene trash Louise's good name. "If you had one ounce of the decency your mother possessed, she probably would have left you *everything*. Don't you get it?" That happy thought shut her up for a second or two. "As it was, she left you enough to get by on. By the way, should we mail you your check this month as usual, or would you like to have the bank dole it out in ones and fives?"

Marlene swelled up like a blowfish and snatched the

gas gun away from Pal just as he started to insert it into her tank. She aimed it at me, both fingers on the trigger. Pal gasped and the Eggheads scurried backward behind their ambulance. I heard that rat Suggs say in an undertone, "Go for it, babe." He'd probably toss her a match next.

My fist tightened around the gas gun in my own hand.

Before anything happened that could wind up in a newspaper, a horn tooted in merry fashion and a white vintage Mercedes-Benz pulled up right behind my car and on the other side of Marlene's Mustang. Stewart rolled down her window and waved at everyone like she'd been appointed grand marshal of the parade that day. "Hello there!"

Pal and the Eggheads gawked at her, pillars of salt. For a long moment, nobody moved, not even Marlene, then a figure slowly oozed out of the garage. Suggs moved in a daze toward the Mercedes, hypnotized. He shuffled right up to the window and actually spoke distinguishable words, not the usual guttural grunts and nasty, staccato phrases. "Yes, ma'am. May I help you?"

That was all it took to turn on the light. Stewart beamed up at him, a beatific countenance to match the angelic beauty. "Yes, thank you. I'm late meeting my father and need some diesel. Plus, I have a confession to make."

Oh, boy. The Virgin Mary wanted to confess her sins to Beelzebub.

Suggs blinked at the sparkling, deep blue eyes of the vision. "Yes, ma'am?"

"I'm not good at pumping my own gas. We always had chauffeurs so I didn't learn to drive until very late in life. Would you help me out? Give me a lesson?"

This time I blinked. How the hell does anyone in America get past age sixteen without having to pump her own gas? Unless this amounted to a complete fabrication, I couldn't fathom why she'd lie about such a silly thing.

All of Suggs's gruffness dissolved and his bulldog mouth, which bore a perpetual scowl, managed to lift into a half-smile. One hand opened the car door for Her Royal Highness while the other attempted to slick back his crew cut, leaving a greasy skid mark across one ear. He stepped aside while Stewart gracefully slid out of the car. The long eyelashes batted excitedly, as though Ralph Lauren offered to show her a secret design.

The rest of us stood watching this little beauty and the beast show in amazement. The Eggheads crept forward, eyes glued to Suggs and Stewart in a way they'd regard two world-renowned surgeons who happened to drop by the gas station to illustrate an astonishing new way to remove splinters. Marlene forgot her vicious intentions and Pal gazed at Stewart as intently as he would a shiny, new carburetor, as fascinated as anyone by a woman exotic enough to attract a stalker.

Suggs escorted his pupil to the diesel pump where I stood and proceeded with the lesson, using me as a prop.

"You see how Flip has her finger on the pump trigger there? It doesn't take much strength and any dolt can do it." His neck flushed pink and he stammered at her. "Not that you're a dolt." I guess that only left me.

Stewart's ladylike giggle put him at ease. I wondered if I could laugh like that if I tried. "But I am a dolt because I've never learned how to do this very well. I always douse myself." She shined her light on me. "Hi, Flip! It's good to see you again! You don't mind being part of my gas pump lesson, do you?"

"Oh, no," I replied, completely disarmed by her courtesy. "Knowledge is power. But I'll step aside so you can have a better lesson."

I cut short the fill at ten dollars even and handed the gas gun to Suggs. Pal came to his senses long enough to take the ten bucks from my outstretched hand.

While I screwed on the cap, Suggs reset the counter and started the lesson from scratch, explaining to Stewart everything you never wanted to know about diesel and how to get it into your tank. Pal and the Eggheads listened with all ears like he was a tour guide at the Ford plant. Even Marlene paid attention. She hadn't seen this side of Suggs any more than the rest of us.

I lingered, pretending to sort through cleansers and rags, intensely curious about Stewart. With a natural good humor, and an open, even vulnerable manner, she had a knack for bringing out the best in everyone, which made her easy to like, easy to be with, and hard to work up any jealousy over. She stood next to Suggs, nodding politely at his amazing gas pumping insights, brows knit in earnest. She had all the appearance of an engrossed student. I imagined she looked much the same thirteen years earlier when she sat in Tom's class. She obviously had a talent for giving a man her complete attention, no matter what the subject, business law or petroleum.

One thing rang clear, she'd picked up four new male members of the Drooling Over Stewart Larkin Fan Club.

After daintily handling the gas gun, eyes dancing at Suggs, asking "Like this?" two or three times, the lesson ended. She paid in cash and considerately backed out so I wouldn't have to move my Volkswagen. The testosterone quadruplets waved farewell in unison and returned to normal life. Pal waited on Marlene; the Eggheads climbed into their ambulance, distressing each other over Stewart's dangerous situation; and Suggs's scowl returned. He slouched back into the darkness of the garage, a rodent into its hole.

Nobody noticed or cared that I still stood there, stupidly dusting the smile off the face of a bottle of Mr. Clean, eyes tightly focused on the white Mercedes-Benz as it drove away. And nobody else noticed or cared when a small, nondescript gray car slowly pulled out of a side street and followed the Mercedes until both disappeared from sight.

CHAPTER 7

❋

I TRIED TO reach Tom on Wednesday night to tell him about the suspicious gray car I'd seen, but without success. Granted, nothing but pure instinct propped up my worry. I dialed again Thursday morning, but by then he'd set up a message informing the general public of his absence from town for a few days. Because of a stubborn, old-fashioned streak, he often "forgot" his cell phone, or simply turned it off. Seeing someone answer a call in a quiet restaurant or carry on a cell conversation in a store or on an elevator flung him into a foul humor for hours.

Not knowing what else to do, I sat on the information about the car, since it probably amounted to nothing, anyway. With Tom away for a long weekend, my time would be better spent focused on something practical, like a major self-improvement project.

Stewart's arrival in Solace Glen and the instant effect she had on the general male population (Tom, unfortunately, included), prompted me to carry out two tasks I rarely performed—get a haircut before six months elapsed and buy something glittery.

Sally agreed to take me on that Saturday with Tina in standby position, ready to launch an assault on my fingernails.

"What's got into you, chickadee?" Sally smacked her gum and threw a bib over my shoulders. "Oh, shoot. That's one of the twin's. Here's a clean one. You bored with Tom out of town?"

"Nope. Thought I'd do a little something different to keep *him* from getting bored when he gets back."

"Oh. I gotcha. Need that *Sports Illustrated* supermodel look, huh? Keep him on his toes." She raised my chin with her forefinger. "You nervous about him helping that pretty Stewart Larkin with her troubles? Being stalked or something, right?"

Solace Glen had no need of a newspaper. "Yeah, she's had a pretty hard time of it out West."

"And she used to know Tom, right?" The tone carried a forced nonchalance.

"Yeah, years ago. So," I switched back to the subject at hand, "I want to do something different today."

Tina squealed with delight and started begging. "Can I paint your nails hot pink? Please say yes, Flip, pleeeze."

I hesitated, but recognized the pleasure it would give to do such a silly thing. "Sure, Tina. What the hey."

She practically collapsed with joy. "I'll pick out something right now! Oh, I've wanted to get hold of your hands for years!"

"I wouldn't say that in public," Sally quipped and swung me around to face the mirror. She picked up a strand of dull brown, shoulder-length hair. "Usual cut? Two inches all around?"

I stared at the woman in the mirror—the all-too-usual hair, the all-too-common features, the all-too-plain skin tone. Stewart held an advantage by only seven or eight years, yet she managed to maintain a shininess, a copper quality of being bright and new that I'd definitely let slip, if ever I possessed such a thing. Suddenly, that's what I wanted. I wanted Tom to look at me and see something shiny and new, to feel proud of my appearance. I wanted to see more in his eyes than a comfort zone. I wanted to see fire and adoration.

My hands gripped the chair arms. "Give me layers and highlights."

Sally stopped popping her gum and Tina froze in midair over bottles of nail polish. "Good Lord."

"And . . ." I could hardly bring myself to say it, "I need some new makeup."

"New?" Sally bent down and looked at me like I had purple skin. "Since when did you own any makeup at all?"

"I have some lipstick," I said weakly.

Sally's laugh filled the room. "Roll out the whole line, Tina! This girl is a woman now!" And she launched into song, happily tearing up tinfoil and mixing together a foul-smelling glop that would soon cover my fearless head.

MUCH LATER, IT seemed like forever later, I left the two miracle workers. Sally and Tina stood framed in the doorway of the beauty parlor, holding each other up after their exhausting three-hour operation, peeling plastic gloves off each other's fingers.

"Remember, now, hon," Sally coached, "you're like a soufflé right out the oven. Let people see you while you're still fresh 'cause this heat is sure to make you fall flat any minute."

I used my pink nails to tap goodbye against the car window, causing Tina to go into spasms, and started the car. Before Tom returned the next day and beheld the flatter version of this glamorama, I wanted to add to my meager collection of earrings. Not born with an excess of gorgeous features—brown eyes a little too almond, nose a tad crooked in the center, lips a bit too thin—I had to make do with the leftovers. If I had to rank body parts on a chart, I'd count my ears as number one and my neck second on the list. As a result, dangle earrings remained a weapon of choice.

I checked out the amazing new me in the rearview mirror and headed over to Connolly's Jewelry Store, anxious to hear two different opinions on the big transformation.

Melody and her husband, Michael, waited on a couple of out-of-towners when I breezed through the door. Melody heard the tinkling of the shop bell and barely glanced up, calling, "Be with you in a minute, Ma'am."

Michael finished ringing up his customer and looked my way only to gape.

I fluffed the highlighted locks and struck a catwalk pose. The approval in his Irish eyes made my day and he humored me by tilting a mirror so I could primp and strut to my heart's content. He flung a thumb at Melody, grinning, as if to say, wait'll she gets a load of you!

Melody finished up with her customer and turned,

donning her best saleslady smile. "May I help you find . . ." Her eyes popped wide and she screamed. "Is it YOU? Is it really *you*? My God, Michael, grab a tiara from the safe, the Queen has arrived!"

"Do you think Tom will like it?"

"Are you kidding? Look at Michael. He's speechless. He's practically drooling." She knocked him in the side with an elbow. "Stop drooling."

Michael, ever the gentleman, though hardly ever speechless, retired to a corner and busied himself with ring displays.

"So," Melody reached a hand out and fondled a curl that dipped into my chin, "who else has seen you? Besides Sally and Tina, obviously."

"Nobody else. I came straight to the ones who matter. I figured I'd pick out some earrings and then hit the Bistro."

"New ear attire, too? You're really putting on the dog. How come?" Melody sidled up to me.

"No reason."

She squinted her eyes, the color of coffee beans, and reared her head. "I smell competition and her name is Stewart Larkin. Oh, I've heard the talk. You think you have to compete with her, sweetheart? You think Tom is a man to be swayed by appearances?"

"Obviously not if he's engaged to me."

Melody slapped a hand to her side. "There you go again, running yourself down, something you've been doing too much of lately. Heavens," she picked up one of my fingers, "you even got a manicure. Flip, where's your confidence?"

"Melody," I winced, "you hit the nail on the head. I've lost it. And as far as Stewart being competition,

I don't know. How do you compete against such a beautiful woman who is also an incredibly nice person? It's depressing."

She squeezed my arm and led me to a glass counter. "Well, maybe your instincts are right and this day o' beauty is just what you need as a confidence booster. But you really don't have to worry about another woman stealing your guy. He's building you a house, for God's sake."

"Yeah, he wouldn't want to squander an investment. Speaking of houses, I have a settlement date with Stewart on Monday."

Ever the businesswoman, Melody replied, "So it's nice she owes you money."

Life could have continued as usual from that point on with chitchat over jewelry and nail polish, with the worst of my worries being whether highlights in mousy hair could fend off a beautiful woman, with the slow ticktock of summer in a small town.

But the door to the shop opened with the tinkling of a bell, and Stewart's arrival in Solace Glen became mere prologue.

"You won't find it in here! Good God, you know you can't find anything *worthwhile* in this feed-and-seed town!" Cecile Crosswell, the infamously rude C.C. we thought we'd gotten rid of six months before, compliments of Screamin' Larry, cemented her bony back against the door, refusing to follow Leonard one step further.

Leonard Crosswell, dapper as always in a custom-made linen suit and rakish black tie, didn't bother to turn around when he said, "You never know what you'll discover in these quaint, country boutiques."

Melody's coffee-bean eyes blackened and she hissed, "Did that fox just call our jewelry store 'country'?"

The fox slid straight for the diamond counter and lowered his gold-rimmed glasses halfway down the elongated snout. "Mr. Connolly! If you're not too busy, I'm in the market for a bracelet. It's our silver anniversary, if you can believe that."

Michael appeared from the back room mumbling, "How about a pair of silver bullets?" He silently nodded a greeting to Leonard, who never raised his eyes from the display case, and unlocked a sliding glass door next to the diamonds, drawing out a couple of nice sterling pieces for Leonard to fondle.

C.C., who stood a good twenty feet away, howled, "No, no, no! Not what I had in mind at all." She crossed her well-toned arms together, immutable as an Apache warrior awaiting enforcement of her decision.

"Mmmm." Leonard eyed the one bracelet in his hand as if it contained traces of Ebola virus. "Perhaps not." He inspected the other bracelet in much the same fashion and shoved it back at Michael, pointing at a short strand of diamonds.

C.C. huffed and raked a set of fuchsia nails through cropped, raven hair. Her rolling pupils rolled my way and her brows twisted, as if I looked vaguely familiar but she couldn't pinpoint the face. Suddenly, it dawned. "Flip Paxton! My Gawd, is that you? What did you do to yourself, hit every Hair Cuttery east of the Mississippi?"

"On behalf of all their employees, I thank you." I raked my own pink nails through a lock of highlights.

"Oh, look, Leonard," she drawled. "Our maid finally discovered the joys of an emery board. Doesn't she look . . . different?"

Before I could bark, "I'm not your maid any longer," Melody growled, "I'd like to jam an emery board up her . . ."

"Stop babbling," snapped Leonard, fingering the diamonds. "Can't you see I'm trying to concentrate?"

But concentration was not the watchword of the day. C.C. squawked as the shop door behind her abruptly opened, jolting her forward into the middle of the floor. Grace Kelly entered the room wrapped in a full-skirted, white cotton dress, clear-eyed and fresh as a new bar of soap. I caught a whiff of White Linen.

The special olfactory nerve Leonard must have nurtured over the years for other women kicked in because he immediately transferred his rapt attention to Stewart. "Why, Miss Larkin!" The fox eyes gleamed bright as the jewels in his paw. "What a surprise! And what a pleasure!"

As he strode toward the squeaky-clean goddess in white, I remembered the charm he exuded in Lee's direction months before, when he hungered for something she possessed. I wondered what he wanted from Stewart, and felt a strange protectiveness toward her.

C.C., Leonard's awful mirror half, reconstituted herself from the floor and intercepted the pass. She jumped in between Leonard and Stewart. "Stooo-wert. What an odd coincidence. Are you alone?"

Before Stewart could respond, the shop bell tinkled again and a tall, platinum-haired man stepped into the store. He wore a crisp, navy blue suit. A navy and red silk tie anchored the center of his white dress shirt. It struck me how incongruous he and Leonard appeared in this little shop, like two corporate tycoons who'd stepped off a Learjet to buy a slushie at a 7-Eleven.

"Conrad!" C.C. multitasked; she poked out her flat

chest, sucked in a nonexistent stomach, and directed a sarcastic comment in Stewart's direction. "You must be doing a little early shopping for Daddy's day."

Stewart remained in perfect Snow White mode while C.C. snagged Conrad's arm and coiled around it, rising on tiptoe to plant a kiss on his clean-shaven cheek. Leonard, too busy ogling Stewart to notice his wife's equal interest in the father, sidled closer.

"So that's the famous industrialist," Melody whispered. "Not bad looking, if I do say so myself."

"You always do." Content to have the focus switched off my trip to the beauty parlor, this little sideshow captured our full attention.

Leonard extended an arm toward Conrad Larkin's free hand. "Conrad, whatever are you doing in *this* little town? I've never seen you outside a major city."

"Then you missed my entire childhood," Conrad smoothly replied, the tiniest smile playing across clamped lips. "Stewart and I enjoyed the party your firm hosted in Washington last month." Given Stewart's age, I figured he hovered in his mid sixties. But for the silver hair, Conrad looked more like a man in his mid forties.

"I bet a surgeon gave him that good-looking face," I whispered to Melody.

"I don't care where he got it."

I turned and beheld a Melody I'd never seen before. Her dark eyes, positively mesmerized, latched on to Conrad Larkin as if he were the Hope Diamond. Perhaps all the women in town would go as gaga over the father as the men had over the daughter.

"*We,*" C.C. emphasized the word as if she meant the royal we, "are actually making plans to move back to this area, but more in the country. We made such a killing on the sale of our former property, what with the fire insurance, that we just made a bid on another little estate down the road."

To hear her tell it, Solace Glen crawled with ritzy "estates."

"Where might that estate be?" Michael asked casually from across the room, pretending to polish a ring.

Both Leonard and C.C. tossed wrinkled noses in the air as if to say, none of your beeswax, buck-o, but Leonard murmured loud enough for all to hear, "North of here. North of Frederick, close to the Monocacy and that charming, old covered bridge at Loy's Station."

"You mean you bought a family farm that somebody can't afford to hold on to anymore," Michael said quietly, but also loud enough for all to hear.

"I always suspected you'd make a good robber baron," Conrad deftly disentangled himself from C.C., "watching how you've managed your business interests all these years. You've done quite well with your holdings in my network."

"Until recently. But you do have some very attractive holdings." Leonard's fox eyes practically bore holes through Stewart. He shifted them away long enough to say, "I tried to see you a couple of weeks ago when I found myself in L.A., but you'd been called to Philadelphia unexpectedly. I've tried reaching you several times, in fact, to discuss some questions I have about the latest financial report of L.C.S. Something doesn't compute. You're a difficult man to get hold of."

Before Conrad could respond, Michael called out, "Mr. Crosswell, are you still interested in that bracelet you're holding, or would you like to see something else?"

In a liquid move, Leonard slipped Stewart's arm

through his and clasped the diamond strand around her wrist. Conrad arched a brow, cooly amused at Leonard's blatant flirtation. Not so cool, C.C. looked like every stitch of her face-lift might pop out.

"Mr. Crosswell," Stewart began uneasily, "I think your wife is a better model for such an exquisite piece." She started picking at the lock, but Leonard held tight.

"Leonard, Leonard, Leonard. How many times have I begged you to call me Leonard. You're no longer a child." His eyes raked her up and down.

"No, she's not a child." Conrad stepped in, still mildly amused but responsive to his daughter's discomfort. He snatched the bracelet off, dropping it into C.C.'s outstretched palm. "She's *my* child," he said drolly.

The beautiful woman in her mid thirties with the dual degrees didn't flinch at the word. She rather seemed to enjoy it, and matched her powerful father's twitching lips and arched brow—a shared joke. She lightly rubbed her wrist and walked away from the grown-ups, peeking into display counters, searching for a new toy.

Having spared his daughter from the linen-suited predator, Conrad turned on the charm and engaged in innocuous small talk about the local area, shared business interests in the Mid-Atlantic, and the rising cost of real estate and oil.

Half-listening, I grew more interested in the body language between father and daughter, the way Stewart occasionally glanced Conrad's way and flashed a smile, holding up a trinket as if it symbolized a whole other realm of private jokes. The duel mannerisms, the indulgent flick of a wrist, the wry rise of a well-groomed brow. With my mounting interest, envy also surged.

I wondered, would it have been like this with my father? Would we have read each other's thoughts with a quick glimpse across a room?

C.C., who by this time wore the diamond bracelet clamped firmly around her right wrist, raising Melody's and Michael's hopes, led the talk in the direction she wanted. "I didn't realize you and Leonard had so many mutual business connections. So is that why you and Stewart are here? Business?"

Conrad peered down at her patronizingly. "Partly. Stewart just bought a house here in Solace Glen."

"Oh, rrrreally?" Leonard followed Stewart's movements around the shop.

"Stewart bought the house?" C.C. couldn't hide her disbelief. "What about you? Is this a house for the two of you?"

Stewart answered the question as she browsed over watches. "No. It's my house. I have my own place in L.A., so it makes sense to have my own home now that I'll be helping Daddy with some of his dealings here in the East. Now he'll have a place to park when he's jetting around. Even the best hotels can be sterile and unfriendly."

"Splendid!" Leonard sounded almost giddy. "But why Solace Glen, of all places?"

"I went to Hood, remember? I have old friends here," she replied, very matter-of-fact. But a fact that mattered to me. "Besides, a small town is less stressful. I wanted to return to a place and time in my life where everything was simple. No traffic. No crime."

C.C. whipped her skinny body around to face Stewart in the ring. "But what house could you possibly want in this fly pit?"

That's when I tossed my hat in the ring, just for the

pleasure of jerking C.C.'s chain. "My house. She bought my house, C.C."

C.C. stared at me as if I'd said Jesus stood outside and wanted a word with her.

"WHAT?"

"That's right." Stewart coolly checked out a jewelry box. "I bought Flip's charming little cottage and we have settlement on Monday, don't we, Flip?"

She smiled at me conspiratorially, pals with a shared secret.

"Gawd!" C.C. could hide nothing—not rage, not astonishment, not impatience, not judgment. Astonishment came tumbling out now. And jealousy, a jealousy much more palpable and real than the slight dip in self-confidence I had experienced of late. "You're going to live in that house *alone*?"

"I'll be around, and Stewart will have other protection." Conrad spoke in a firm voice, addressing Leonard exclusively. "Stewart's well-being is always at the heart of my actions."

"So you'll be visiting her often?" C.C. slunk back toward him, absentmindedly tapping each diamond on the bracelet as if doing a headcount of children. "Staying at the house with her?"

"Visiting," Stewart answered again, making sure the answer belonged to her, not her father, a small way of asserting some degree of independence. "Daddy's business is expanding in the East. He's had to spend more time here."

Conrad ended the discussion. "We need to be moving along, Stewart. Pick out a little something and let's get on to the airport. We don't want to keep Mr. Parker waiting."

Stewart swiftly plucked the nearest gold watch from a rack and signaled the price to her father. He withdrew a billfold from his breast pocket and laid out the cash for Michael to ring up. The two nodded fare-thee-well's to all around and hurried out. I watched them cross the street where a driver in a limousine leaped out and opened a door. It struck me what a cocooned life Stewart led. How could someone so protected be the object of a stalker's threat? Or was the cocoon drawn around her as a result of the threat?

"So Stewart's moving to Solace Glen," the fox repeated gleefully to himself.

"And she bought a very nice watch." Michael nodded appreciatively, a Saturday in the store not wasted.

"And she's going to live in *your* house." C.C. scowled at me, the great betrayer. "Ugh! I despise this bracelet!" She tore it off her wrist and slapped it on the counter in front of Melody and me, eyes glaring coal hot at her husband. "It's been used before."

Chapter 8

"Where's Screamin' Larry when you need him?" Melody groused, and went about her business.

Larry's renewed harassment of C.C. offered us some consolation at least. If he could drive her away once, he could do it again.

The rest of the day spanned out in pretty tame fashion. Following Sally's advice, I made sure everybody in town got a good gander at her handiwork, making a dramatic appearance at the Bistro. Margaret and Miss Fizzi made the appropriate amount of fuss, flapping big eyes at each other and saying the word, "Finally!" about a million times. Garland burbled, pacing around in circles like I was an important Civil War monument. Hilda said I looked so spectacular she'd consider getting her own transformation, and pitifully slid questioning eyes at Officer Garrett to see if he'd offer an opinion. Nothing.

My new hairdo also generated the typical dueling Egghead reaction.

"Whoa, Flip. What'd you use on your head, Selsun Blue?"

"That's for dandruff, dummy, she doesn't have dandruff, not that we know about, she got lights put in. What'd you use, Flip? Grecian Formula or Summer Blonde?"

"Greek Formula is just for men, dumbo. You didn't use something just for men, didja, Flip? Might make ya go bald or something."

Like anything they say is worth responding to.

At the Presbyterian Church on Sunday, everybody devoted themselves to topics less superficial than hair, like the big farewell party for Reverend McKnight, the new interim pastor, and how the heck would we raise money for the youth group's summer trip to Montreat without McKnight's barbershop quartet? Word had also spread that the gorgeous California babe (already closely connected to Tom and spotted at several Solace Glen establishments) was, in fact, in hiding. Many church members, mostly women, fretted that the man who stalked Stewart would follow her to Solace Glen and crime would jump one hundred percent.

"Moving from California to Maryland is pretty drastic stuff," one lady whimpered as she wrung her hands. "It means nobody could catch him out there, even with all the Larkin money. So how's she going to be protected if this criminal shows up here?"

"How are any of us going to be protected?" Another woman took flight on the subject. "What if this man decides to stalk other women he sees? We're not prepared for cloak and dagger in this little town. Nobody even owns a burglar alarm. It's terrifying!"

I kept my mouth shut about the suspicious gray car I'd seen, the hysteria level already accelerating at fever pitch.

Ivory interrupted the nervous chatter long enough to point out the fresh lemonade, then swished back into the kitchen singing the brazenly pagan "Aquarius" with lyrics of her own making. I poked my head in the door to remind her to think about a salary number and that we'd talk in the next day or so. She winked at me, drumming fingers on the counter, experimenting with words that rhymed with *Aquarius*. It was a wonder she got so much work done given the amount of time she spent entertaining herself.

Per usual, my thoughts wandered during the service. I started out thinking about a salary figure for Ivory. Before I could work that one out, I puzzled over how Garland, sitting two pews ahead of me, could have stayed married to Roland for so long. He sat across the aisle from her, refusing to give up the Bell family pew, the only one sitting there now. Since Garland left him, Roland had aged ten years, growing grayer by the minute. Gray skin, hair, eyes, personality. Everything about him gray as a summer storm. I couldn't believe I used to be so intimidated by him. Next, I wondered what time Tom would make it home and why he hadn't called me even once since Tuesday. Finally, the silent prayer time found me completely wrapped up in Leonard's open lust for Stewart (he usually maintained a pathological secrecy), and his business connections with Conrad. From what I could glean, Conrad used Leonard's D.C. law firm on occasion. As a result, Leonard and his partners had enjoyed some lucrative investments the past couple of years. I didn't trust Leonard myself, and wondered if Conrad Larkin had any doubts. But I did not expect the doubts and suspicions Lee generated the next morning.

"WE'RE BACK! WE'RE back! We're back!"

Lee Jenner Gibbon flung her athletic limbs across my back as if jumping into a pool of water rather than leaping onto my bed.

"Ummph! Jeeze! You scared the hell out of me! What time is it?"

"Oh, about seven." She rolled to the side and plumped a pillow up behind her head. "I was so antsy to get back that I made Sam drive to Frederick last night. We had a nice dinner and stayed in a B and B. Frederick's so close, you never think to visit it like a tourist, but that's what we did for the last night of our wonderful honeymoon."

"Wonderful, was it?" I yawned and turned over to inspect Lee. "You don't look like a married lady."

"Wow," she whistled approvingly, "you don't look like the town domestic. Love the hair, girlfriend. Even with pillow head I can tell it's gorgeous." She remained the gorgeous one, however. The same as ever, a natural knockout with thick auburn hair hanging in a long, loose braid over one shoulder, skin clear and peachy, lips covered only in Vaseline. Small-town Lee could give the sophisticated Stewart a run for the money any day. "And I'm married all right. Married and working hard on a family."

"Nice work if you can get it."

"And you can get it. . . ."

"If you try," we finished together in a jazzy duet. Larry would have been proud.

"Oh, it's good to have you back. Sam, too, of course. Where is your long drink of water?"

"My demon lover is downstairs making coffee and catching up with Plain Jane and Dear John. He wanted to bring them on our honeymoon, you know, just in case we ran out of things to say to each other."

"Did you?"

Lee smiled dreamily, her happiness spilling over. "There are more ways to communicate than just talk. Speaking of all talk, no action, how are you and Tom?"

I sighed heavily. "Thanks. And no, we still don't have a wedding date set except 'sometime in the fall,' or 'when the house is ready, dear.' "

Lee patted my head. "Poor Flip. You can't take the lawyer out of the bachelor, or the bachelor out of the lawyer. Maybe you should dump him for Brad Pitt."

"If he doesn't dump me first," I muttered.

Lee's ears picked up the worry of truth. "What are you talking about? Something happen while we were away?"

"Not some*thing*, but some*one*." I spilled out my tale of woe without mentioning names, just feelings, the fears and loss of self-confidence. Lee listened and after awhile, gathering more detail, her face clouded.

"This woman. Her name's Stewart Larkin, isn't it?"

I nodded. "Yeah. You knew her in college, didn't you?"

"Did I ever." That's when she told me about Stewart. And Charlie.

"Charlie Scott!" Sleepy eyes wide awake, my jaw came unhinged. "I never knew you were in love with Tom's brother!"

"Nobody did, not even Tom. It was my last semester in college. Charlie worked for the *Frederick* Paper and was older, you know, by a good ten years. We didn't want everybody in town all revved up and excited, gossiping about wedding bells, so we kept our relationship strictly under wraps." She let out a deep breath and I could see tears welling up in her hazel eyes, remembering. "God, I was so in love with that man."

"Everybody loved Charlie." Three years ahead of me in high school, Charlie Scott wore Gatsby shoes. Achingly handsome, wealthy, athletic, witty, adventurous to a fault. I didn't know a girl in school who didn't have a crush on him, even a couple of young teachers. "What happened?"

"Stewart happened." Lee examined one set of short fingernails. "She was my best friend at Hood senior year. We shared a room. We shared secrets. But I didn't expect to share Charlie. She knew how much I loved him. What I learned too late is that Stewart always wants what isn't hers and once she overcomes the challenge, she's history. She loses interest and moves on to the next challenge or thrill. Designer clothes, the fastest car, or the next man. Poor Charlie didn't know what hit him."

"Why didn't you get back together after Stewart dumped him?"

"Because he really fell for her. Hard. The break-up left him a different man—angry, bitter, mad at women. He said if he stuck around, he'd end up killing himself or her. That's when he decided to travel."

"The get-the-hell-out-of-Dodge syndrome, to use a favorite Sallyism."

"Exactly. It did prove he wasn't as serious about me as I was about him, but I ended up hurt and devastated. He ended up hurt and devastated. Stewart went her merry way and never looked back. Until now, that is. What's she doing here?"

"Getting away from a stalker. Tom says it's life or death. The theory is if she moves clear across the country to our little pothole in Frederick County, the guy who's threatening her can't find her, or will find her and expose himself. No anonymity here, as we all know."

Lee rolled her eyes. "Why doesn't this surprise me? Mark my words, it's a disgruntled ex-lover. She's probably made as many enemies in her life as her father's made in twice the time."

The image of the suavely handsome Conrad Larkin surrounded by enemies didn't make sense, but I remembered Miss Fizzi's words about him—"something scandalous happened . . ."

"Why's he got so many enemies?"

Lee flipped over on her stomach and hugged the pillow into her chest. "He's like the J.R. Ewing of California. Mr. Mogul Tycoon, except more playful and charming. The type who designs mazes for fun. He loves jokes and games and puzzles, but always gets what he wants, like Stewart. Combined, their beauty, charm, and brains have landed them on the cover of *Fortune* and *Forbes*. I admit, there's a lot to admire. But God help you if you cross them."

"Why? What would he do, strangle a CEO with his Armani tie?"

"Close enough. The story goes—and this is straight

from the horse's mouth, too; Stewart told me all about it—Conrad figured out that her fiancé, a brilliant corporate computer whiz, the guy she 'loved' right before she grabbed Charlie, was stealing from the Larkin till. Big time."

"What did Conrad do? What did Stewart tell you?"

"That her father figured out the fiancé's scheme and, despite her pleas, crushed the guy like a bug. He ended up in prison and Stewart's loyalties were completely torn. Apparently, since then Da-Da and Babe have made up. Unlike *moi* and Babe."

"Oh, Lee, honestly." The log in her own eye stuck out. "So the guy got what he deserved. Obviously, he was using her for financial gain and Conrad found out. Scandalous, yes, but like a good daughter, she came to her senses and realized her father acted in her own best interests. So, no more fiancé. She probably turned to Charlie for comfort, then simply realized he wasn't right for her."

Lee's hazel eyes narrowed into slits. "Where is my best friend, and what have you done with her, O Ye Who Defends Sirens? She has that effect on men, but I didn't think *you'd* be drawn to the rocks."

"I'm not. I'm just trying to make you see your own prejudice. As for the rocks, you should have seen the song she sang to Suggs. He turned into a smitten kitten in her hands. Pal and the Eggheads didn't fare much better."

"God, that just leaves Screamin' Larry. And . . ." Lee tipped one brow, "Tom?"

"The jury's still out on that one. Right now he sees her as a lady in distress, and I have to admit she is." Something didn't sit right with Lee's venomous portrait of Stewart and I pursued the subject. "Really, you make her sound almost evil. All because of Charlie. I just don't see it. She's been nothing but kind, generous, and polite. She looks like an angel and seems so vulnerable."

Lee spat her words, the old jealousy rekindled. "Vulnerable! Listen here, Flip. Steer clear of that woman. If somebody out there is really gunning for her, she and Big Daddy will use and abuse any living soul to protect their own interests. The greater the stakes, the greater the thrill. Seriously, a friendship with either one of them could be dangerous."

I scoffed and climbed out of bed, thinking Lee's past history colored the current overreaction, her jealousy even extending to me befriending Stewart. "Calm down. Chill out. Get a grip. Thirteen years is a long time to nurture sour grapes." In blatant self-interest, I added, "Do you mind if I tell Tom about the Charlie episode?" Tarnishing Tom's shiny image of the goddess just a tad wouldn't hurt.

"Use my sordid past for whatever twisted purpose you desire." Lee sprang up and briefly checked herself out in the mirror. "What else is on your agenda today?"

"Cleaning Lindbergh Kohl's house, then Miss Fizzi's. Upbraiding my fiancé for neglecting me for almost a week. The settlement on my house with Stewart."

Lee gaped. "*She* bought your house? You told me some man bought it."

"That's before I knew anybody named their baby girl Stewart."

Lee shrugged. "Well, at least you get some money out of her."

"That's how Melody sees it."

From downstairs, we heard a familiar voice. "Sweet-iekins! Coffee's on!"

"Thank you, darling," Lee yelled.

"Not you. I was talking to Flip."

My eyes met Lee's and we smiled at each other like two puppies from the same litter, separated for the longest time, reunited at last.

Unashamed, my voice cracked when I said, "It's great to have you home, Mrs. Gibbon."

PART TWO

❊

Bodyguards and Beaux

CHAPTER 9

✳

I LEFT SAM cuddling Plain Jane in his lap and Lee re-
pairing the damage I'd wrought on her herb garden.
Before heading to Lindbergh's house, I dropped by my
own favorite piece of real estate. Abner Diggs greeted
me with his usual excitement.

"Flip." He dipped his head slightly.

"How's it going, Abner?"

"Fine."

"Good. Just checking."

Abner kept his eyes on the busy workmen in front of
us while I babbled to fill the social void. "Tom got back
to town yesterday, I guess." Since he hadn't bothered to
call, I could only guess. "So I expect he'll be out here
soon and go over stuff with you."

"That'll be fine."

"I'll see him this morning." Like Abner needed to

keep tabs on my schedule. "I'm settling on my house today. You know, my little house in town?"

"Can't say that I do."

"About a month ago I sold it to a woman who I thought was a man, and we're settling today. Her name's Stewart Larkin. Funny name for a woman, huh?"

The deadpan demeanor melted. Abner's crinkled eyes widened, the jaw flinched.

"Abner? You know her? Her father's Conrad Larkin, the famous industrialist?"

I had never seen such fire in those placid eyes.

"Abner . . ." But he whipped around and hurried away, waving at a workman to stop sawing up the wrong section.

What in the world? I thought. Did Abner know Conrad from Chicago? Then again, Chicago only signified another rumored guess in Abner's murky life. He could just as easily have hailed from Australia. Or Los Angeles.

I waited for him to return, but he ran in fifteen different directions, apparently too busy to satisfy my curiosity. Or doing his best to avoid the subject. I slid back into the car and watched him from a distance. Wherever Abner Diggs came from, whatever the empty blanks of his life, one blank had just been filled.

He hated Stewart or Conrad Larkin, maybe both. More than he could say.

My MIND WHIRRED as I drove to Lindbergh's house, Screamin' Larry's Buddy Rich drum program adding to the tension. Maybe Stewart breathed easier in Solace Glen, but her father better watch his back. Lee was right. The man had made his share of enemies, touching even our little corner of earth. Leonard didn't hesitate to badger Conrad over financial matters, and Abner couldn't hide his contempt for the man or his daughter, I couldn't tell which. Perhaps one of Conrad Larkin's many enemies took his revenge by stalking the daughter. Then again, given Lee's account of poor Charlie, maybe Stewart's cauldron bubbled with plenty of her own victims. Could Abner Diggs, thirty years her senior, be one of them?

"Oh, Flip," I lectured the face in the rearview mirror, "stop it right now. You are too ridiculous."

Lindbergh Kohl greeted me in the familiar beige sweater vest, deerskin slippers, and gentle smile. His white sideburns fanned out on either side of his face like lamb's wool.

"Good morning, Mr. Kohl." I stepped into the house hearing the first, faint strains of a Mozart violin concerto, and glanced quickly at the title of the book he held. "Good Lord, you're reading that trashy book about Princess Diana?" I winced and drew up sheepishly. "Oops. Sorry. None of my business."

Surprisingly, Lindbergh didn't glower or scuttle away. His voice, as soft and soothing as the warm moccasins, replied, "I suspect much of what I read *is* rather trashy. When someone else pieces together a life, the unsavory bits we would have thrown away ourselves are unhappily retrieved from the bin and glued on the canvas along with the better parts. The frustration I have with autobiography is the self-editing. Going through the trash is much more enlightening and fun, wouldn't you agree, Miss Paxton?"

"You know," I flashed a smile, maybe even a little

flirty, "you better call me Flip because you can't call me 'Miss' much longer."

"Is that so?" He slipped into the spirit of my humor with complete ease. "Dare I ask who my rival is? No, wait. I believe the talk I've heard links you to that impertinent whippersnapper, Tom Scott."

"Why, Mr. Kohl, I didn't know you fell in for gossip."

"Call me Lindbergh. No one's ever given me a decent nickname. Lindy's a little too cute for a serious scientist. And I don't really fall in for gossip, outside my trashy biographical interests. Gossip, however, sometimes falls in for me, and accosts me in the park, at the grocery store, even the barbershop. One can't help but hear."

"No," I agreed, "one can't."

Thus began the first real chapter of my personal biography of Lindbergh Kohl, all previous knowledge but a brief and shallow introduction to the core. In no time at all, I understood Tom's admiration for the gentleman, and Lindbergh's reputation as an enigma. He opened doors when and where he wanted, and if one opened to you, you felt the unique honor of it. He could talk about anything, even music (unlike Margaret). His brilliant mind held not only intricate facts, but also the ability to connect, analyze, and arrive at astounding conclusions.

At one point, as I swooshed a rag across a shelf of books, I observed, "You have some Civil War books here. *Lee's Lieutenants. A Stillness at Appomattox.* Do you have a biography of J.E.B. Stuart?"

"Ah," the gentle eyes twinkled, "the dashing general with the plumed hat. A favorite of yours?"

"We share some DNA." He'd like that explanation, being a scientist.

"Tell me all." And he perched on the arm of a wing chair while I proudly launched into the story of my newfound heritage.

At the end of the tale, his little eyes twinkled even brighter and he shook his head. "I am amazed. For Leona and all the Bell women to keep such a secret, to hide old love letters to protect each other that way, along with your mother. It's really quite touching, isn't it? Where are the letters now?"

"At the Historical Society. I'm living there until our house is built and Tom finally finds himself at the altar. Drop by anytime for a peek. Lee has a great book collection. Novels, biographies, essays, and of course, reams of local history. The lives of the ordinary folks who've lived here in Solace Glen are just as fascinating and racy as any trashy Princess Diana concoction."

Lindburgh chuckled. "You think so? It never really occurred to me, Flip, that the living souls around me, especially in Solace Glen, could make for an entertaining or instructive study. But your lovely tale has begun to convince me otherwise."

"You need to get out more," I advised. "Date."

Naturally, this would light a fire under every Circle Lady in town. They'd be forever in my debt.

I took not a minute more to clean the whole house, even though Lindbergh followed me from room to room, and we talked the entire hour and a half.

As I pulled out of the driveway, memories of solace and belonging stirred, the way I used to feel after spending time with my "mothers," Louise, Leona, and Marie. Their presence lingered, and I ached for each one, including my own lost mother. Yet the face that leaped to mind from the depth of all that love carried no feminine feature. I saw my father, head thrown back, laughing, full of life. I saw him walking down a church aisle, arm linked with mine, anxious to deliver a wedding toast, delighted to dance with the bride. Yearning overwhelmed me; the vision quickly burst. My eyes filled full with grief at the remembered sight of a flag-draped coffin, the remembered fact of a life cut short.

I PULLED UP to Miss Fizzi's and tried to refocus on the task at hand and the day ahead. Her stuffed Victorian house awaited a thirsty mop. After that, I could clean Tom's office (in between kisses, I hoped, though I couldn't decide if anger at his neglect outweighed lust), and conveniently sit down for the settlement on my house. I found Miss Fizzi in the kitchen rolling out pie dough with a scrolled champagne flute.

"Top of the day, dear." She paused to wipe a floured hand across her forehead. "I don't know where I buried my rolling pin. Oh, well. This works quite nicely even if it has taken all morning. Drink a little, roll a little, drink a little, roll a little."

I had to admit the dough looked smooth and undisturbed, unlike Miss Fizzi.

"News flash. Lee and Sam got back from their honeymoon."

Miss Fizzi clapped her floured hands together. "Tell me all! Did they have a nice trip?" She lowered her voice as if the walls had ears. "Is she expecting yet?"

I started wiping down the messy kitchen counters. "Didn't get a chance to hear much about their rampant sex life except the litany she spouted. 'Oh, Oh, Oh, wonderful honeymoon! Wonderful, wonderful!' They already have the look of two comfortable, old shoes together. And if she's not pregnant, it ain't from lack of trying."

"Don't use the 'p' word dear. It's vulgar."

"More vulgar than *ain't*? Anyway, you might want to back off the questions regarding the 'p' word. They were only gone two weeks."

Miss Fizzi plopped into a Windsor chair with her doughy champagne flute and poured from a pitcher of orange juice. "I see that look you're giving me, Flip. It really is just orange juice."

"Glad to hear you're not getting sloshed before eleven."

"I'm eighty years old, no reason I shouldn't." She smiled vaguely and sipped the juice while I worked. "By the way, I remembered what that scandalous thing was about Stewart's father."

I wiggled both brows. "Besides throwing his daughter's fiancé behind bars?"

Miss Fizzi's powdered face crumpled. "Hell's bells. You ruined my fun."

"Sorry." I poked a lip at a cast-iron skillet solid with bacon grease. "How you've lived this long eating pounds of animal fat, I'll never know. Anyway, I found out from Lee about the Conrad/fiancé thing."

"Yes. Who knows the truth? Guilty or not, it happened a long time ago." She puzzled over her orange juice, memory flickering.

I stopped scrubbing. "What do you mean 'guilty or not'?"

Miss Fizzi pursed her pink lips. "I mean, Stewart staunchly supported that young man and believed in his innocence. It's amazing she and her father have found common ground again after such an upsetting and *public* display."

A charter member of The Old School, Miss Fizzi considered a birth announcement, wedding write-up, and tasteful obituary the proper limits for any lady's name in print.

I pictured the eager expression Miss Fizzi would wear when she heard a different spin on the story. "I wonder if Abner Diggs knows the truth."

"Abner Diggs?" She was all ears. "What does he have to do with the Larkins?"

"I don't know. I do not know, but . . ." I slowly started scrubbing again. "I've never seen the man react with such emotion as when I mentioned the Larkin name. Something really serious must have happened, something that left such a deep wound it's never healed. Because it was clear to me Abner hates Conrad or Stewart or both with a passion."

"I wonder what happened! Oh, I simply must find out." Miss Fizzi's creaky wheels began to turn and she fell into the limitless space of her own imagination.

I fell in right beside her, wondering, puzzling. I should have been chiding myself on becoming the worst gossip in town, poking around in everybody's dirty laundry. Literally.

After a while, we both broke into lighter chatter while I finished cleaning the clutter she called a kitchen. I told her about running into C.C, Leonard, and both Larkins at the jewelry store. And about the amazing reaction Suggs exhibited over Stewart.

"I tell you, what a transformation. I didn't know Suggs had it in him to act civilized. That California beauty can charm the socks off anyone."

Her tiny eyes widened and she exulted, "Do tell! Maybe there's hope for a grand niece-in-law yet! Oh, I'll have to give a party!"

The idea of Grace Kelly hitched up to our version of Jud Fry threw me into convulsions. On that note, I swept through the rest of the house and sprinted over to Tom's, spritzing perfume on my neck in the car as the radio played "Do Nothing Till You Hear From Me."

Well, Tom Scott was going to hear from me now.

CHAPTER 10

❋

I FLEW UP the stairs to Tom's office and into the secretary's outer room, where I drew up fast.

"Hey, Flip, whatcha up to?" Tina straightened her back, taking on an officious tone. "I mean, do you have an appointment with Mr. Scott, Madam?"

"I'm no madam yet," I said in my best Mae West, "but I'm working on it. Well! You and Tom finally got your act together. He needs a good secretary. Just remember, his bark is worse than his bite."

I started to brush past her desk, but she said, "He's got people in there. Want to wait out here till he's done?"

I huffed. "Oh, poop. We haven't seen or talked to each other in almost six days now. I may as well make an appointment myself!"

"Thursday's good," Tina said brightly, flipping through the appointment book.

I wondered how long she'd last working for Tom. I plopped down on a nice leather sofa for about ten seconds before springing up and grabbing a pair of rubber gloves. "Heck, I can't sit here waiting. The least I can do is clean something."

"Good. That dog of his leaves a nest of hair in every corner. Good thing I'm not allergic." Tina shifted in the small office chair. "That man's going to have to spend some money on me if I stay. First thing to go is this squeaky chair."

"First thing to go would be you. Tom hates spending money." I dusted and emptied the trash around the outer office while Tina and I indulged in harmless babble. Mostly, she wanted to describe her latest diet, lots of stewed fruit and dry toast, which sounded perfectly grotesque to a woman who enjoys sugar on her butter sandwiches. I grabbed the spray bottle and paper towels and started in on the windows. About that time, the door to Tom's office opened and I whirled around, dirty paper in one mitt, spray bottle in the other, ready to fling arms wide and leap into my lover's arms.

Instead, the arms I beheld gleamed with tasteful gold bracelets and an expensive watch. Stewart stared at me as if she'd stepped through her looking glass into a bizarre world where women wore aprons and used cleaning products. The stare vanished at once, though, and she chirped, "Oh, hello, Flip! Ready for settlement? Or do you need to finish what you're doing?"

Like I was halfway through a spa facial and shouldn't be disturbed.

Three faces framed her entrance—her father, an unknown man, and Tom. Tom's eyes wore an unsettled, agitated appearance, as if the sight of me with the tools of my trade suddenly rankled him. Again, reality or my own paranoia?

Conrad Larkin spoke up. "This is the seller, sweetheart? Ms. Paxton, a pleasure to see you again. That was you in the jewelry store Saturday, wasn't it? I'm Stewart's father, Conrad."

He pressed forward to greet the town maid like a gentleman, allowing me to place the spray bottle down before taking my rubber-gloved hand. "You have a delightful home. Stewart's lucky to have found it. It's perfect for her, an easy commute to Baltimore or Washington, and so reminds me of my childhood home in Missouri. Simply sitting on the front porch swing brings back happy memories for me. You have a cleaning business? Isn't it wonderful to own what you do in life? Hats off to you. You must be quite resourceful. You must walk us through your house after settlement and point out all the special touches, and let me buy you lunch. You and Stewart should become good friends."

So many questions, flattery, and subtle demands lay packed into his little introductory speech that all I could do was nod and smile.

"Conrad," Tom finally found some words of his own, "would you, Mr. Parker, and Stewart please wait out here for a few minutes? We'll get things set up for the settlement."

The three courteously stepped into the waiting room. Before seating himself, however, Mr. Parker, a squat, pedestrian-looking man wearing a raincoat even though it wasn't raining, and a hat that covered half his face, sized me up with a lengthy, hard glare.

Tom added in a formal voice, "The realtor should be

here in about ten minutes. Flip, would you step into my office, please?"

With that warm, inviting request, I slowly peeled off the rubber gloves, making him wait a few long seconds, and tossed around the question of whether to plant a whopper kiss on his mouth when the door closed or kick him in the shin. The question evaporated when he closed the door and practically threw my back out with a hot kiss that left me a plop of melted jelly on his desktop.

He ran both hands through my highlights and breathed in the perfume at the nape of my neck. "Promise you'll do a rubber-glove striptease like that every day of our lives."

"You like that, huh? Wait'll you see my little trick with a feather duster." I pushed him off and struggled up. "Like my hair, too? Yeah, well, fine. Why the hell couldn't you pick up a phone from Wednesday until to-day? And why were you looking at me out there like I'm an embarrassing relation?" I jabbed him in the chest with a pointed pink nail. "Tell me, that, Mister."

Eli yawned in the corner. Not your star attack dog.

"Hey!" He grabbed my hand and kissed it. "You got a manicure, too? Tina must have paid you."

"Answer the question, counselor. And thanks for hiring her, although I doubt she'll last long with a recreant like you."

"No name-calling allowed. I told you, it upsets Eli. For your information," he circled my hips with his arms and drew me close, "I did call, but you were out."

"I didn't get any message."

"I didn't want to leave one. I just wanted you. In the flesh." He nibbled my ear. I breathed in his shaving lotion and realized I'd missed even that. "Plus, I've been slightly busy. Right before and after Richmond, I met with Mr. Larkin's PI in Washington, the man you saw out there, Jackson Parker. Not to mention other work and clients. And Richmond—yow! Endless seminars on trusts and estates, mechanics liens, and federal tax law."

"No wonder the sight of a rubber glove got you so hot and bothered." I tried out a sultry pout and walked two fingers up his chest.

"As for looking at you as a poor relation, you misread what you saw—not an uncommon occurrence. Actually, I was taken aback by the discovery of a glamorous creature with shimmering hair, armed with glass cleaner, right here in my office." No misreading the gleam in his eye now.

"If you come over tonight, I'll show you the feather duster, and give you a good dusting."

He started to kiss me again, but Tina blasted through the door, announcing excitedly, "The realtor's here! The realtor's here!" As if Richard Simmons had discoed into the waiting room to give her a private lesson.

Tom sighed heavily and rolled his eyes heavenward. "Tina. We knock when we enter the boss's office."

"OK, Tom. I mean, yes, sir!" She saluted. "I'll herd everybody into the conference room, okie-dokie?"

"Yup." He let out another woeful sigh. "I might not kill her in one day, but two has possibilities."

I shoved the carryall to the side and picked up my purse. "So that man who gave me the royal once-over, he's an investigator for Conrad? Is he local or an import?"

Tom rustled through some papers on his desk. "He came from California and has been in Larkin Industries' private employ for several years. He's Stewart's personal bodyguard, so you know Conrad trusts him implicitly."

I knew I shouldn't ask, but curiosity's a terrible thing to waste. "Do they think she's still going to be in danger now that she's made her East Coast move? Is there anything I can do?"

Tom's dark eyes narrowed skeptically before he read the sincerity in my face. He paused, no doubt mulling over what he could properly divulge and what must remain private. "The latest correspondence to her California address, received the day she and Conrad flew here, suggests this man knows she's trying to get away from him. He's let it be known he'll stop at nothing to find her and harm her."

"Harm her?" I pressed. "You mean kill her?"

His forehead creased, eyes downcast as he gathered up documents, but I read the answer in those dark eyes.

"Do they have any idea who's stalking her?" Now that she roosted in Solace Glen, a haven of nervous Nellie's, the question took on some importance.

"The police aren't sure, but they have two or three suspects. If one of them does show up here, he can't exactly blend into the crowds the way he could in L.A." He lightly kissed my cheek. "It's nothing for you to worry about. Come on."

We walked into the conference room together, a room I'd mundanely cleaned a thousand times, a room where the depths of grief lay raw and exposed, and my name echoed off the will of my parents, Leona's will, and Louise's will. But this was also the room where I read the first hint of love in Tom's eyes.

Seated around the familiar cherry wood table I

counted Stewart (the lady in distress, smiling brilliantly at Tom), her father (smiling proudly down at Stewart like she'd just won Best of Breed), Jackson Parker (sitting in a corner, alternately glancing out the window and stealing looks at the realtor), and the realtor who, surprisingly, I did not recognize. Tina acted like she knew what she was doing, and she probably did. She had Tom's place neatly arranged with settlement documents, a pencil, and a calculator. She asked if anyone wanted coffee. When the realtor spoke up, she hustled out. He wasn't the man I'd dealt with before, but did wear the logo of the real estate company on his green blazer.

"Excuse me," I piped up, "I don't believe I know you. I thought Mr. Furgeson would handle this."

He sprang up, self-ejecting from the comfortable, padded armchair, hand extended, displaying every tooth, the perfect salesman. Suspiciously dark hair slicked back, and almost chinless, his skin bore a tan-from-a-bottle tint that made him look older than fortyish, not younger.

"Fergie's attending a monster settlement at our Deep Creek office today." His voice carried the slightest lisp (endearing on some people, not on him). "That's where I usually work, but I've asked for a transfer to Frederick for my poor mother who's in ill health. This way I can keep my job and take care of the dear love, too. Works out well for Fergie. I'm sure you're familiar with the price of real estate in the Deep Creek area? Oh, my, I could go on for hours on that subject!"

Too bad. He and Officer Garrett could get together and bore each other to death. He rolled back his head and whistled, quite pleased with himself for some reason.

"Been living in Deep Creek long?" I small-talked,

noticing the huge diamond ring he dragged about on his right hand.

"Oh, for *decades*." He waved his hand in the air, a gesture guaranteed to show off the size of the stone.

"That so?" I continued to chitchat while Tina gently set a foam cup of coffee by his side and whisked back to her office. "We've certainly heard about the big multi-millionaires snatching up lakefront properties and building hotel-sized homes. We have an off-duty police officer from there, Sidney Garrett. He marvels at it all the time. Do you know Officer Garrett, Mr. . . . ?"

A second. A pause. A slight hesitation.

"Worthington. Horace Worthington." He peered intently into my eyes, hunting for something. If he'd been looking sixty seconds later when I bent down to tie a sneaker, he would have found it—a spark of recognition. He could be *Marlene's* Worthington! My jaw went slack and I stared wide-eyed at the carpet before skimming over the well-dressed laps and legs of Stewart and Conrad to focus on Horace Worthington. Naturally, I would have to make a full report to the Ladies. He wore khaki pants and a tightly tucked pink Polo shirt underneath the green blazer. Pink. They'd eat that up. Wiggly white toes poked out of black leather sandals. The Ladies would also adore that little detail.

I poked up my head and found everyone waiting for me to begin. "Sorry. They don't make shoestrings the way they used to."

"I dare say," said Mr. Worthington, cheerful in his sandals.

Tom's face bore his standard conference room expression: no-funny-business-will-be-tolerated-missy. I straightened my spine, eyes front.

Stewart sat directly across from me. A JD, an MBA, years in the tough business world of her father, and yet she wore the demeanor of a teenager out to take her first driving lesson. She glowed happy as a sunbeam before the discovery of a tiny chip on one nail caused instant distress, but managed to listen in rapt attention when Tom spoke. As he sorted through documents, she excitedly squeezed her father's hand now and again.

I could not for the life of me detect the sins Lee attributed to her. In fact, I liked Stewart more and more in spite of myself. There really was something innocent and vulnerable about her, a sweetness and trust that couldn't be manufactured.

Jackson Parker wrapped his raincoat tight. He sat too close to the air-conditioning vent. The ferret eyes dashed around the room, taking in everything, including what, if anything, occurred down in the street below.

Horace Worthington rolled out the pleasantries. After all, his only role consisted of picking up a commission check for his company. I started to follow up on my light cross-examination when Jackson Parker rudely butted in.

"You say you've lived in Deep Creek for decades, Mr. Worthington? Where exactly?"

"Beg pardon?" Horace rose in his seat, surprised by the voice at his back.

"What was your address in Deep Creek?"

Horace sputtered. "I-I fail to see how my private residence is any concern of yours. You don't need to know my address. You're not even a party to this transaction."

Conrad stepped in. "Jackson is my personal assistant and my daughter's bodyguard. He sometimes performs his duties with inappropriate zeal. Apologize to the man, Jackson. He's just the realtor."

Horace bristled, waiting for the apology that never came. Jackson merely glared and grunted before staring out the window again.

I wondered if it was lost on everyone but me that Horace Worthington couldn't come up with an address, and had never said he knew Sidney, who had lived in Deep Creek all his life.

I smiled at Horace, my new best friend. "Do you like your work?"

He appeared thrilled with me. "Oh, my, yes! Such beautiful properties you see. Such interesting houses. You meet the nicest people. *Some*times." The eyes behind his round, black-rimmed spectacles dipped sideways at Jackson. "There's definitely money to be made in Maryland."

"You don't say! Did you live somewhere else before moving here?"

Again, he hesitated, carefully choosing the words. "I *was* out West for awhile. But Maryland drew me back. There's nothing like our colonial and Civil War history, or our rolling hills and Chesapeake Bay."

A drop of information with a wave of small talk.

"Where out West?" Jackson interrupted gruffly. "Give me an address."

In answer, Horace pursed his lips and sniffed.

"How's your poor mother doing?" Sympathy dripped from my every pore.

This innocuous question sent Horace into a rambling soliloquy on the pitfalls of the elderly. Four seconds later, nobody listened. No true value could be found in it for me; Tom busily added up numbers; Stewart entertained herself watching Tom's fingers fly over a calculator; and Conrad, I noticed, withdrew a pocket notebook and busied himself with some sort of design, probably a maze, smiling, a thousand miles away.

Jackson barely tolerated Horace's babble. He displayed unmistakable signs of a man anxious to dash off. He also, I saw, wore a gun holster inside the raincoat. The sight of the leather strap sent a chill down my back until I remembered his job. Poor Stewart, having to live like that.

With all the documents completed, signed, and copied, Tom issued checks left and right. I contemplated the number, pleased, but a little sad, too. I'd lived almost forty-three years in the little Paxton house, ladybugs and all. My childhood birthday parties took place in the backyard, usually under a sprinkler. My mother helped snap the hooks of my first bra in the upstairs bathroom. The tabby cat we called Chigger lay buried under the Japanese maple, my father's rough carving of a Celtic cross dignifying the tree.

Tom noticed my pupils start to float away and presented a handkerchief. I waved it aside. "No, no. The end of the old. A new beginning."

Stewart sighed in empathy. "A new beginning for me, too." She wrapped two milky white hands around Tom's right arm. "I'm so grateful to my old professor."

The green monkey could have struck with a vengeance, but all I read in the sapphire eyes was admiration and gratitude, not lust. Nevertheless, just to play it safe, I wrapped two not so milky paws around Tom's left arm. "He is sort of an old professor type, isn't he?"

Tom's arm muscles tightened as he slowly rolled his face toward mine, lips cemented together.

"You know," I continued generously, "you need to meet some of the eligible young men in town, Stewart."

She looked rightfully confused.

"Oh, *you* know, like that nice Suggs Magill you charmed the socks off of the other day."

Tom's welded lips slowly unhinged and his arm tensed harder.

"And those gallant Eggheads. S'cuse me, Jesse and Jules Munford, our brave rescue team. We can't forget Pal Sykes, either. After all, he does own his own business. That's a fine thing, isn't it, Mr Larkin, for a young man to have his own business? Like you say, it's wonderful to own what you do in life. Even if all you own is a little dirt and axle grease."

Conrad lifted a steel gray brow, not certain what to make of me.

Tom couldn't take a second more. Before I could wax prosaic on the virtues of Screamin' Larry, he shook the women off each wing like Eli shimmying water after a cold bath. "Stewart. Flip. I believe we're all done here."

Apparently, Stewart didn't think so. As closely guarded as she'd been, living the life of a pet turtle, the real estate settlement took on all the glamour of a Hollywood premiere.

"Flip," she said almost earnestly, "you must tell me where you get your hair and nails done."

I heard Tina snort in the next room.

"Sure," I trilled, like I made a daily pilgrimage to the place, "I go to Sally's Salon."

I made a show of folding my new check into teeny, tiny pieces and depositing it into a change purse, prepared to spend every penny on eye shadow and pedicures.

Stewart honestly did not want to leave. "In fact, you'll have to show me everything about Solace Glen."

"I'd love to." I couldn't resist adding innocently, however, "But I thought you'd been here before. Years before."

Tom cleared his throat, a warning sign of inappropriate nosiness.

Stewart's cheeks momentarily flushed a deep rose. How I coveted those cheekbones. "Yes, but it was so long ago. Things change. People change."

Something to remind Lee of. "You were visiting the Bell house, right? Lee Jenner? Well, now Lee Jenner Gibbon."

"Oh, you know Lee." The perfect features lit up, then gradually darkened as if the truth, remembered, tasted quite bitter.

"Yes, she's my best friend."

My words evoked an almost apologetic response. "You see," she used both hands gracefully as she spoke, "I haven't seen or talked to Lee in ages. She might have told you about our college friendship, and the reason we parted company. It pains me to even think about it now. I'd give anything to see her again and start over. To have happy times again."

Her blue eyes wandered to the window where Jackson perched, her burden and protector.

Conrad squeezed her hand. "There, there. Happy times will come again for you. This, too, shall pass."

Suddenly, Horace woke up and began to chatter as he neatly tucked the commission check into the breast pocket of his blazer. "Miss Larkin, why so sad? Have you had a recent loss?"

"In a matter of speaking," replied Stewart, restrained and dignified. "I seem to have lost my freedom."

"Stewart, do you think this is wise?" Conrad asked under his breath.

She must have thought so because out spilled the beans that had already sprinkled across half of Solace Glen. "I'm being stalked. At least I was in L.A., and the threat was growing so great we thought it best I make a rather dramatic move, if only temporarily."

Horace listened with the experienced ear of one addicted to soap operas. "Heavens to Betsy! You poor thing!" He leaned toward her, speaking empathetically. "Do you have any enemies? Or," the eyebrows zoomed up and the questions flew out, "does your father? Or is the stalker simply an eager entrepreneur out to make a perverse buck? Is the stalker making any untoward demands? Money? Jewels? *You?*"

Stewart flushed and stuttered, "I-I really can't talk about that."

Jackson Parker barked, "No, you really can't! And I . . . hey." He leaped up and pressed a nose to the windowpane, a hound on the alert. "Excuse me." He rushed out of the room, throwing Conrad a turbulent glance.

"Oh, my goodness." Horace's diamond hand fluttered to his throat. "Do you think he saw the you-know-what?"

No one spoke for a minute as we listened to Jackson's shoes skim down the stairs to the street below. Stewart grew pale and real fear crossed her eyes. She gulped and turned to her father who protectively wrapped an arm around her.

"Do you know who is stalking you?" Now that the plot quickly thickened, I repeated the question posed earlier to Tom.

Stewart gazed mutely at her father, as if seeking

permission to speak. Instead, Conrad answered, "No, Miss Paxton, the police aren't one hundred percent sure. They have two or three suspects in L.A. they've been watching very closely. But *I'm* sure who's behind all this misery. One of Stewart's ex-suitors. No matter how he's tried to disguise his voice on those disgusting messages he leaves." His hand cupped Stewart's chin. "Not to worry, dear. Jackson jumps at the snap of a twig, you know that. I'm sure it was nobody."

At that moment, the conference room door swung open and a handsome, disheveled man blew in loaded down with canvas carry bags and oddly shaped black containers. But it wasn't "nobody."

It was Charlie Scott.

CHAPTER 11

✻

Tina came bustling into the conference room waving her flabby arms in the air. "I'm sorry, Tom! I was in the ladies' room and this gentleman . . ."

Charlie took off his Jack Daniel's baseball cap and ran a hand through wavy, sandy hair, grinning from ear to ear. One of which was pierced.

"*Eeeeeik!* Charlie!"

"Charlie!" I gaped.

"Charlie," Tom said, as if they'd just spoken on the phone for an hour. "You're wearing an earring."

"Charlie?" Stewart pushed off from Conrad like an Olympic swimmer and stroked straight toward Charlie. She drew within inches and wavered, accepting the unseen wall between them. "You didn't tell me you'd be coming out here, too."

"Hello, Stewart." The voice sounded friendly enough,

but he pulled away, his gray eyes, as penetrating as Tom's, staring as if a rare hummingbird hovered close by and he wondered what it would do next.

In response, the rare creature broke into a lovely smile and breached the wall. She reached up to stroke a wisp of sandy hair off his surprised forehead.

Horace burst into applause. "Oh, honey, *The Way We Were,* part *deux*!"

"Yes," I murmured, "we should charge admission."

Charlie quickly retreated, uncomfortably clearing his throat. The Girl Who Stomped on His Heart years earlier slipped back behind the wall, a little out of breath. Something remained of the old feelings, both the attraction and the heartache. The whole scene left me wondering why neither seemed especially shocked to see the other.

"You two know each other?" Tom stepped between them, unaware of their history, while Eli hoisted up his old bones and acted like a puppy, wagging a long tail and frisking at Charlie's feet. Tom shook his brother's hand. "Nice of you to drop in. And let me know you were coming."

An awkward pause, then Charlie laughed that same old, easy chuckle that affected anyone within earshot. He wore a faded blue cotton shirt with the sleeves casually rolled up, boat shoes without socks, jeans with no belt. He'd let his sandy hair grow out, and it hung just over his shirt collar. Hardly noticeable, streaks of gray tinged his temples. He and Tom stood side by side, polite and civil like strangers at a party, but hardly warm, the same six feet in height, the same aristocratic nose, the same flat, if slightly large ears. *Charlie, Charlie,*

I thought, memories shooting back to high school—*you Gatsby, you*.

And there she stood—his Daisy. Capable of mowing a man down and driving off without a backward glance, according to Lee. But *so* beautiful.

"Yes, Tom, we do know each other." Stewart's smoldering blue eyes encompassed Charlie.

What was she thinking, I wondered? *Which way would the river run?*

"We dated. Don't look so shocked. Years ago at Hood. We ran into each other recently at a gallery opening."

"In L.A.?" Conrad asked sharply. He turned suspicious eyes on Charlie, glancing away only briefly to read his daughter's face. "You never mentioned it to me, sweetheart."

Stewart shrugged her slim shoulders, beaming. "No need. Just a chance encounter a few weeks ago. It's been nice to renew an old friendship, if only through e-mail. I really had no idea you would be here, Charlie. You should have told me."

"Well," Charlie stumbled over the words, "it was spur-of-the-moment business."

In the space of another awkward pause, Tom took Charlie's arm and led him toward me, murmuring skeptically, "A business trip? Here? You remember Flip, don't you, Charlie?"

"Flip?" He took both my hands and pulled me up for a big hug. "Look at you! You look great, kiddo!"

Kiddo. He must have been thinking of someone else. "Thanks. You, too, Charlie." I flipped a wave of hair seductively behind one ear and peered over his shoulder at Tom. "Did you tell him our good news, darling?"

"Wait a minute. Whoa." Charlie let go of me like I was a lit firecracker. " 'Darling?' '*Our* good news?' "

"If you phoned more than every six months, you'd know by now. Flip and I are getting married."

Stewart half-gasped. "Married! Congratulations! Why didn't you tell me?"

Good question, I thought, making sure Tom caught my accusing eye.

"Married! A Scott man wants to get hitched?" Charlie grabbed me for another hug, talking all the while. "How'd you do it, Flip? This guy has trouble deciding which one of his twenty pairs of black socks to put on in the morning."

Tom remained unperturbed. "Flip makes all those executive decisions for me now. How long have you been in L.A.?"

The question hung in the air as Stewart gleamed bright enough to throw off prisms. "Tom." She wrapped a friendly arm around Tom's elbow. "Charlie." She tentatively offered him her other arm. He hesitated, but slowly reached out to cup a palm around her elbow as if he balanced a nest of robin's eggs. "Who would have thought, after all this time, we'd end up here, together? It's so wonderful! Why don't we all go for a nice lunch at that sweet little Bistro down the street? What say we head there right this minute?"

She looked straight at me during this invitation, as if to say, *Please, I need friends. I need nice people around me. I need you.*

Who could refuse her anything?

Tom opened his mouth to speak, but Conrad put the stamp of approval on the suggestion, obviously touched by his daughter's emotion, anxious to deliver any tidbit of delight he could. Anxious, no doubt, to learn more about Charlie Scott. "What a wonderful idea! And after lunch, Miss Paxton can give us a special walk-through of the house."

Stewart practically melted into the floor in ecstasy.

Conrad stood, issue settled despite Tom's clear reluctance to leave the office for even an hour in Tina's inexperienced hands. Conrad extended an invitation to Horace to come along with our cheery little group. Horace, of course, jumped at the chance to hobnob with the rich and famous.

"Oh, yes, I'd *love* to!" he twittered. "I want to discuss your businesses, Mr. Larkin, one company in particular. And Stewart, you must tell all about your stalking horrors. I can't imagine . . ."

"Stalking?" Charlie froze in mid-step, but kept his tone nonchalant. "What's this about stalking?"

"It's nothing, really." Stewart didn't want the moment ruined. "Nothing for you to worry about. It had barely started when I ran into you in L.A."

Before the words left her mouth, Jackson Parker burst into the room, out of breath. "I think I saw him, Mr. Larkin, but I lost him."

Stewart froze, pale skin doubly blanched.

"Who? Who?" Horace squealed. He rose on his toes, a spectator at his new favorite sport. "Who do you think you saw?"

Jackson ignored him and addressed Conrad stoically. "The man who's been stalking your daughter."

NEEDLESS TO SAY, our little settlement party ended abruptly. Conrad whisked Stewart away until Jackson could determine if he'd really seen the L.A. stalker whose name no one volunteered. If so, the plot to draw him out of the safe anonymity of big city crowds had quickly worked, but now the threat had to be faced. Charlie offered to accompany Stewart, but Conrad, distrustful (Charlie wearing the noxious "ex-suitor" label), nixed the idea. To her father's annoyance, Stewart promised to call Charlie later for a rendezvous. To her annoyance, Conrad asked me to meet them at the house the next day to go over it with a fine-toothed comb.

"I'm so sorry, Flip," she apologized. "I know this must be terribly inconvenient."

Charlie gathered up his luggage and cameras and took off for the Scott's old stone house. An elderly couple popped into Tom's office for an emergency will writing, so I finished cleaning his office and departed. It occurred to me later that poor Horace Worthington missed his golden opportunity to lunch with the lofty Larkins, and I missed my opportunity to ask him if, by the way, he had ever been married to Marlene. That niggling mystery would have to wait.

I threw myself into work the rest of the day, trying not to dwell on Stewart's terrible situation and Lee's warning of danger by association. Instead, I replayed the memory of Tom's fiery kiss and flipped through recipes in my head for what I hoped would be an equally fiery, long overdue, sinfully romantic evening.

Now. Where *did* I put that feather duster?

Chapter 12

NEVER UNDERESTIMATE THE power of your best friend to show up at exactly the wrong moment with her vacation-charged husband, refuse to take subtle and not-so-subtle hints to leave, tell every "awesome," "soooo funny" detail of her honeymoon, and keep your already work-exhausted fiancé up so late that he begs to drive back to his house, falling asleep at a stop sign a mile from home where Officer Garrett finds him and has to tug-boat him into the driveway. So much for Operation Feather Duster.

Lee, never one to squander a micro-smidgen of energy, showed up at the Historical Society before seven the next morning, intent on packing some boxes to take to the Bell house.

When I opened my eyes, she leaned over me, an excited child ready to visit the carnival.

"You just left," I groaned. "What are you doing back here?"

"But a lot of me goes such a little way. Aren't you glad to have me all to yourself for awhile?" She bounced onto the bed and began braiding her long hair into a single strand.

"You mean you've already abandoned your more considerate half? Or did he leave you once he discovered what a pain in the butt you are so early in the morning?" I rolled over, turning my back to her.

She bent down and whispered in my ear. "I don't think that's what he'd call it."

That made me giggle. "OK. I might as well wake up because you're not going to let me sleep, anyway, but don't expect me to load boxes. I have a full schedule today. I've got Margaret's house, and the McKnight house is nearly empty now, and needs a complete overhaul top to bottom. . . ."

"Empty?" She didn't know about the family leaving so soon. I filled her in on that tidbit and everything else on the list—how I'd hired Ivory, C.C.'s and Leonard's unwelcomed return, Tina's new job with Tom, the business connection between Conrad and Leonard, Abner Diggs's weird reaction to the Larkin name, the possibility that Horace was Marlene's ex, and the Big News.

"Charlie's back in town."

Lee went ashen. "Charlie?"

I shook her shoulder. "Lee Jenner *Gibbon*. Now hear this. You are a married woman now, right? Working on a family, et cetera, et cetera?"

"Don't misread my shock." The color returned to her peach skin and she poked me in the rib. "I love, adore,

and worship the ground Sam stumbles on. I'm just surprised Charlie would blow in right now. Quite a coincidence." She wrapped a hair band around her braid,
mulling over the news flash. "Don't you think it's odd
timing?"

I pictured Charlie's face when he first saw Stewart,
the penetrating gray eyes. "Maybe not so odd at all. He
says it's a sudden business trip, but interestingly he's
been living in L.A. and ran into Stewart a few weeks
ago. They've been e-mailing."

"E-mailing?" Lee wrinkled her nose. "That's it? A
little this-is-what-I-had-for-lunch e-mail? Stewart must
have lost her touch."

"Naw," I shook my head, "she's got the Midas thing
down pat where men are concerned. I think the problem
lies with Charlie. He doesn't want to drift close enough
to get singed again."

"Who can blame him? And yet, he's here." Her pupils
floated into space a few moments, but I could practically
hear the clink-clank of wheels turning. "So it's no coincidence he's back in town. And Stewart's here. And is
being stalked . . ."

"Lee," I took a cautionary tone, "you are not suggesting Charlie is stalking Stewart, are you? Tell me you're
not going there, because Jackson Parker, her bodyguard,
said he saw the stalker from L.A. right here in town."

"Saw him here?"

"Well, he said he thought he saw the guy, but lost
him."

"Why didn't you tell me that last night?"

"And interrupt your nonstop honeymoon mono-
logue?"

She opened her mouth, happy to take up where she'd left off, but I placed a finger across her lips. "Let's get back to Charlie. Why would you think for even a second that he's capable of stalking a woman?"

"You didn't see the mess Stewart left him in when she broke it off. He was a crazy man."

"But that was thirteen years ago!"

"Time doesn't heal all wounds. Maybe he's been plotting his revenge. Maybe that's why he moved to L.A., and now suddenly decides to 'visit' his dear older brother while 'on business.' Those two have never been close, you know."

I stuck a hip out. "Stop this. Stop it right now. You're substituting evil intentions in place of your own hurt and rejection. Ancient history. I don't believe Stewart is the witch you say she is, and Tom's baby brother is not capable of stalking and threatening a woman. But you, Mrs. Jekyll and Ms. Hyde, have been known to offer opinion as fact to stir up trouble."

Her mouth dipped. "When have I done any such thing? I mind my own business and stick to myself."

"Ha! Not always. What about the time you told everybody Screamin' Larry had fathered a love child with Marlene?"

"He thought it was funny. Even played 'Yes, Sir, That's My Baby' on the radio fifty times. Remember how mad Marlene got? That baby I saw her with looked an awful lot like both of them."

"And how about the time you spread it around that Roland had a brain tumor with six days to live because he had a lump on his head?"

"I was hoping. Anyway, how was I to know the klutz knocked an iron skillet off a shelf?" She jutted her jaw.

"You're not so pure. What about the time you told me Tom was a ladies' man sex maniac so I'd go out with him?"

I clutched a breast and looked skyward. "Truer words were never spoken. My point is, if you start insinuating Charlie is some kind of insane stalker out for revenge, Conrad is liable to slap him in jail."

"He's been known to. No respect for Stewart's lovers, especially the felons. But I bet Charlie would simply disappear, shanghaied to Timbuktu. That's Conrad's sense of humor."

"At least he has one." I started getting dressed, same old bewitching ensemble I wore to work every day in the summer: khaki cotton pants, T-shirt, and sneakers. "Conrad says the police have more than one suspect, but brilliant, natural detective that he is, he's sure the stalker is a particular old beau of Stewart's."

"What did I tell you! Didn't I say 'mark my words'?" She reveled in her own genius and continued playing with the pieces of this new puzzle. Lee couldn't help herself, she loved a good story. Margaret always said Lee would make a great novelist if she could only sit still for two seconds to write a complete sentence. "You said Jackson *thought* he saw the stalker. Mmmm. Little did he know that the real stalker, Charlie Scott, walked among them in—of all places—a law office, during— of all things—a real estate settlement. Very smart of that Charlie 'the Stalker' Scott. Very wily."

"Oh, Lee, honestly." I zipped up my pants. "You might as well accuse Abner Diggs and Lindbergh Kohl while you're at it. Now, I've got work to do and you've got to get packing. I'll fill in Jackson and Conrad on your remarkable and oh-so-verifiable theory when I see them today at the house."

"Good. And I'll start circulating the story that Charlie and Stewart had a love child in college that Conrad sold into white slavery and is now a teen rock star."

"You do that." I ran a brush quickly through my pillow head and hustled into the bathroom. "From the way Stewart fastened her eyes on Charlie in the conference room yesterday, a love child wouldn't be out of the question."

Lee hawed. "Wouldn't Daddy Conrad just *love* that! Poor Charlie. Poor, poor Charlie the Stalker."

CHAPTER 13

✷

T HERE ARE DAYS when lunch is not an option.
I hurried through Margaret's neat-as-a-pin home
and got completely bogged down at the McKnight
manse. The preacher's boys had done a number on that
house the past twelve years. With most of the furniture
and wall hangings gone, and just enough of the basics
left to tide the family over for a week, the damage and
blemishes lay exposed. Football plays scrawled in
Magic Marker on oak floors, filthy windowpanes, ini-
tials etched in glass with their mother's jewelry, a rain-
bow of Kool-Aid–stained carpet, shoe prints on walls.
How I managed to overlook this disgusting list of cleaning nightmares for twelve years, I could not fathom. But
I got busy. The new interim minister would arrive soon
enough, probably a picky, germ-paranoid widower with
allergies.

By the time six o'clock rolled around, I threw the last paper towel in the trash and dumped a vat of moisturizer on my dry, red hands. My engagement ring, a square emerald set off by two small diamonds (a favorite of Tom's mother), got creamed in the process, but I was in a hurry. Conrad Larkin would not be kept waiting.

Outside my old house—a white two-story wooden box with a wonderful L-shaped front porch and a large yard screened all around with thick evergreens—Stewart and her father bent over architectural plans spread across her Mercedes. Not that the old Paxton estate (to coin C.C.'s favorite depiction of local ground) counted as a handyman's dream. The place stood in fine stead. But I figured the Larkins viewed the move to Solace Glen as a temporary measure, safety first and all that, and while they resided in the area, they might as well tack on some fancy additions to inflate the price when the time came to sell. Stewart could then soar back to the swanky L.A. nest she'd left and continue to attract men like flies.

Jackson Parker sat on the porch swing and immediately popped up when he spotted my car. Not out of politeness, of course, but merely doing his job.

"Miss Paxton!" Conrad delivered his patented gracious greeting. I supposed all industrial tycoons behaved in a like manner, the better to disarm you when they wanted something. "Right on time, a commendable virtue."

"That's me. A beacon of virtue." I shook his hand and sent a friendly smile toward Stewart.

She out-sugared me, though. "Hello! How are you, Flip!" She wrapped her hands around my arm the same way she did with Tom and Charlie, a regular chum. "It is so nice of you to come walk through the house. I don't know any of the interesting little secrets and quirks of the place, so you'll have to show me everything. Where would you like to start?"

"How about the front door?" I gently pushed her hands off my arm, but she took no offense. "After you."

She skipped up the porch steps and swept into the house. Conrad signaled Jackson to follow while he remained outside, pencil in hand, tinkering with the house plans. Once in, I quickly walked Stewart from room to room, Jackson trailing behind, a paid spy, trying to blend into the walls. She ooo-ed and ahhh-ed, asked questions, and zeroed in on the most amazing trivia. Have you ever painted your outlet covers? Do you think a pastel print would benefit that corner? Does the floor squeak when you get up to go to the bathroom in the middle of the night?

"I don't know" and "I never noticed" served as my mantras for the hour. At some point while we toured the upstairs, Jackson concluded it was a useless waste of time to listen to window curtain and lampshade talk, so he slunk away. That gave me the opportunity on the way downstairs to point out one curious feature I'd always loved about the house.

"See these bookshelves built into the wall? My mother showed me something once." I couldn't believe I was doing this. "Now I'm showing it to you as the new owner. When I turned five, we were walking upstairs to run my bath when my mother stopped halfway up, right here, and said, 'Shhh. Look.' I watched while she reached in and pulled two thick books out. Then she put her hand back here against the wall, like so, and pulled up this plank." Stewart watched, fascinated. "*Voila*. You have a secret hiding spot for money or jewelry or important papers."

I pressed the plank back into place, eyes watery. "I've never told anybody about this. It feels strange and sad."

The moment was not lost on Stewart. She nodded solemnly and said, "I have a ring my mother gave me on my thirteenth birthday. It's my dearest treasure. She knew she was dying. She said, 'Stew, I want you to keep this ring safe. It belonged to your great-grandmother, her engagement ring, and I want you to wear it on your wedding day and think of me.' I promised her I wouldn't wear it until then, and I would keep it safe. This looks like the perfect spot for it."

She reached around the back of her swan neck and unclipped a gold chain. At the end of the chain necklace hung a beautiful platinum and diamond ring. She softly kissed it and pulled the plank back, carefully planting the chain in my hiding spot, now hers. I helped her reposition the wood, and a look passed between us, a look of shared secrets, shared memories, and a shared trust. *Had I,* I wondered, *just seen the core of Stewart Larkin?*

"Some things should only be shared between two people," she whispered. "This will be what we share. I'll never tell a soul. I promise."

I could hardly get the words out. "Thank you."

"Flip," she said, "you go on downstairs. I'm going to go splash some water on my face."

"Sure." I gave her shoulder a pat. "You go right ahead."

I slipped down the stairs and started to head out the

front door when voices rose in the parlor. I froze at the foot of the steps; the voices so tense, I shamelessly decided to eavesdrop.

Conrad spoke in a loud hiss to Jackson, his tone authoritative and conspiratorial. I edged closer to the outer wall of the parlor and strained to hear every word.

"Let me make myself clear. You told everyone you *thought* you saw him."

"Yeah, but I'm positive that was our guy."

"OK, fine. We can move ahead. Nothing gets by you, Jackson, and this isn't exactly L.A. or New York. But when you see him again, don't broadcast it."

"Excuse me?" Jackson hissed back. "Not even to Stewart? Not to the police?"

"Especially not the police. Don't tell anyone but me, and don't attempt to grab him. He mustn't yet know *we* know he's here. As for Stewart, leave that to me. We're going to handle this thing my way, without the red tape. *My way,* got it?"

I heard nothing more because Stewart started to come down the stairs. I quickly headed out the front door in time to witness Suggs Magill fooling around with something at the back of Stewart's Mercedes.

"Hey!" I shouted at him, well aware of Suggs's sleazy history, that strange protectiveness of Stewart resurfacing. "What the hell you think you're doing, Suggs!"

Before he could answer or bat an eye, Jackson tore out of the house and arm-wrestled Suggs to the pavement.

Stewart rushed past with Conrad on her heels.

"What's going on?" she cried. "Who is that, Jackson?"

Jackson jerked the stocky Suggs to a standing position and pulled his arms back so that his enraged face lifted.

Conrad glowered at Suggs. "Who are you, young man, and what were you doing around my daughter's car?"

Stewart relaxed when she saw Suggs. "It's you. Suggs Magill. The nice gentleman from the gas station, Daddy, remember? I told you about that."

Suggs's rage and distorted bulldog features faded into worshipful adoration at the sight of her. "Hey, Miss Larkin," he said respectfully. "How are you today?"

If you heard only his voice, you'd never know the man stood clenched in the grip of a painful vise, a vise Jackson appeared unwilling to relinquish. "You know this man, Miss Larkin?"

"Yes, I do." Stewart gallantly approached Suggs and tapped Jackson's fingers from their mighty hold. "Were you admiring my old car again, Suggs?" she teased.

"It is a classic, but no ma'am, not exactly." Suggs turned pink. "I was walking by and, you know, I'm in the business so I notice everything about everybody's car, and I saw this." He pointed at the rear license plate. "It's blocking your numbers." Tucked inside the frame lay a piece of folded note paper.

Stewart's skin whitened drastically. She slumped against her father's chest. "Oh, no. He *is* here. It can't be. It just can't be. Oh, Daddy, I can't do this all over again!"

Suggs, helpless in his adoration, stood silently by after Jackson released him. The investigator carefully pried the paper out with the edge of a handkerchief. He opened the note and perused it before handing the paper to Conrad, who carefully handled it with the handkerchief. At a glimpse, I could see words pasted together.

"Read it." Stewart's voice trembled. "I have a right to know."

Conrad cleared his throat, glancing with some consternation at both Suggs and me. He read the note in a hesitant, faltering voice.

Welcome home, Stewart,
I've left a housewarming gift in your car. The usual theme.

Yours,

The Locksmith

"The Locksmith?" I looked questioningly at Stewart.

"That's what he likes to call himself." Her head drooped against Conrad's chest. "You'll know why when you see what's in the car."

Chapter 14

※

Jackson Parker knew what he was doing. He whipped a plastic bag from a raincoat pocket that held several clean handkerchiefs and a pair of medical gloves. He slipped on the gloves, drew out two handkerchiefs, and stuck a pencil from his breast pocket behind his ear. He opened the back door of the car.

"It's on the floor of the back seat, Mr. Larkin. As usual."

"Stewart!" Conrad couldn't conceal his exasperation. "If you insist on buying these vintage models without keyless entry, can't you at least remember to lock the car yourself? How many times have we gone over this?"

"I thought I had locked it." She sounded like a six-year-old. "I don't know." Her eyes, dull and vacant, stared at the car. "Take it out, Jackson. Open it up."

"Wait a minute!" I'm no genius, but the thought did occur to me. "Aren't you going to call the police? This is evidence."

But Jackson had already removed what looked to be a half-pound box of candy, holding it deftly with the handkerchief and gently pulling the blue ribbon bow loose.

"Miss Paxton," Conrad addressed me in his trademark polite-but-formal tone, like I was a foreign dignitary ignorant of local customs. "Jackson will see to it that any evidence goes to the appropriate authorities in Los Angeles who have been working on this case. We want all the evidence in one facility."

Jackson nodded curtly and pried open the top of the box with a latex-covered finger. Expressionless, he placed the top on the back seat of the car and lifted the object from the box with the pencil.

Stewart's face crumpled and I flinched.

"Handcuffs?" Suggs asked flatly. "What kind of sicko gives a girl handcuffs?"

That was the pot calling the kettle black. "Suggs," I said, "don't you have some place to go?"

He didn't budge, brimming with sensitivity.

Jackson, a human plastic dispenser, sealed up the "gift" in yet another bag and hurried into the house, explaining curtly over his shoulder that he had a call to make.

To my surprise, Suggs started talking to Stewart, if you could call his short, blunt phrases talk. "You need more protection than that soft shoe."

"Gumshoe," I corrected.

"Soft shoe," he snarled. "You looking to hire another bodyguard?"

Stewart's forehead wrinkled, but her father answered the question. "Not at the moment, Mr. Magill. Jackson is quite capable. And a professional."

"Get it, Suggs?" I couldn't help rubbing in the point. You couldn't trust Suggs to filter through subtleties.

Stewart left her father's side and placed both hands on one of Suggs's arms. "That's an incredibly sweet thought. I'd appreciate it if you just kept your eyes and ears open for me, Suggs."

Suggs practically sprouted wings because he sure looked ready to float skyward. He wagged his thick head repeatedly and gradually snailed away from his center of worship, finally disappearing around the corner.

Conrad and Stewart, eager to confer with Jackson, bid me a fond farewell, grateful for the house tour.

I almost had the car seat belt buckled when Stewart came running back toward me. "Flip! I meant to ask, could you add me to your client list?"

I was about to say, "No way can I clean another house," (even my small, familiar old home), when the protective feelings I'd developed for Stewart kicked in. She needed more trustworthy eyes than Suggs Magill's. And I remembered Ivory and her two extra hands. "Sure, after Monday I can take you on."

"How about start the Wednesday after next?"

"Fine. If you're not at home when we get here, some clients give me a front door key to keep." Her face told me she hated that idea. "But most hide the key someplace." She hated that idea even more.

Common sense prevailed.

"I suppose," she spoke slowly, rightfully hesitant, "you should keep a key. I'll get one to you after we change the locks."

"I think that's smart."

She bent down, placing both hands on my arm as she had with Suggs. "I'm so glad you were here when we found that awful package. I didn't feel so alone. At first, I was always alone when the notes started arriving, then the packages and the telephone calls. He seemed to know the times I'd be all by myself. Now I'm never by myself, but it feels even lonelier."

"Stewart," the question bothered me, "if your father thinks he knows the guy who's doing this, why hasn't he been arrested?"

"Because there's no proof. Nothing." She lowered her voice as if the stalker lurked in the back seat of my car. "He's been questioned by the police. He volunteered to have his apartment searched, turned over phone records, even submitted to a voice analysis. Nothing came of it. On my father's orders, Jackson broke into his apartment and made a thorough search." She shook her head sadly. "I'm afraid Daddy has fixated on this one man at the expense of finding the real stalker. He's so sure it's someone *I* know when it could just as easily be one of *his* many enemies."

I wondered exactly how many people held an ax to grind over Conrad's head. "I have to tell you, Stewart, those handcuffs sent a chill down my spine. I can't imagine the effect they must have had on you."

"Oh, he's sent handcuffs before. That's his gift of choice, usually sent in a flower or candy box. He also sent a leg chain once and a neck shackle. They're always in the locked position because he is, after all, the Locksmith. The man with the key, in control."

I didn't know what to say except how sorry I felt. I also threw in a warning about Suggs, but she brushed it off. I drove away dejected, but even worse, feeling lame and useless. There was, however, one thing I could do that might prove helpful, and I decided to do it right away.

TAKING THE CHANCE that Officer Garrett would be eating his supper at the Bistro, I drove straight to Garland's. Maybe Conrad didn't want the local police involved, but I'd made no promises to keep my big mouth shut. It wouldn't hurt to give Sidney a heads up in case of trouble down the road, a real likelihood given the scene I'd just witnessed. The fact that Suggs wanted to interject himself into the situation bothered me no end. Other than lust, love of money, or hopes of grand larceny, what possible motive could he harbor to "keep an eye" on Stewart? Miss Fizzi, of course, would be thrilled at his chivalry. She couldn't see the dirt on a muddy boot.

Sure enough, Sidney Garrett sat at his usual back table against the wall, the closest table to the kitchen. From this vantage point, he could keep tabs on everyone without having to twist his head around. As I walked through the door, Hilda glided past, lips scrunched to one side, concentrating hard on delivering a loaded tray to another table. When her knee gave way and she almost dropped the tray, Sidney swooshed into action and arrested the catastrophe in midair. He set the load firmly on the fold-out tray table, mumbling, "No trouble," and headed back to his chair before Hilda even caught her breath to stammer, "Thank you." She stood there a moment, batting her eyes and smiling foolishly, hoping to transform a minor event into a major opportunity. But Sidney's BLT held a greater attraction for him.

I marched over and grabbed hold of him. "Officer Garrett. Sidney!"

He snapped to attention. "Yes, ma'am!"

"Sidney, I need to talk with you privately."

Hilda's batting eyes, the lids slimed in sparkly bright green, flashed question marks, but she dutifully turned away and served her customers.

"Finish your supper and listen up," I whispered, stomach rumbling at the sandwich, "but try to act like this is a friendly little talk about stoplights and nothing serious."

He nodded and picked up the sandwich. Now we would see what sort of stuff Officer Garrett was made of—a lazy, no-good freeloader like his predecessor, or a decent cop.

I launched into the entire saga of Stewart Larkin— past, present, and ominous future. I brought up the small, gray car I'd seen (you never know when your instincts are on target), and closed with the note and the "gift" I'd witnessed. Sidney listened intently, crystal eyes narrowing at the appropriate moments, his demeanor professional. At the end of my tale, he admitted he'd heard the talk about a stalker, and asked a few brief questions, all of them to-the-point and intelligent.

"You know, Sidney," I said admiringly, "I underestimated you. You're going to make us all proud."

He glowed from the compliment, but humbly replied, "It's my job to help out. In my opinion, Miss Paxton, the department ought to be in on this, especially now that there's real evidence. They have special units that are trained to handle this sort of thing."

"Call me Flip." I sighed and reset my ponytail. "I agree with you, Sidney, but that's Mr. Larkin's call, and we can't really intrude. Besides, they've got a PI and the L.A. police in on it. They don't want the attention of the local authorities just yet. I suspect Mr. Larkin has his own strategy." For the time being, I'd keep the conversation I'd heard between Conrad and Jackson private, unsure what to make of it myself. "Anyway, I wanted you to be aware. There may come a time when you're needed."

He seemed satisfied with the logic and finished the last bite of his dinner. At that moment, Garland approached us.

"Hello, you two." She wiped her hands on a bright-yellow apron with red cartoon crabs scampering across the fabric. Her brown-and-gray–streaked hair curled from the kitchen steam. "I'm telling everybody who comes in about the big shindig Friday night for the McKnights. Be here about seven o'clock. Don't miss it, now, because the whole town's turning out for this grand affair." She cocked a brow at Sidney. "There'll be dancing."

You could practically see the blank space in his brain where Garland itched to write HILDA. A mother's imagination always contains a dance floor, spotlight on a handsome young couple whirling past an enchanted audience.

"Dancing," Sidney repeated firmly. "So you think there might be trouble."

I grinned wide as a bread box and nudged his elbow. "We certainly hope so."

He turned redder than Garland's cartoon crabs, afraid I was making a pass.

Garland lightly smacked him on the shoulder with the back of her hand. "You gonna tote along a date, or would you like one on the house?"

I boldly leaned over and smacked Sidney's other shoulder. "One on the house! Now, Sidney, that's an offer you can't refuse!"

Garland and I burst into laughter, leaving poor Officer Garrett flustered as anything, wondering what in the world we crazy women were getting at. Until finally, at long last, Hilda caught his eye. And held it.

Chapter 15

Although playing matchmaker with Garland lent my day a dusting of frivolity, I didn't rest any easier that night after talking to Tom. He called from the office, chained to his desk. Earlier, Conrad had filled him in on the chilling reappearance of Stewart's stalker, and refused Tom's advice to bring in Maryland authorities. Balancing my penchant for eavesdropping and general nosiness, I confessed to Tom that I'd heard Conrad say he wanted to handle things his own way, "without the red tape," but didn't tell him I'd been presumptuous enough to spill the beans to Officer Garrett. He'd no doubt sock me with the lecture on sticking my shiny nose in where it didn't belong.

"I guess Conrad pretty much said to you what I overheard him say to Jackson Parker. He's bent on letting Jackson and the L.A. people deal with this stalker.

Though how the L.A. police can help from there is beyond me, except maybe matching up evidence. I'm worried about Stewart."

Tom sat silent on the other end of the phone. When he spoke, irritation infused his usually unruffled speech. "It is more than bothersome that Conrad won't bring in the local police now that we know the stalker has tracked Stewart to Solace Glen. I can only advise him; I can't divulge what he wishes to keep private. Stewart isn't any more cooperative. She has a lot of faith in her father, and Jackson's ability to protect her and trap the stalker."

"Jackson's not the only one who wants to protect her. Our local sociopath offered his services."

"Suggs?" Tom groaned. "I hope they didn't step into that one."

"Well. They stuck a toe in. Stewart thought it resembled a sweet gesture and asked him to keep his eyes and ears open. Who knows? Suggs might redeem himself by acting as a second pair of eyes."

Only the rattling of paper and Eli's bored yawn in the background broke Tom's silence.

"What happens now, Tom? Other than you working yourself to death with everything you've got on your plate, plus worrying about some crazy man running after Stewart."

"I just keep plugging, I guess."

He sounded so tired and beat down, I wanted to race over to his office and take him in my arms.

I started to make the suggestion when he abruptly added, "I'm swamped, so don't expect me over tonight. I've got to get my desk cleared, which will help clear my mind, and then I'll grab some leftovers at the house."

"Leftovers? You actually have something left of an original cooked product?"

"Blame Charlie. Charlie cooks. He whipped together an incredible lunch for us today. Add it to the list of things I didn't know about my brother."

A subject worth exploring. "You really don't know Charlie very well, do you?"

"No." Tom stifled a yawn. "There's always been a wall between us. A kind of awkwardness. He's a few years younger and we didn't share many of the same interests growing up. He played football; I ran. He liked photography; I preferred chess. We grew up in the same house, but not the same room. And he's been on the road for thirteen years. Hardly ever calls since Dad passed away."

"Was he close to your father?"

"No. Charlie's never been close to anyone that I know of. Except Stewart, and I only found out about that yesterday."

"Mmm. Funny, him running into her in L.A. What's he been doing there?"

Tom couldn't hold back another yawn. "He's been working on a book—his travels and photographs. The publisher's based in L.A."

Sounded innocent enough. "Oh, really? How long has he lived there?"

"Several months. Why all the questions? You know I'm beat."

"I know, sweetheart." I poured on the honey. "Just one more itty bitty question. What do you think the chances are of Charlie and Stewart getting back together again?"

"I don't know, Matchmaker, Matchmaker. She seems

interested enough, but he's pretty wary. In fact, she told him she may be stopping by later for a visit, with Jackson lurking in the shadows, I'm sure, gun sights trained on Charlie."

Sneaky me, I added, "Well, he's *so* attractive. Like his brother. Did Charlie give you a reason for his visit other than 'business?' Any details?"

"That's two questions too many. Now good night. I want to finish up here and go home to a nice dinner."

Oh, I thought, the green monkey poking his brazen eyes over the tip of my shoulder, *you can go home to a little dinner with Charlie and Stewart, but I'm supposed to hop into bed all alone with a* House & Garden.

"Fine," I huffed, with a pinch of frost. "Sweet dreams."

He didn't catch the iciness, or if he did, didn't care. "Good night, Flip. See you tomorrow, maybe."

When he hung up, I fumed at Jeb, who coiled around my ankles, wanting attention. " 'See you tomorrow— *maybe!*' Is this the kind of life a lawyer's wife has to lead? Does he even realize how long it's been since we've been to-ge-ther?"

How different, I wondered angrily, *might married life be with a photojournalist? Or a nice, old scientist?*

THE NICE, OLD scientist presented himself early the next morning outside the Historical Society. Lindbergh appeared from out of the blue, taking his A.M. constitutional. Before jumping into the car, I invited him to go into the old 1794 brick house and linger as long as he liked. Then off I sped.

Sam and Lee begged me to stop by early to help with

a cleaning, so at seven I drove up the circular driveway. The 1855 Bell mansion stood majestically on a small, grassy hill within the town limits, surrounded by evergreens and flowering trees that waved and rustled in the June breeze like glinting sails on a lush, emerald sea. I knocked on one of the massive, double oak doors and barged through, loaded with cleaning gear.

"Hey, it's me! Make yourselves decent!"

Lee's throaty giggle carried down the stairs. "You ruined the moment, Flip!"

Sam yelled out, "The hell you did! We'll be down in a few minutes!"

I blushed and trudged into the kitchen. The least I could do was brew coffee and mop a floor while waiting for whoopee time to come to its natural conclusion.

After about fifteen minutes, Lee shyly peered around the kitchen door looking a little more than rumpled. Her auburn hair held knots and tangles; her neck appeared raw and chafed beneath an oversized nightshirt.

"You look like you've been necking with a squirrel. He leave any nuts and berries in that hair?"

"No," she answered pertly, "but maybe he left a sweet little baby someplace else."

I handed her a cup of coffee, feeling right at home in this house I'd cleaned for more than twenty years. "The way you two have been going at it, your Valentine this winter could be wearing diapers."

She turned up her nose smugly, as if such a possibility already amounted to a fait accompli.

"So. You want the regular cleaning, or do you need some special job here and there due to the move? From the looks of the downstairs, you've been busy. You're pretty much unpacked."

"Yeah," Lee whipped a hairbrush from her nightshirt pocket and started the detangulation process, "we got a lot done before the honeymoon. Did I tell you about my honeymoon?"

"Oh, for God's sake, keep a lid on it. I've got work to do."

Sam made an entrance and headed straight for the coffee, whopping Lee's backside in a territorial manner as he shuffled by. "Good morning, Flip. You're here mighty early."

"You invited me, you fool."

"I am a fool. A fool for love. What's been going on that the oblivious honeymooners should know about?" He crossed bare ankles and leaned his sinewy back against the kitchen counter, both hands cradling the coffee mug. The rusty hair stood on end. "I haven't seen you in three whole days."

"Been bored and missed me, huh?" I sipped from a mug with a particularly ugly photo of Jeb printed on one side with a big red X drawn from ears to whiskers. "What you two need is a good party to get you out of the bedroom. I mean, the house."

Lee started to protest. "You throwing us another party? You and Tom have really done enough."

"With his schedule lately? He doesn't even have time to . . . well, never mind. The party's for the McKnights and the whole town is turning out Friday night at the Bistro to say good-bye to the old and hello to the new. Ivory told me a new interim minister made the Presbytery's list at the last second, highly recommended, and the search committee made a grab."

Sam yawned and stretched his long arms. "I tell you what. Nothing like a Presbyterian changeover to make everybody schedule a big drinking binge and some dancing."

"You're just jealous 'cause you're Catholic." Lee pulled a spool of hair from the hairbrush. "We wouldn't miss it. What else is happening?"

"When did I see you last? Tuesday morning? That's right. So you don't know about Stewart."

Lee stuck a finger down her throat. "Bleck! That woman! I don't even want to hear her name! Whatever you have to say about her, keep to yourself."

This comment, of course, only encouraged Sam and me. He stood up straight. "I'm interested. Hear she's a real looker. Always good to have a backup, ya know, where wives are concerned. Otherwise, they get uppity."

Lee slit her hazel eyes his way. "OK, what about the perfectly perfect Miss Larkin? And I'll try not to puke."

"Your envy is showing, dearie." I waited a second or two before spilling the news; more dramatic that way. "The stalker followed her here."

"Get out! It's definite? You're kidding!"

"Sounds serious enough to me," Sam murmured.

"Yep, I was there when it happened. Right in front of my old house."

"What *did* happen?" Sam and Lee could never live anywhere but a small town. Every event, no matter how catastrophic or mundane, sparked their imaginations. Every incident provided fuel for their running motors.

"Well! It was like something you read about in Baltimore. Suggs came walking along. . . ."

"Suggs! What's he got to do with this? Don't tell me he's the stalker."

"No, Lee, use your head. But he volunteered to be her guard dog. That's a whole other story."

Sam winced. "Suggs Magill? Good God."

"If He is good, He'll protect her from Suggs. But let me get on with it."

They both shut their mouths, sleepy eyes wide awake and attentive.

"Suggs was the one who spied the note on the back of Stewart's car. The stalker left a note and a 'present' on the back seat. He calls himself the Locksmith. Gives me chills. Guess what the present was?"

They shook their heads solemnly.

"Handcuffs. Locked handcuffs."

Lee gasped and Sam's jaw clamped tight. "Oh!" she exclaimed. "Now I've got chills, too! She must have really done a number on this guy."

Sam scoffed. "There you go again, blaming the victim. She didn't ask for any of this."

Lee maintained her anti-Stewart stance. "Neither one of you know her like I do. Trust me. Whatever she's going through now, she brought it on herself."

I shook my head slowly back and forth. "Noooo. I completely disagree. I've been around her a lot more than you have recently. You knew her twelve or thirteen years ago, Lee. People change."

"And some don't. Those zebra stripes aren't gonna rub off. Period."

"Now, Lee," Sam tried a hand at reshaping his bride's harsh opinion. "Flip's right. People do change. I wouldn't have married you if that weren't true. Why, I used to juggle women like crazy."

Lee's eyes flew to the ceiling. "Yeah, yeah, yeah."

"Point is, you haven't seen Stewart in many years. You never know. You two might strike up your friendship right where you left off."

Lee tossed her head and snorted. "It 'left off' where Stewart Larkin *left* on the arm of my boyfriend and then *left* him high and dry. That's what she does best."

I coughed. "You might be interested to know what's going on there, too."

"What, with her and Charlie?"

I smacked my lips. "She invited herself over last night."

"Ugh! Don't tell me he's that stupid. That man needs a reminder, and I'm just the one to do it."

"Leeeeee," Sam gritted his teeth at her. A professorial expression crossed his face, wisdom dealing with youthful folly. "Leave well enough alone."

"But it's not well enough, precious. It's a disaster waiting to happen. I'll just plant a little bug in Charlie's ear at the party tomorrow night. Does he know I'm married?"

I laughed at her. "You are such a vain creature. Yes, Tom told him, and Charlie said he's very happy for you and would love to meet the lucky guy."

Lee leaped across the room and flung her arms around Sam's neck. "Good! And I hope he's excruciatingly jealous of the lucky guy!"

They appeared on the verge of tousling each other's hair again, so I disturbed them long enough to say I'd start cleaning upstairs, thank you kindly, and the honeymoon could continue on the clean kitchen floor.

Grunting under the weight of the vacuum I lugged up the staircase, I wondered if my own honeymoon would ever begin.

CHAPTER 16

✳

STRANGER THINGS HAD happened, but Tom actually made himself available for the big blowout at
the Bistro Friday night. He said he'd pick me up at
seven-thirty.

I lay in wait, anxiously counting the slow chiming of
the Historical Society's mantel clock, armed with the
feather duster to bring a grin to his face. As I stared at
the empty chairs vacated by Plain Jane and Dear John,
visions of the new house floated through my mind.
When I'd stopped by the building site earlier in the day
to check the steady progress, Abner was nowhere to be
found. The foreman simply shrugged his shoulders, as
ignorant as anyone else of Abner's sudden departures
and whereabouts.

The knock at the door jolted my reverie and I raced

to the entranceway, feather duster at the ready, a semiseductive tilt to my glossed lips. But. Nothing is as it should be. Tom stood straight and tall, dignified in his rolled-up shirtsleeves. Before I could leap into his arms, he pointed over his shoulder. Charlie and Stewart dawdled on the sidewalk behind him, and across the street, deeper in the twilight shadows, skulked the outline of the ever-present Jackson Parker. Goodie. A double date with a chaperone.

The feather duster disappeared behind my back, but not before I caught the gleam in Tom's hawk eyes and the rise of his upper lip, appreciative of the gesture. He honored me with a kiss on the cheek. "Someday, we'll get back to dusting," he whispered.

"Maybe tonight?" I whispered back, and called, "Hello, everyone!"

The evening air of mid-June didn't require a sweater, so I threw the feather duster on the kitchen counter and locked the door behind me.

"I've been missing you," I said in an undertone, before we approached Charlie and Stewart.

Tom took my arm in his and wrapped it tight against his side. "And I you. Don't worry. This, too, shall pass."

"That's a favorite expression. Especially lately."

Stewart greeted me brightly, a torch that rarely fizzled out. She looked splendid in a red cotton halter dress with a long, slim skirt. "Hi, Flip! How's it going? Isn't this a beautiful evening? Gosh, it's nice to be out, doing something *normal*. Charlie's being very kind to indulge me."

She reached for his arm with both hands and clung tight. He didn't retreat. In fact, he didn't seem to mind at all. Old wounds healed quickly, no ugly scars left behind. Or so it appeared.

The four of us fell into an easy gait toward the Bistro, Stewart and I in between the men. We chatted as we walked.

"Things are going well, thanks, although I haven't seen as much of my fiancé as I'd like. We can't have everything, I guess." I tossed a little pout Tom's way. "But the real question is, how are things with you? Has Jackson made any progress?"

We all involuntarily cast a backward glimpse across the street at the figure that doggedly trailed us. Jackson wore a light jacket, even in the summer weather, discreetly concealing his weapon.

Stewart's bright countenance dimmed. "No. No progress at all. In fact," her worried eyes met Charlie's, "I haven't even told you yet, but I received a call this morning and a note this afternoon."

Charlie stopped dead in his tracks. "This guy called you? What did he say? Don't you have caller ID or something?"

"Yes, and Jackson immediately checked it out. The call came from a public phone in Frederick." Her hands dropped in a helpless gesture. "Now I'm sorry I told you. I really don't want to ruin everybody's evening out."

"The last thing you should be worried about is ruining our evening," Tom replied. "Why didn't you call me?"

Stewart's cheeks flushed. "Daddy, of course. He was so disappointed with the outcome in L.A. after all the time, energy, and technical hoopla that went into the case. You know how he wants things handled here in Maryland, even if you don't agree. He thinks if we lie low with as little involvement by the police as possible, we'll have a better chance of drawing this man out. He may make a mistake and be careless, and Jackson will be there to grab him."

"Unless he's smart," Charlie muttered.

"Stewart," I gently placed a hand on her upper arm, "has this man threatened your life? Has it come to that?"

Tears welled up in her eyes. "I can't believe it myself, but yes. There's real anger in what he says now. The call—that horrible, muffled voice he uses, and the note . . ." She couldn't continue. "Oh, please. Let's talk about something else. Anything else. I need to put this awful situation aside, if only for a couple of hours."

Exhaustion seemed to overtake her for a moment, and the three of us sent the same, silent message to each other—*the least we can do is give Stewart what she needs.*

Charlie, I noticed, gave her arm a light pat.

"OK," I said, taking a jab at bright conversation, "let's talk about a date for our wedding."

"Oh, good Lord," Tom choked. "When the house is ready, dear."

Both Stewart and Charlie laughed in relief, but I didn't find anything funny about it at all.

PART THREE

❈

Parties and Peril

CHAPTER 17

✳

EVEN WITH EVERY table shoved against the walls to allow for dancing space, the Bistro burst at the seams. Practically the whole population of Solace Glen crammed into the first floor of the old, nineteenth-century warehouse tastefully renovated into Garland's dream restaurant. The beer and wine flowed freely, and the staff hustled from one customer to the next. Hilda collected the one-price-fits-all admission money at the door, and pointed out the two long buffet tables along each side. The McKnight family huddled toward the back, accepting the good wishes of the people they'd come to know so well in the dozen years they'd been a part of the community. Ivory, dressed in a glittering silver pantsuit that made her look like an orbiting satellite, held her own court beside them, bragging loudly about her new "partnership" with me in the cleaning business, assuring members of the congregation that she'd still show up for Sunday services.

"You can take the sexton out of the church, but you can't take the church out of the sexton! Are we doin' karaoke tonight, 'cause y'all know how Ivory loves karaoke."

Pal and the Eggheads sucked on beers nearby, and the word *karaoke* caused a minor eruption.

Pal spurted, "Hear that? We're doing karaoke tonight, just like on a cruise ship!"

"Cruise ship?" yelled one Egghead. "Like *Love Boat*? I've seen every rerun. Best show ever. Remember the one where Gopher . . ."

"Nah," the other Egghead argued back, "it doesn't hold a candle to *SpongeBob SquarePants*. Now that's a good ocean show. That little guy tripping around the ocean with the crab? I die laughing every time."

My attention wandered from the Ship of Fools to the small stage erected in one corner. Sound equipment filled the platform and loudspeakers blared Tommy Dorsey and Glen Miller. In the center of it all loomed Screamin' Larry, a hulking Buddha on his throne, plugged into earphones and surrounded by empty bottles from his favorite microbrewery. By the end of the evening, he'd surely have collected a case.

I spotted my favorite group of ladies, clucking like a flock of peahens at one table. Miss Fizzi showed signs of enjoying herself with a half-empty glass of white wine, and the women surrounding her—Margaret, Melody, and Tina—chattered all at once. To my delight and theirs, Lindbergh sauntered over and pulled up a chair. Every spine zinged straight, every hairdo got finger-fluffed.

Garland swooped from table to table, checking on her guests' comfort. She drew up short when she ran into Roland, her soon-to-be-ex, slouched over a beer next to Marlene, the other most popular person in town. The two grouches no doubt showed up for the booze and public relations, both their businesses suffering lately from a lack of local concern. Garland wisely pressed her lips together and made a U-turn.

Swinging her shoulders and swaying her hips in rhythm to the music, Lee yakked up a storm with Sally. She sported one of Sally's twin baby boys on a hipbone, getting in some practice. Sam hovered nearby, talking sports with Wilbur, who occasionally punctured the air with the Longhorn signal, and Abner, who, as usual, did all the listening and none of the talking. I wondered where he'd disappeared to this time and knew after a couple of glasses of wine, I'd be brazen enough to ask.

"Oh my God, is that Lee?" Stewart stooped down to my ear so I could hear over the Big Band music. "That's not her baby, is it?"

"No, she's just trying him on for size. Are you going to speak to her?" I hoped Lee could bury the past. The way things lay, with Lee married and Charlie perhaps close to freeing old battle wounds, it made perfect sense to let bygones be bygones. Knowing Lee's tenacious hold on a grudge, though, Stewart faced an uphill battle.

"Of course, I'll speak to her." She gazed at her old college chum a few moments. "She hasn't changed a bit, has she? She's so beautiful."

"And well-loved. She's everybody's favorite."

"Which one is her husband?"

I pointed to Sam. "The tall, gangly one. He's a history professor at Hood. He's talking with Wilbur Polk, who owns a landscaping company, and that's Abner Diggs. He runs a construction company."

I turned to confirm that she heard me over the din and caught a puzzling look on Stewart's face. Lips parted and eyes wide and staring, a night creature captured in a harsh light. She stared straight at Abner Diggs.

"Stewart? Are you all right?"

She immediately shook the expression. "Why, yes. I think I'll go over to Lee. Could you tell Charlie? He's getting me a drink. Oh, and before I forget, here's my house key." And she slid away.

Puzzlement quickly changed to curiosity as I strained my eyes to see how this reunion would play out, much more interested in Lee's reaction at the moment than pestering Stewart about Abner. I stood by and anxiously watched. Happy scenes of the three of us enjoying Friday night dinners together with our husbands flitted through my imagination. Thanksgivings at the fire pond with me chasing their children away from the water. Caroling together at Christmas.

Stewart slowly approached my best buddy until I saw Sally quit talking and Lee stop swaying. Her face revealed everything. The jaw tightened and rose, the mouth bent down, the hazel eyes projected a chilly formality. It pained me to see Stewart, who had been through enough for one day, almost groveling, trying so hard to break the ice and find safe footing. But Lee would give no quarter.

"It's ridiculous," I muttered to myself, and felt Tom's warm hand caress the small of my back.

"What did you say?" He brushed his lips against my temple.

"Nothing, nothing." I took the glass of white wine he offered. "The Ice Queen forgiveth nothing."

He followed my gaze and caught the drift. "Oh. Too bad. Charlie filled me in on the untold history." He lifted his shoulders. "Charlie and Lee. I never would have guessed that one."

"Yes. Charlie and Lee. Add it to the list of things you didn't know about your brother. They both look happy enough now, though, don't they?"

Charlie wove his way through the crowd to Stewart and handed her a drink, a subtle sign to Lee that the two of them were cozying up again. Maybe. Then he turned to Lee and they shared an awkward nice-to-see-you-again hug. Their tepid embrace propelled Sam away from sports talk. He stepped into place beside his new bride, politely introducing himself to both Stewart and Charlie.

About this time, I heard Pal exclaim, "Suggs! What the heck you doing here? You never come to parties."

An Egghead answered, "Oh, we know the real reason he's here. She's wearing a red dress and has a guy's name. Starts with an 'S.' "

"And it ain't Sally!" the other Egghead threw in. "Hey, don't you think Sally shoulda named the twins after us instead of Dale Earnhardt and Kyle Petty? I mean, we delivered 'em in an emergency. Saved her hide, so t'speak."

Pal ignored him and pressed Suggs. "You know, you have one paying job, Suggs, not two. Miss Larkin already has a bodyguard. Something's gotta give. I can't afford to have it be the Crown. You barely made it to work on time this morning. Suggs? You listening?"

But he'd skulked away, drawing closer to the woman

he could not tear his eyes from. Fortunately, he cut his engine after a few paces, content to play guard dog from a respectful distance. I wondered if he'd stepped on Jackson's toes yet.

Screamin' Larry ended one song and introduced another, his deep, radio voice booming as brash as ever, the words taking on a slur that would only worsen as the night progressed. "This goes out to . . . I am hesitant to say . . . or should I say *forced* to say because I am getting paid for this gig," he waved a nearly empty beer bottle at the crowd, "all you young lovers out there. Bluck!" He clutched his throat, gagging, and pointed the bottle at Garland. "OK! I said it, dammit. Now, everybody leave me alone and do not ask me to do any more of these stupid, juvenile dedications. And keep the beer coming, dammit!"

With that, the romantic strains of "Moonlight Becomes You" filled the room and Garland rushed to plug in a couple of fig trees she'd decorated with twinkling white lights. Men and women coupled off and began to slow dance. With gentle prodding, Garland guided Officer Garrett toward Hilda. She motioned her embarrassed daughter to leave her seat by the door while Garland took over the job of collecting funds. She and I smiled conspiratorially as Sidney took Hilda's hand and the two of them made for the dance floor. I had to admit, after the initial giggling over which way their hands went, they made a fine-looking young couple.

Tom and I melted into each other, balancing our wineglasses as we slowly shuffled around the same six inches of floor space. Lee handed off the baby to Sally and threw her arms around Sam's neck, forcing him to bend low. She abruptly turned her back on Charlie and

Stewart, who merely blinked and slid into each other's arms. Stewart immediately buried her face against Charlie's neck and my heart went out to her.

"Really," I huffed. "I'm going to have to have a talk with Lee. She's being stubborn. And rude."

"Hush," Tom chided in my ear. "You're distracting me from my true intent."

His free hand inched slowly down to my hip and I pretended to mind.

"This is a Presbyterian party, remember? The Frozen Chosen?"

Ivory orbited by shamelessly leading an Egghead, a stiff mannequin, blabbing in his face nonstop. "Loosen up, boy! You dance like you're takin' my blood pressure! Why don't that man play some decent music for once? You wanna sing backup for me at karaoke time? You like the Righteous Brothers?"

Over Tom's shoulder, I spied Abner moving toward the door, unable to handle the over-stimulation of a party. Before he walked out, he paused. The usually serene, crinkled eyes zeroed in on one object. Stewart. His face betrayed a hard, hate-filled anger. Then he vanished.

Recalling Abner's reaction at our building site days before, I prodded Tom. "I think Abner knows the Larkins but won't admit it. Do you know any reason why he might hate Stewart and her father?"

Tom reared his head back, delivering one of his patented, patronizing expressions. "You have the longest nose of any woman I have ever come across."

"Thanks. I owe it all to rhinoplasty. Seriously, now, I mentioned the Larkin name to Abner the other day and he suddenly looked like one of those pro wrestlers ready to maim and kill."

"I don't know." He dismissed the subject. "Someone with Conrad's power picks up enemies everywhere. Let's talk about feather dusters. Do you have one in red and black? You know, Terp colors."

"*Tom.*" I stood poised on the edge of a lecture when the silhouette of a familiar form automatically changed the subject for me. "Ha! Look who just joined the party. It's that goofy real estate agent. What in the world is he doing here?"

Tom focused on keeping his rhythm to the music and slurping from his wineglass at the same time. "Beats me. Maybe," his voice rose dramatically, "he hates Stewart, too, and has come to do her harm. For a nice, Presbyterian party, vicious woman haters abound."

His silliness bounced off me and I twisted my head this way and that, trying to draw a bead on Horace Worthington as he made his way across the floor. He wore the same outfit he'd donned the other day, green blazer and all, including the funky sandals and huge diamond ring. He vaguely reminded me of Ichabod Crane. Naturally, I started checking Marlene out, to see when she'd notice him and to gauge any theatrical reactions. Just when Horace moved close enough for Marlene to spit at, Tom whirled me around.

"Good Lord, there's Leonard and C.C.," he announced with a smile. "Now the party will really start hopping. Larry's drunk enough to light a fuse without a match."

Sure enough, in sashayed C.C. with Leonard bringing up the rear. She wore a slinky, black little number with more straps than you could count and glittery earrings as long as two cigars. Leonard, even in a plain, tieless Oxford shirt, appeared ready to launch a board meeting at the drop of a hat. C.C. spotted Marlene and immediately waved an arm over her head, silver bracelets jangling, to draw attention.

"Mar-lene! Mar-lene! Look! We made it!" An Egghead, torturing one of Hilda's friends around the dance floor, slammed into her, prompting C.C. to screech, "Good God! Do I have to be assaulted every time I turn around? Get off me, you boorish pig!"

The boorish pig apologized in minimal fashion, untangled himself, and gallumphed away, leaving C.C. to roll her eyelined orbs and stomp toward Marlene. Leonard trailed behind, head rotating methodically in search of the nearest bar or waitress.

When I refocused on Marlene, she'd inched out of her seat, a welcoming grin on the fleshy lips, so happy to have her rich, best friend join the party. Suddenly, the smile froze and the fish eyes almost popped out of her head.

She'd seen Horace! Thrilled that for a split second I alone knew her secret, I squealed.

"I have that effect on most women." Tom took a deep swig of wine. "You know, this is awful stuff. Chateau Grotesque."

"Tom! Horace Worthington is Marlene's ex! Look at her!"

Marlene had, in fact, come unglued. Piece by nasty piece, she seemed to break apart. Her shoulders collapsed, her knees buckled, she slumped backward into the chair, arms flopped to her sides.

Horace, however, merely sneered, eyes slit, a cat on the prowl. Calmly, deliberately, he paused directly in front of the collapsed heap, then crept away, having made his silent announcement: *I'm back, dearie.*

When C.C. reached Marlene, she started the normal blather, noted Marlene's frozen attitude, and shook her shoulder. When Marlene didn't respond, C.C. actually grabbed the boorish pig Egghead who'd run into her, using words like *stroke* and *aneurysm,* and had him check Marlene out. She finally emerged from her shocked state and kicked the Egghead away as she might a stray dog.

"Leave me alone! I've got to get out of here. I can't breathe."

"Should Leonard drive you to the clinic, darling? You don't look well."

"No, no, I'm fine. I just have to get out of here." Marlene grabbed her purse. "I'll call you later."

She rushed past without a backward glance, but my jaw dropped at the expression she wore. Terror. Sheer terror.

I zoomed in on the mysterious ex-husband who drifted toward the little bar set up in back, looking as innocent and guileless as a middle school student. Presently, he engaged in conversation with Leonard, who'd aimed for the booze the moment Marlene raced out the door.

The lilting, romantic music dissolved and Larry started spinning jazzy, upbeat songs like "Let's Do It" to the delight of Reverend McKnight, who loved to boogie. He stole Ivory away from the one Egghead brave enough to dance with her, and hit the floor. Officer Garrett and Hilda reluctantly pulled apart at the end of the slow stuff, and now sheepishly stared at each other and the dancers jiggling around them. Lee picked up her discussion with Sally, juggling the second twin on her knee. Charlie and Stewart somehow managed to corner Sam, no doubt attempting to persuade him to talk some sense into his unforgiving bride.

"I'm going for a refill, OK? Want me to get you one?" I took Tom's empty glass. "Why don't you help those two gang up on Sam? If we all pull together, Lee might at least find it in her heart to act more civil."

I turned on my heel and scurried away, an ulterior motive in mind. Sidling close to Leonard and Horace, I presented empty glasses to the bartender and stuck an ear in their direction.

"Why, yes, Mr. Crosswell, I do remember you. We met briefly at the Larkin Industries Headquarters in L.A., am I right?" The affected flamboyance, the effeminate personae worn earlier in the week, evaporated. Monday's face did not jibe with the face I'd witnessed minutes before—the face that chilled Marlene to the bone and sent her scrambling.

"Yes, you're right. About two or three weeks ago. We discovered we'd both made appointments to discuss our investments in L.C.S., but Conrad was called away." Leonard made small talk with but one purpose in mind—ammunition for future destruction. "For some time now, I've had some very—how should I phrase this?— unsettling concerns. Perhaps we could compare notes."

Horace barely lifted a brow and dunked a celery stick into some dip. "I've noticed a few irregularities myself. As a matter of fact, I had a messenger drop off a package to Conrad a few months ago spelling out a list of problems I saw on the horizon. He ignored me, so I made an appointment with the great man, which is where I ran into you. Needless to say, I left his office rather frustrated."

"We both did. Are you from L.A., Mr. Worthington?"

"Not originally." He added to my disbelieving ears, "I had a real estate business there that floundered, thanks to investing in LCS. I just this week moved to Frederick. An associate in Deep Creek convinced me there are financial opportunities to be found here that could not be pursued in California."

At that moment, Horace noticed me standing close by. He instantly changed his tune. "So voila! Maryland, my Maryland." He dotted a spot of dill dip from the corner of his mouth and sipped at his wine like a teetotaling old lady.

I took the two full glasses of wine the bartender offered and slipped to the side with one thought in mind—*what in the world?*

At the settlement in Tom's office, Horace said he'd lived out west for a short while, but insisted that Deep Creek, Maryland, where he'd lived "for decades," amounted to home, hearth, and burial ground. Now the one true thread in his story seemed to be a recent move to Frederick. Was the lie about Deep Creek designed to mislead Stewart and Conrad? Or was the L.A. business story a lie designed to impress wealthy Leonard Crosswell?

Leonard continued with the business meeting, his most comfortable arena. "Conrad can be annoyingly evasive. It's hard to gather information through the regular channels, which is why I'm delighted to see him and his charming daughter here in Maryland for a time. Have you ever met him?" The fox eyes suddenly glinted as Stewart wafted by on Charlie's arm; the snout flared at the scent of her perfume.

Horace elaborated on finally meeting Conrad. "I ran into both of them earlier in the week, as a matter of fact, at a real estate settlement I attended to help out my

Deep Creek associate. Mr. Larkin doesn't know who I am, though. I've always used a company name in my business correspondence. More impersonal that way. But you were saying?"

Leonard kept his sharp eyes clamped on Stewart as he spoke, admiring her shape. "I was about to say that I've reached a crisis point with at least two of my concerns, and may be closing out all investments shortly. If Conrad wants to play hardball, so can I. He has no idea how hard."

He sniffed the air behind Stewart's back and inched forward, unable to resist running a paw down her bare back as he greeted her with warm, friendly words. She jumped at the touch, already nervous as a trapped mouse.

Suggs appeared from out of nowhere. "You need anything, Miss Larkin?" He shot Leonard a look with needles in it.

"No, thank you, Suggs." She smiled sweetly, if nervously, and introduced Suggs to Leonard as a "friend and protector."

"But where is the loyal and true Jackson? Surely, *this* man can't be your only lifeline tonight."

Suggs glowered and Charlie twirled around, clutching two drinks. "Why, no, old chap, he's not. I don't believe I know you. I'm Charlie Scott, Tom's brother."

Leonard mutely appraised him, slow to accept the offer of a handshake. "Tom's brother, eh? Another lawyer?"

"Nope. I'm a professional bum. Got a license and everything."

Humor was wasted on Leonard. "In town for long? Or for good?"

"Not for good," Charlie replied vaguely. "Will you excuse us, please?"

"Stewart, before you go," the paw again strayed to her bare skin, the thumb slowly rubbing swirls on her shoulder blades, "will your father be around tomorrow? I'd really like a word with him. You should be there, too, I think. Yes, definitely, you should be there."

Stewart nodded, eyes imploring Charlie to whisk her away from Leonard and his demands. She was not up to this tonight.

Tom made a sudden appearance, Velcro on my hip. "What have you been doing all this time? Flirting with the Eggheads again? That your second or third refill? I bet you've been drinking mine, too, you sneaky two-timer."

The smell of wine and something else, unnamable, hit me. "Tom, have you had anything to drink besides wine tonight?"

He pointed across the room. "Charlie. That Charlie. He brought this stuff home, they make it on an island somewhere in the Pacific. *In* the Pacific? *On* the Pacific? Hell, I dunno. *Under* the Pacific."

"So you either drank it or swam in it."

"You . . ." He fell into my chest full force. "I think I'll marry you."

"That's it." I set the glasses firmly on the table. "Knowing Charlie, whatever he brought back is illegal. But illegal or not, you've had enough."

"Oh, no, no, no. Wanna dance? Larry! Why'd the music stop?"

At that moment, Ivory, who could not contain herself a second longer, launched a loud assault that quickly escalated.

"Who died and made you musical czar? You don't

play nothin' but Big Band and jazz, and some of us are damn sick and tired of it! You ever heard of Sha-Na-Na or Elvis?"

Larry cracked open another beer and guzzled half of it. "I know you. You work at one of those religious insta-tutions. And you are not even in the choir."

"So what? You are not even sober."

"So what? I am a trained musicologist, sober or not. At present, I prefer not. Now get out of my face."

"The hell you say! How 'bout you get your butt out of that chair, and gimme the microphone!"

As tall as Larry, and of equal girth (most of it mus-cle), Ivory could throw around her weight when she wanted to. She bustled around the platform, grabbed the handheld microphone, and tugged on his chair. "Time to end your little swan song, Mr. DJ." She appealed to the audience. "Who's gonna help Ivory? Come on! Who wants to sing karaoke? Let's put some pep in this party, people!"

The Eggheads couldn't resist any call for help, sensi-ble or not, and a plea for karaoke sounded sensible enough. They tramped over to Ivory and took position on either side of Larry.

"One, two, three—heave!"

With Screamin' Larry roaring like a hurricane, flail-ing massive arms in a useless attempt to knock out one of them, the Eggheads managed to heave the chair backward until it teetered on the edge of the platform.

"For Pete's sake, stop swinging at us, Larry! Duck!"

"No, you duck!"

Simultaneously, they abandoned the chair to save themselves, and the crowd watched in awe as the chair tilted back in slow motion.

Ivory's head poked up from behind. "What are you fools doin'? I can't hold this man up by myself!"

The madness that contorted Larry's face suddenly subsided, replaced with a pleased, beatific smile. The squinty eyes lit up. He raised his beer bottle heavenward, threw his head back, and poured the liquid in a splashing stream into his open mouth. When his head leaned back, the chair leaned with it. For a brief moment, it seemed to totter in midair, enough time for people to moan, "Oooooooooooo," before it crashed over Ivory like a Buster Keaton vault falling from the sky.

The Eggheads stared, astonished, and raised accusing fingers at each other.

Ivory screamed and grunted, squashed under Larry and splintered pieces of broken chair. "Wait'll I get my hands on you! You did that on purpose! I know the stories about you, sinner! Somebody better help Ivory!"

This brought the Eggheads to their senses. They leaped off the platform to render professional service. Pal and Officer Garrett ran over to help.

Ivory bugled in Sidney's ear. "Arrest him! I want him arrested for salt and battery! Look! Ahh, he tore my new silver evening attire! See that! I'm bleedin'! This blouse is ruined. I'll sue his butt! Where's Tom? You crazy, mean, son-of-a—damn, this is a church party, I can't talk evil. Damn, I said damn. Listen what you made me say, devil!"

The four men dragged Ivory to her feet, leaving Larry on the floor, gagging, he was so happy.

Tom blinked, as if he'd witnessed a tiger disappear into a top hat and was trying to figure it out. "Did I just hear my name?"

"No." I pulled on his arm. "Let's go home."

"Home? Which one? Yours, mine, or ours? Wait. Ours isn't built yet, is it?"

"The Historical Society, remember?"

"A-ha."

"Good. You're not as drunk as I thought." I pushed Tom toward the entranceway. "We're gonna have that stuff Charlie gave you analyzed."

As we made our way to the front door, Tom drew to a halt to congratulate Garland on an elegant evening affair. Her eyes crossed at the elegant spectacle playing out behind us.

"It's hard to accomplish anything dignified with this crew," she groaned. "Oh, well. On another painful subject, when's my divorce hearing scheduled, Tom?"

I discreetly stepped aside so she and Tom could discuss it in private.

Giving the room one more sweep, I took in the general hysterics. Ivory, hands clamped on her hips, straddled Larry, who lay wriggling beneath like a giant beetle. She leaned down as close as she dared and gleefully asked, "Hey, slob, did you know your best friends, C.C. and Leonard, are moving back? That's right. That shut you up good, didn't it? And I'm gonna help that woman do whatever she wants done with you. You hear me?"

The usual antics with the usual array of town characters. Except one.

Leaning against a wall not ten feet away, quietly blending into the woodwork and shadows, I noticed a handsome, blonde stranger who, somehow, looked vaguely familiar. He flattened his entire body tight against the pinewood, quietly watching, intent eyes searching the crowd. He licked his lips a lot, and silently motioned approaching waitresses away. I found myself edging closer, curiously scanning the faces in the crowd to catch the first "Oh!" of recognition, but none came. Nobody stepped forward to slap him on the back and exclaim, "Look everybody! Cousin Fill-in-the-Blank is here!" Nobody drew out a camera and demanded, "Say cheese!"

I studied the pale features, the intent, roving eyes that suddenly locked into place. A line of vision hard as a steel cable that led straight to Stewart.

As Tom rushed up and threw an arm around my shoulders, hustling me out the door with a crowd of revellers, I distinctly heard the stranger's words—"So there you are."

CHAPTER 18

✳

LYING IN BED the next morning, waiting for the sun to rise, I retraced events of the night before. How I'd blurted to Tom out on the street that Stewart might be in danger, and tried to push my way back inside. How Tom, fuzzy-headed and slow, doubted I could hear anything above the noise. How Jackson suddenly cut in and dragged me through the crowd to identify the stranger but he'd disappeared. How Stewart and Jackson listened to my description of the man and exchanged a furtive glance, Stewart suddenly very tense. Yet both denied they knew anyone who fit the description. How Tom lectured me all the way home about how noses that grow too long get chopped off, then got woozy in the herb garden and fell asleep on the garden chaise.

I'd thrown a blanket over his feet, carping like a fishwife, and stomped upstairs.

Now at break of dawn, along with the chirping of birds, I heard a pitiful moan from the garden below.

"Uhhh. Oh, good Lord. I'm gonna kill Charlie. I can't feel my teeth."

I slid out of bed and hurried downstairs to start the coffee. "Eggs and bacon?" I called sweetly. "Jelly doughnut and fried scrapple?"

Tom shuffled through the door, wan and pale. He eased up behind me, draping limp arms around my waist, and lay his head on my shoulder. "Was I awful last night?"

"Yes. You were."

"Can you forgive me?"

"Yes. I can." Tying one on isn't exactly a deal breaker in Solace Glen.

"Would you make the coffee faster?"

I rotated around to embrace my brilliant, if hung over, love. "I'm good, but I can't work magic. After you've gotten some coffee in you, we need to talk."

"Sounds serious." He fought to keep his head from drooping.

"Life and death. You said so yourself. Now, go wash the dew off your face."

When he'd cleaned up, half-awake after a cup of black coffee, I presented my case, laying out every fact and suspicion at my disposal. "So that's my conclusion. The stalker, that blonde guy I saw last night, has been purposely lured out here to Maryland so Conrad can take care of him in his own way. No fuss, no muss. No L.A. police looking over his shoulder."

Tom took his time, a little slow this morning. "Well, *lured* is a pretty strong word. It's no secret that Conrad and Stewart knew that if the stalker did show up here, he'd stick out like a sore thumb in such a small place. By the same token, Conrad couldn't exactly get away with murder with every Circle Lady in town zeroed in on his every move."

Good point. Nothing got past the Belles of Solace Glen. "Maybe *he* wouldn't pull the trigger. Maybe he's ordered Jackson to have a little 'accident' when the time is right."

Tom snickered, rolled his eyes, and winced at the pain in his head. "If that's true, why not simply have the 'accident' in L.A.?"

This was the problem being engaged to a lawyer. Too much logic.

"That's something I haven't quite figured out yet." A dab of theatrics never hurts. "Why *here*? *Why* Solace Glen? Maybe to make it seem more legitimate. You, the town legal eagle, have an aura of respectability—except for last night, of course—and you knew and admired Stewart. Waaaay back when, past tense. Plus, the more open they are about the danger Stewart's in, the more accepting all the small-town dummies will be when the bad guy turns up dead. Everyone will cheer for Jackson, especially Screamin' Larry, who thinks stalking is a sport. Stewart may or may not go along with this devious, evil plan. She loves her father, but she's also scared to death of this blonde guy. And I swear, Tom, when I described the man to Stewart and Jackson, they knew exactly who I was talking about. I could see it in their eyes. But when I asked, they denied it. Conrad's behind this. I know he is."

"Well, I don't know that he is." Tom placed a thumb and forefinger between his eyes, grimacing. "He may be a gamesman and a risk taker in the business world, but I

can't see him dangling his own flesh and blood like a
carrot stick to trap a stalker."

"Unless," I pointed a finger in the air, "the gain out-
weighs the risk."

Tom drained the last of the coffee. "You realize how
hard it is for me to think this morning. Let me ruminate
a while."

"Ruminate away. What's on your agenda today?"

"I'm going home. I'm taking a shower. Then I'm going to kill my brother."

I agreed it was a good plan.

AROUND MID-MORNING, I found myself standing in
front of the new house, watching Abner's workmen
scurry about like carpenter ants. Abner emerged from
the hub of the activity, his focus on a particular section
of roof.

"Abner! Hey!" We met halfway across the yard. "It's
really looking good! Tom and I are very pleased."

Abner nodded in mute satisfaction, proud of his
work.

I'd arrived with compliments, but also with a short
list of questions. "Nice party last night, huh?"

"Yeah, pretty nice."

"You didn't stay very long, I noticed. Were you feeling OK?"

He hesitated a moment. "I felt OK."

"It was kind of crowded, though, wasn't it?"

"There were a few too many people there, yep."

"Anyone in particular?"

The crinkled eyes widened at me. "You got a point to
make, Flip?"

I wet my lips. "Don't take this the wrong way, Abner, but I saw the look you gave Stewart Larkin on your way out."

He didn't respond, merely stared into space.

"Want to tell me why you hate her? It won't go any further."

His jaw set firm as concrete. "I never said I knew her."

He hurried away, leaving me with a list of questions that continued to grow.

SINCE IT WAS a Saturday, I sprinted around town, running errands, and ended up at the Bistro for a quick sandwich. Garland and Hilda worked the room, noses to the grindstone, all evidence of the big party wiped clean. I grabbed a seat at a small table and spotted Hilda just as she arrived at Officer Garrett's table with a heaping plate of fried chicken. The evening before had wrought its magic. The two of them joined in a flirty, spirited conversation that left silly grins on both their faces.

They weren't the only ones. Lindbergh had been charmed into the warm, communal bosom of the Circle Ladies. A pack of them clustered around the old boy like fussy nannies over a newborn. "Want part of my sandwich, Lindy? I must watch my figure, you know." "Do you like this lip color? How about this scent?" "What are you doing for dinner tonight?" Poor Lindbergh.

Marlene and C.C. huddled at a corner table, talking earnestly. Occasionally, C.C. reached out and patted Marlene's hand. I would have given anything to be a fly on their bud vase so I could hear Marlene's tale of woe. She had to be talking about Horace.

The Bistro held the usual large Saturday lunch crowd, so you could hardly hear yourself think. I caught a glimpse of Charlie and Stewart taking turns at a plate of something and wondered which one made the date. I suspected Stewart, who glowed bright as a Christmas star in June, more than happy to revamp an old relationship. The concoction Charlie shared with Tom the night before hadn't affected him in the least. He appeared to enjoy the company he kept, immune, for now, to misery of any kind.

"Hey!" Lee plopped into the chair beside me. "Where's your steady boyfriend? Got a little headache, maybe?"

"Oh, you noticed his sedate behavior last night. Yeah, I think he downed a couple hundred antibiotics and is sleeping it off at home. Where's your worse half?"

"Same sorry state. He and Wilbur ended up doing melon shooters at our house after the party. Sally and I called it quits long before." She plucked a tortoiseshell comb out of her hair and refastened it. The hazel eyes roamed toward Charlie. "By the way, I had a quick dance with Charlie last night after you left."

I frowned. "What did you say to him? Poor man."

"I said exactly what anybody with a grain of sense would say. 'Don't be a fool twice. She burned you bad once and she'll do it again.' I don't think Charlie came back here 'on business,' either. I think he's flirting with fire."

"Oh, Lee, really. Leave well enough alone. Look at the two of them. They make an attractive pair, and they're both adults. Keep out of it."

"I also told him, 'You can't relive the past.' There. I said my say, and that's all I'll say."

"Good. Now perhaps you'll see that you're wrong. Wrong about Stewart and wrong about the two of them getting back together."

"Oh, yeah," she replied, with more than a hint of sarcasm. "History never repeats itself."

Just then, the door swung open and who should wander in but Leonard with Horace sticking close to his heels like a dachshund. They made their way toward the table where C.C. sat empathizing with Marlene. Leonard gave C.C. an obligatory peck on the cheek for public show that made C.C.'s face-lift contract an inch. But it was Marlene's face that interested me.

Marlene turned white as a snowflake when she looked up and saw Horace standing at her table.

"Horace," Leonard drawled, "I don't believe you've met my wife, Cecile. Cecile, this is Horace Worthington, and this is Marlene Worth—"

Marlene sprang up. "No introduction necessary. He's my ex-husband." The whites of her eyes resembled one of those wild Chincoteague ponies fighting its way crosscurrent.

Lee practically blasted out of her chair. "No way!" she wheezed. "Is she serious?"

"You can't be serious!" C.C., who had extended her hand for Horace to shake or kiss, now whipped it back, fast as a rattlesnake. "This is the monster you've been telling me about?"

The monster clucked his tongue and smiled disarmingly. "*C'est moi, cheri.* Darling," he slit his buggy eyes and raked them over Marlene, "what have you been revealing?"

"Only the truth." Marlene's voice shook as she backed up against the wall. I'd never seen her so frazzled. "What are you here for? You promised to leave me alone."

"I couldn't help myself." Horace scraped a chair from the table and eased down. "Opportunity knocked, and is still knock-knock-knocking. And," his head tilted sympathetically, "I heard poor MaMa died. Didn't you get my card?"

"You know I didn't."

"Tut-tut. Must have gotten lost in the post. E-mail will be all that is left us one day."

Leonard and C.C. didn't quite know what to make of this new turn of events. Apparently, C.C. had gotten an earful from Marlene on the intimate details of the marriage from hell, while Leonard harbored hopes he'd found a fellow investor who could help gang up on Conrad. Lee and I sat still, glued to the melodrama.

C.C. scrutinized every detail of Horace, from the slick, black hair down to the wiggly white toes poking out of the black sandals. Her thickly lined eyes narrowed, mouth scrunched to one side. You could read the doubt playing across her brain that this oddball specimen could be the hideous ogre Marlene described. Leonard, too, gave Horace an intense once-over. The fact that this man had actually married a woman as physically repulsive as Marlene meant he must have clouded judgment, not an appealing trait in a business colleague.

"Of course," Horace addressed his comments to C.C. and Leonard, "I never actually met Marlene's dear MaMa. Our marriage was short, but oh-so-sweet. When I heard she passed, I simply had to rectify an old wrong, and find my way to Solace Glen to pay my respects. Is she buried somewhere, Marlene? Or are Louise's ashes scattered over the Bistro and through the woods?"

"Don't defile my mother by speaking her name." You could have pulled the chair out from under me. Marlene, who hated Louise most of her life, treating her own mother like a leper, suddenly grew lioness fangs and claws, defending the fine woman who bore her.

"My, my," Horace clucked. "What a change in tune, Marlene. You used to tell me you couldn't wait for the dear, cancerous soul to kick the bucket so you could inherit the . . . three million, was it? Or has the principle and interest grown by leaps and bounds? You must be sitting pretty high right now, generous angel I know you to be."

"Is that what you're here for, then?" Marlene threw her head back and howled with laughter. "You think I inherited loads of money? The same way you thought I had money before?"

Horace played it cool. "My darling ex-wife, rest at ease. Your inheritance is, I'm sure, a nice little egg in the nest for you, but I have larger horizons to conquer. That is where I think, Leonard, you and I can be very useful to each other." He suddenly stared at Marlene as if he'd just that second noticed a cockroach in the building. "Oh. Were you leaving?"

"You'd better believe it," Marlene snapped. "You coming, Cecile?"

C.C. appeared torn, wanting to support her only friend in town, but curious as hell about the mysterious Horace Worthington. In the end, she joined Marlene, figuring she could beat any information out of Leonard later on.

Leonard frowned at his wife's back and turned his attention to Horace again. "How do you think we can be useful to each other?" he asked in his bored manner, but slowly sat down, one eye straying toward Stewart. He lowered his voice, and the two men bent heads together, with Horace doing most of the talking.

"What do you know about that!" Lee whistled. "Marlene married that weasel?"

"He does have a high rodent factor. But I'm more interested in his beef with Conrad than Marlene's beef with him."

"Oh? Another member of the human race who has a bone to pick with the great industrialist? And how did Horace get to be so palsy-walsy with Leonard all of a sudden?"

"Greedy minds think alike. Leonard's got a lot of money invested in a couple of Larkin companies, just like Horace. I overheard them talking last night."

"You? Eavesdropping?" Lee spooned a piece of ice out of my water glass. "Next thing, you'll be confessing you gossip."

"Pardon my many sins, Jezebel. All I know is, Horace and Leonard are up to something. Then again," I watched as both men sneaked quick, intent, glances at Stewart, "they'd better be careful if they're out to hit Conrad Larkin where it hurts."

CHAPTER 19

✸

REVEREND MCKNIGHT PREACHED his last sermon on Sunday, or at least half of one. The new interim preached the other half, a nice sort of lead-in for all concerned. Most members of our little congregation expressed joy and relief that we'd finally come into the twenty-first century, and could now boast a woman in the pulpit—a spunky, petite fifty-something widow with a string of degrees after her name, Reverend Martha G. Gessup. A sprinkling of not-so-enlightened members complained that the world as we knew it imploded, and the whole Presbytery would be sucked into a black hole of chaos and debauchery.

"I never thought I'd live to see the day," Roland whined to anybody who'd listen. "When she starts marrying Jane to Joan and cats to dogs, don't say I didn't warn you."

"Shut up, fool." Ivory sloshed lemonade in Roland's direction, splattering yellow drops on his Sunday shoes. "She's gonna be just fine, no help from you. Reverend G.G.—that's what she likes to be called, ya know—she's a nice lady. Got more energy than six of Ivory put together. She'll win you over. You'll see. She's gonna hire my cousin Lolly as sexton, too, help pay her way through college."

Everyone murmured approval except Roland, the original caveman.

True to character, our talk drifted from saying nice things about Reverend G.G. to making unsportsman-like comments about C.C.'s and Leonard's return, which led to unsavory impressions of Horace and Marlene, which somehow led to angst over Suggs and his latest obsession, Stewart. That, in turn, led to a fervent discussion of the stalker. Everybody had heard about the notes, the calls, and the handcuffs, and I was bursting to tell of the blonde stranger. But because nothing had been confirmed, since Stewart and Jackson denied knowing the man, I kept my jaw clamped tight and listened.

"How do you think he got the note and the box in the car without anybody seeing him? We usually notice strangers around here."

"Unless he's not a stranger. Maybe it's somebody we know."

"Oh, get out. This started in L.A."

"People from Solace Glen do travel, ya know. And we're getting more and more tourists thanks to the Bistro, so we don't always notice a strange face."

The Bistro. The Bistro! My eyes boinged open. That's where I'd seen the blonde stranger before! I knew his face looked familiar! He was sitting at a table the day Stewart and Tom ate lunch together. Sitting at a table, hovering behind a newspaper. The day after Stewart arrived. *So soon after she arrived.*

"Well, I'm getting a burglar alarm."

"I'm getting a shotgun."

"I'm getting a dog."

"I'm having my mother-in-law move in."

The *baa*ing of the sheep grew frantic.

Stewart must not have seen him that day, didn't realize that early on he was already in town. He'd known her destination. He'd followed her to Solace Glen. At least now I had something to go on. Time to get back in touch with Sidney.

MONDAY MORNING, BRIGHT and early, Ivory rapped at the kitchen door, laden with a big bag of scrambled eggs stuffed in biscuits and foam cups of hot black coffee. She wore a creative imitation of my summer working garb, a short khaki skirt that showed off her thick, muscular legs and wide thighs, topped by an Hawaiian shirt swimming with orange sharks.

"Fuel up, Flip. Whose house do we hit first?"

"We hit Lindbergh Kohl's first, then Miss Fizzi's. After that, we take a lunch break at the Bistro," where I hoped to run into Officer Garrett, "and then head for Tom's office. Come on, I'll entertain you with the Flip Paxton cleaning method on the drive over. My equipment's already in the car."

Ivory rolled her eyes around the house. "Where's Tom? He sneak out already?"

"You insult my well-documented virtue. To tell the truth, he hasn't been able to do much sneaking around lately. Too busy."

She could hardly miss the dejection, and said, "Oh, child, I know you'll be glad when y'all are legal. Men shouldn't be running around loose."

"No, they shouldn't. At least after we're married, we'll be under one roof."

"One roof. That's the answer. Like the song says, Flip, 'When this bad, old world starts gettin' ya down, right smack dab in the middle of town, climb up on that new house roof, and poof, your cares are blowin' in the wind.' There's room enough for two up on that Mr. and Mrs. Scott roof."

"You think so?" Ivory's good-hearted attempt to lift my spirits worked, and I gladly gave in to her positive thinking, almost whistling as we started the day.

Lindbergh met us at the front door, one thumb holding his place in a book called *Biographical Writing and Interview Techniques*.

When I raised my brows, he said, "See what you started, Flip? You got me thinking, and before I knew it, I began talking to people, asking about their lives. You have no idea what you can learn in a barbershop. Then I spent time at our fascinating Historical Society, and again, before I knew it, I began to see connections between the past and the present. Do you know how many trees are growing out of the Historical Society right before our eyes, and the amazing fruit of their many branches? Right now, I'm on a quest to discover how I can help make the connections. I am going to write the definitive history of Solace Glen, and it will be a living history. Isn't it wonderful?"

The cheeks under the soft, lambs wool sideburns radiated.

"I'm thrilled for you, Lindbergh. And for Solace Glen. Sounds like you are actually going to do what any number of people have talked about for ages. I'll be happy to help, but the Circle Ladies are really the ones you can count on. They know *everything* about *everyone* in this place."

"Oh, yes, they've been most enlightening. Especially Margaret." The glow burned pinker. "I've never been so well-fed. This project should leave me fifty pounds heavier."

Ivory whooped, "Oh, Mr. Lindy, you the smart, sly dog. You remember Ivory, don't ya?"

"Of course, of course. The grocery store. We fought over an eggplant." He gazed at the bucket in her hand as if she might have brought a peace offering. "Are you . . . oh, I see! You are working with Flip now. Yes, I thought I heard something about that."

"I'm sure you did," I answered wryly. "You're our first experiment."

Sure enough, Ivory pegged it. Two more hands made for light work. She attacked the upstairs while I tackled the first floor, Lindbergh nipping at my heels, reading from a notebook he'd started writing detailing the lives of the local color. My comments generally ran the way of, "No! I never knew that about so-and-so." Which made Lindbergh cock-a-doodle-do every time.

"Know what's great?" I marveled at one point. "I don't feel the least bit guilty talking about people like this. It's not really gossip. . . ."

"It's biography," finished Lindbergh, a spark in his eye.

After the grand experiment at Lindbergh's, Ivory and I proved lightning could strike twice with a successful run through Miss Fizzi's large Victorian home. Miss Fizzi roosted on a kitchen stool sipping something bubbly and suspicious, cheerfully treating our cleaning visit as if we'd shown up for a Sunday brunch party. She went on and on about Lindbergh, matching him up with every widow and spinster in town, calculating the chances of success with each coupling, even graphing out the best honeymoon spots for the ladies in question. I noticed more and more travel magazines on her side tables.

"Margaret's always wanted to go to London, although I'm partial to the Scottish Highlands myself, but she doesn't drink whiskey. Tina would love the spas at Walt Disney World, although a lot of those rides sound like a stress test. Or maybe an Arizona resort where she could sweat off the food she ate. Bite my tongue. *Sweat* is such an ugly word, isn't it? Our grandmothers were right."

"You're setting up Lindbergh with everybody but you. Why can't you marry him?"

She looked at me as she might a talking ladybug. "I'm ten years older, dear. I'm too much woman for him."

She didn't stop talking the whole time we cleaned. And Ivory laughed, worked, threw in a question or a comment, sang, worked. Here we were, only on our second house, and hiring her was the best career move I'd ever made. We finished so early, we had time to head for Tom's office before the lunch break.

The downtown square, dotted with old dogwoods and azalea bushes, drew the heat of the mid-June sun into its concrete sidewalks. Children in flip-flops, finally out for their summer vacation, buzzed around the fountain in front of the drugstore, splashing each other and playing chase while their mothers dillydallied in the nearby shops.

Ivory and I trudged up the stairs to Tom's office weighted down with the usual cleaning equipment. Despite our loud groans and heavy feet, I could hear raised voices coming out of the conference room straight ahead. When we reached the top of the stairs, I could see into the room, the door flung wide.

"No! Absolutely not!" Stewart, practically hysterical, face flushed, paced the carpet. "Daddy made it clear, remember? I'm *not* calling the police."

Tom gritted his teeth, in control, trying to reason with her. "This is the second or third time this has happened to you on our turf, Stewart. It is irresponsible, even dangerous, for you not to involve the police at this point."

I stepped into the room, motioning Ivory to head for the bathroom and start cleaning. "Sorry to interrupt. I don't want to invade anybody's private discussions here, but I'm your friend, Stewart, and I'm concerned."

She burst into tears and fell into my arms for a hug. Over her shoulder, I realized the three of us were not alone. Suggs stood by the bookcase at the far end of the room. I followed his eyes to something on the table.

A small cage.

My blood froze. "Is that what was left in your car?"

"Yes." Stewart straightened up, her sapphire eyes as red as her lipstick. "On the back seat this morning. Jackson found it."

I cast a wary eye toward Suggs. "Where is Jackson now?"

"Picking up my father at the Frederick Airport. He was running late when we found that *thing,* and Suggs happened to be walking by. Since we refused to call the police, he insisted I come here. He's even late for work just to babysit me."

Chalk one up for Suggs. Somehow, Stewart did bring out the best in him.

"I don't understand you or your father." Tom threw up his hands. "Some whacked-out sicko is stalking you, getting more and more threatening, and you two treat this like it's a business decision only the two of you can handle. This is no corporate takeover, Stewart. This is your *life*. I don't get it."

"I agree with Tom." Maybe an extra vote would count. "Did he leave another note?"

Stewart nodded. "In the bottom of the cage."

"Suggs," I asked, "could you read it to me, please?"

Suggs reverted back to his sullen self. "You can read it for yourself." He backed away from the table.

It occurred to me that maybe he couldn't read, so I walked to the end of the table and peered inside the metal cage, about the size and type you'd keep a laboratory mouse in. The words on the note had the same appearance as the note I'd seen the week before, letters cut out of magazines:

Stewart,
We always hurt the ones we love. Don't make me
hurt the ones you love.

Yours,

The Locksmith

I cringed. "Do you think he'd do something to someone else?"

Tom shrugged with a worried face. "I don't know. The 'ones you love' could mean any number of people."

"No," Stewart sank into a chair. "No, I can't believe he would go after anyone else. It's me he wants. It's me he wants to lock up and keep for himself. The note's a scare tactic. He's trying to isolate me from friends who would protect me, that's all."

Her eyes welled up again. I went to her, gently patting her back. "You don't have to worry about that. We're a pretty tough lot. Nobody's going to abandon you because of some cuckoo threat on a piece of paper."

Just then, we heard the trampling of feet flying up the stairs and Conrad and Jackson dashed into the room.

"Stewart." Conrad rushed to his daughter and embraced her. "I'm so sorry I wasn't here, sweetheart. Jackson," he pointed to the far end of the table, "take care of that thing."

Jackson whipped out the gloves and raced to more closely examine the new piece of evidence. His forehead wrinkled as he read the note. "Good. He's getting angrier, which means he'll get desperate and do something stupid. Don't lose any sleep over this, Miss Larkin. He's as good as ours."

Stewart tried in vain to smile.

Conrad addressed Suggs. "Thank you, Suggs, for bringing Stewart here and keeping an eye on her. You're proving most dependable."

Suggs shuffled both feet and stared at his shoes. "It was nothin'. Just being neighborly. I gotta go to work now."

Jackson barked, "You didn't touch this with your bare hands, did you?"

Suggs's bulldog jowls shook. "Nope. Did exactly what you told me to do."

Jackson grunted slim thanks, and Suggs left the room.

Tom started in on the police issue again, but Conrad waved him off. "Thank you for your assistance, Tom, but I know what I'm doing. Jackson here is a good man. He knows what he's doing."

"I'm so glad you both *know* what you're *doing*," Tom said evenly, "but I think this stalker knows what he's doing, too. He's eluded everyone so far, yet manages to get close enough to Stewart to leave these nifty little gifts that scare the ever-living daylights out of her! You're putting her life at risk."

Conrad cut him off. "That's enough, counselor. You've gone far enough. Thank you for your help. Come on, Stewart. Jackson, make sure you express that thing to the proper people."

All three hustled out, leaving me upset and Tom furious. As Conrad's attorney, his hands were tied.

But mine weren't. "Tom, don't be mad, but I'm going to talk with Sidney later on."

To my surprise, he replied, "Sooner. Sooner rather than later."

Chapter 20

✳

MAYBE SUGGS TOLD Pal, or maybe Ivory told everybody she ran into, but by suppertime the word had spread like wildfire. I suppose after our talk, Sidney, too, might have dropped a word to Hilda out of concern for her safety. And as we all know, as Hilda goes, so goes the news, with plenty of extras. Her approach to passing along information matched her approach to building a sundae—the basic scoop of plain vanilla piled high with junk, junk, junk.

For the next week, nobody could talk about anything else—a stalker walked among us, the Blonde Stranger, and he posed a threat to anyone who befriended Stewart. Clients pressed me for every detail, clutching their throats as I recited the notes I'd seen, peppering me with questions about the handcuffs, the cage, a description of the blonde man I'd spied at the party. They breathed a sigh of relief that brave Officer Garrett stood ready to pull a pistol, on the alert, but were mad as hell with Conrad and Stewart for their pride, refusing to call in the Frederick police, the National Guard, or the Navy S.E.A.L.s, for that matter. Mothers watched their children more closely; men organized neighborhood watches.

One way or another, Solace Glen banded together to spot and capture the Blonde Stranger.

THE MOST CREATIVE idea to come out of all the hysteria belonged to none other than Reverend G.G. She'd heard the talk and recognized the fear behind it. Pretty smart lady, she hit on a way to help the Presbyterian youth get to Montreat over the summer, and help the community deal with its fear at the same time.

That Sunday, the billboard in front of the church carried the title of her sermon: "Solace Glen Is Going to the Dogs."

"Hell. She's given up on us already," Ivory huffed, perusing the bulletin.

"On the contrary," Garland whispered from the row ahead of us, a knowing smile playing across her lips. She and Reverend G.G. had become fast friends.

"What's this about?" I whispered back.

"You'll see," she teased, and she and Hilda giggled into their hands.

By the end of the service, everybody was giggling. With the big Fourth of July picnic coming up in less than two weeks, when the whole town turned out at the fire pond for food, games, races, and fireworks, Reverend G.G. proposed a unique fund-raiser: a dog auction.

The dogs would not be your average, run-of-the-mill mutts, oh no. Reverend G.G. had already talked to several pure-breed rescue clubs and lined up four dogs to auction. Each winning bidder would be subject to an interview and home visit by a member of the rescue club, and only then would the deal be sealed. If the winning bidder proved unacceptable, or would not agree to any further conditions, such as the right diet or obedience school, then the dog would be offered to the next highest bidder at the original winning price. Bottom line— placing good dogs in good homes, with the proceeds going to the youth group and the rescue clubs.

Reverend G.G. had bright red, white, and blue flyers printed up for church members to distribute around town announcing the auction and naming the breeds, along with a brief description of the dogs' personality traits.

Ivory looked over the list as we walked out of church. "Shoot. I wanted a German shepherd, something big and growly to protect Ivory from the stalker. These are some kinda weird dogs on this list. Lookie here, a Chihuahua! How's that smudge of a dog gonna protect anybody? Don't do nothin' but yip-yap and pee on the rug."

"What's a Puli?" asked Hilda. "Oh! There's going to be an Irish setter!"

"Too much hair." Garland nixed the idea. "I don't know what a Puli is."

"I don't, either." I scanned the list. "And I've never seen a Giant Schnauzer before."

Ivory got excited. "Giant! Giant something, now that's what Ivory wants. I'll go for the Giant. That stalker ain't touchin' me with no Giant in the house."

And so it went. Sometime later, right around twilight, Tom glanced over the flyer, finally taking a break to spend some time with his neglected fiancée. He cracked jokes while puttering in the herb garden, relaxed in his shorts and Terps T-shirt, glass of fine wine in hand. We grilled chicken in the backyard, and talked about our new house before he flopped down on the chaise to read the Presbyterian flyer.

"Hey, this Reverend G.G. has hit on a great idea. You wouldn't believe how many people in the past week have asked me if Eli, in particular, and black Labs, in general, are good watchdogs. But a Chihuahua? And Irish setters may bark a lot, but they're not known as strong protectors. What's a Puli? Oh, a Giant Schnauzer. Now that's a dog's dog."

I switched back to my favorite subject. "Want to go see the house before it gets too dark?"

"Naw, let's go first thing in the morning when Abner's there."

"That's fine, but Abner's not always there. He's gone missing at least two days this past week, and his workers rarely know anything about it." I slid my eyes at Tom. "Who's to say where he goes or what he does."

"Oh, stop it, Flip. Are you implying that Abner Diggs is a stalker? In cahoots with the Blonde Stranger?"

I swirled my gin and tonic. "Noooo. All I'm saying is Abner disappears a lot, and I'm *sure* he has it in for Conrad and Stewart. Whether the two are connected, I don't know. But how do we know there isn't a stalker behind the stalker? Someone who's paying the blonde guy to scare Stewart and her father? Somebody who hates the Larkins. Abner won't even admit he knows them. He about bit my head off when I asked."

"I'm sure you deserved it."

"And Leonard and Horace, those two perfect co-conspirators, are royally mad about the money they've invested, and Conrad's handling of it. They can't get a straight answer out of him. And Lee told me yesterday she thinks Charlie is faking his good will toward Stewart, and has been plotting his revenge all these years."

I expected Tom to laugh, but his forehead creased. "Lee has a wild imagination," he said slowly, "but I'm not sure Charlie's good will *is* genuine! Originally, he said he came back here on business to meet with a D.C. publisher about another book. But he hasn't been anywhere. He hasn't met with anyone. Now he's switched his story. Said he doesn't want to do a second book and he came home for a few weeks, to deepen our relationship. to make up for lost time because I'm his only family except for some distant cousins. But after an initial good conversation or two, he's as distant as the cousins, as distant as he's always been with me. I mean, we're friendly, we share laughs, but the heart of him is something I just can't grasp." His lips drew tight a moment. "I hope this has nothing to do with Stewart."

Inside the house, music from the radio filtered out, Screamin' Larry playing June Christy's "It Could Happen to You." Fireflies got down to business, twinkling across the heather and sage. The soft summer air smelled of roasting chicken, sweet marjoram, and oregano.

Thoughts of Charlie left my head and, heart about to burst, I set the gin and tonic on a side table and curled up beside Tom on the chaise, putting the stalker and all other unpleasantness deep inside a hiding place. His arms around me, all I could think was, *This is where*

I belong. This place, this man, this time. This is where I belong.

EARLY MONDAY MORNING, Ivory rode with me to see the house, Tom trailing behind in his car so he could get to his office and I could get to work more quickly. The moment we buckled our seat belts, Ivory and I started blabbing about the stalker, the Fourth of July picnic, and local politics. Amazing, how much we thought alike.

Abner greeted us in his stoic manner, practically wordless, but pride shone in the crinkled eyes when he turned toward the house.

"Well, Abner!" Tom, who hadn't seen the house in quite a few days, took in the sight. "You've got a real masterpiece here. You and your crew are doing a magnificent job."

Tom rarely threw around words like *magnificent* and *masterpiece,* so the moment held more awe.

"We're very pleased." I tried to sound more sophisticated than I felt, since I really wanted to scream, bounce up and down, and do cartwheels. "When do you think we can move in?"

Tom shut his eyes tight and wrinkled his nose, but grinned. "Abner, just tell her, 'When it's ready, dear.' Come on, Ivory, let's take a tour."

Ivory, mouth agape at the gorgeous house beautiful growing out of the ground, traipsed after Tom to the back of the building.

When they were out of earshot, I tried picking Abner's lock again. "Abner, I'll get right down to it. You have a pretty big bone to pick with the Larkins, don't you?"

He looked me straight in the eye, not pulling any punches. "I'm not getting into this with you." He paused, and added with a curious expression, "Why do you care?"

"I care because Stewart is a new friend. She's having some trouble, and I'm concerned about her."

His upper lip curled slightly. "There're better things to concern yourself with."

"Now what makes you say . . ."

True to form, Abner dipped away, yelling at a worker, leaving me with more questions than answers. There had to be a way to break through his crust.

Instantly, I knew how.

ALL ROADS LEAD to Lindbergh.

Before he could open his mouth to say "Hello," I started scouring for answers and information. Ivory tripped past and headed upstairs, humming "Where the Boys Are."

"Whoa, whoa, slow down. You are in a state of some excitement, I see."

"Lindbergh," I set the carryall down to prove how serious this was, "I need help, and you're just the man for the job."

He shuddered. " 'Job' has such an ugly ring to it. I'm retired."

"You're retired from work, not from life. I think what I have to say is right up your alley."

The corners of his lips rose. "I am intrigued. Continue."

"Do you have Abner Diggs in your notebook yet?"

"No, but I've met the man. We engaged in a little

small talk at the Bistro recently when we were both picking up sandwiches."

"Good. Ask him if you can interview him for your biographical research. Tell him you need more men or something."

"That's a valid point. The notebook *is* heavily female. Is there anything you want to know about him, in particular?"

"Between us," I lowered my voice, "I want to know why he hates Conrad and Stewart Larkin. There's a story there that he's not telling, and I want to know what it is before it's too late."

Lindbergh scratched his woolly sideburns. "Sounds ominous. What makes you think he would tell me, a virtual stranger?"

How to explain a gut feeling to a man of science? "Because you're a man. A peer. If you start digging into his past, he might open up. You might find out just enough to give us a clue. Are you willing to give it a shot, at least?"

Lindbergh's gentle features lit up and he raised a finger high. "I am on the trail, dear Watson, I am on the trail. Wherever it may lead."

CHAPTER 21

※

I VORY AND I started our Wednesday at Stewart's house, the sweet old Paxton wood-frame cottage. No cars in the driveway, no one home, I took the shiny new house key out of a pocket.

No surprise, inside my old home Stewart had made lovely changes. More than once I found myself asking why I hadn't thought of this, that, and the other thing. The placement of a gilded mirror. A bathroom now beautifully papered in shades of gold and pink. New kitchen countertops in a shiny, navy granite. My folksy, English country style succumbed to a sophisticated, metropolitan decor that still managed to look feminine and artistic. Best of all, Stewart's good taste gave me a dozen ideas to use in the new house.

Right before we left, as Ivory carried cleaning supplies out to the car, I paused on the staircase, curious, and slid an ornamental glass egg to one side. I lifted the secret plank in the bookshelf. Stewart's treasured ring still lay inside the hiding spot, sparkling up at me atop the gold chain she'd worn around her neck.

"Guess she'll take it out again when she finally wins Charlie over," I mused, keeping in mind Tom's doubts about his brother. Maybe Charlie felt deeply, but didn't possess the necessary tools to express emotion. Whatever those emotions were. Inevitably, if fantastically, thoughts of a double wedding crossed my mind, and I imagined Stewart and I gracefully waltzing down the aisle toward the two nervous Scott men. Maybe Tom would be more eager to set a date if he knew his brother would be sharing the expense. Better yet, Conrad could pay for the whole shebang. On that happy note, I closed the plank and joined Ivory outside, placing the new house key back inside my pocket.

SCREAMIN' LARRY, WHO could practically list Roland's nasty restaurant as a permanent address, gradually handed over his enormous appetite to Garland and her experienced staff. When an Egghead asked why the switch, Larry complained too many strangers dined at Roland's.

"A damnable trucker trap," he called it. Plus, Roland bored him to death. He wouldn't talk about anything but how Lee stole his inheritance and Garland took the rest.

Larry and Ivory, already off to a bad start, would now cross paths more often since I made eating at the Bistro one of her salary perks. Before Ivory came to work for me, these two local leviathans knew of each

other mostly through reputation, but the night of the
McKnight party changed all that. After their run-in,
Ivory could barely stand to listen to Larry's voice on the
car radio, but I explained that jazz amounted to another
element for me, like air and water. To compromise, I
granted her another perk and bought a portable radio/CD
player. Thrilled to death, she stayed plugged in most of
the workday, singing and humming and dancing with
the vacuum cleaner.

Most of our lunches at the Bistro passed quietly
enough, with Ivory plugged into her music and me entertained mightily by Sidney's clumsy flirting with
Hilda. He hadn't asked her out yet, but was working up
to it. Friday had come at last and the Bistro buzzed.
Every time I walked through the door, now, I scanned
the room for strange blondes, but everyone else in town
did the same, eager to expose our lone criminal and be
crowned an instant hero. But no one had seen hide nor
hair.

Ivory and I grabbed our usual table and waited for
Hilda to swing by while we read the chalkboard of specials.

"Dang." Ivory pulled the earphones off. "The batteries ran out. I get a paycheck today, right?"

"You sure do. You can afford a boatload of batteries.
What do you think, the turkey melt or the pasta salad?"

Hilda showed up and highly recommended the pasta.
"You need some carbs, Flip. Trying to skinny up for
your wedding day?"

"I would, if I knew the date and the time."

She laughed. Everybody always laughed at my wedding bell blues.

Ivory, inspired, started to sing, " 'Tom! I love you so, I always will. . . .' "

"Stop right there!" boomed a loud clap of thunder. Larry rose from his chair on the other side of the room. "This is a No Oldies zone."

Ivory, unplugged, rose to the occasion. "Who you callin' 'old,' fat boy?"

An Egghead chirped, "Did she just call him 'fat boy'?" They discussed running for the stretcher.

"Read my lips," Larry pointed to his wide mouth, full of BLT, "no *Old*-ies. You want everybody to lose their lunch?"

"You crazy," Ivory scoffed, and started to sing, " 'If I had a hammer, I'd use it on you-you-you.' "

Larry countered with "I Should Care."

Ivory, emboldened, gulped a deep breath and sang, "Good Morning, Starshine."

Larry, gagging, belted out, " 'It don't mean a thing, if it ain't got that swing. Do-waa, do-waa . . .' "

Half the room joined in with Ivory, but the other half's singing grew stronger, jubilant, encouraged by Larry's finger snapping and spoon tapping. When Hilda coaxed Sidney into swing dancing with her, the votes swung with them.

Ivory huffed and sat down hard. "Who's he think he is?"

"He is our lunatic DJ Supreme. He kind of grows on you."

"He ain't growin' nowhere on Ivory. Wait'll I get my Giant. I'm gonna train that dog to attack fat, obnoxious DJs."

We got even more mileage out of our lunch hour when

C.C. marched through the door with Marlene. I sat in her line of fire and took the first round. She leaned into my face, red lips flapping, demanding cleaning services for her new house near Loy's Station starting Tuesday.

"But Loy's Station is a good twenty minutes away." I started to list excuses, but Ivory suddenly piped up that we'd *love* to have her as a paying customer again, though the price would be slightly stiffer owing to the extra drive time, and anything we could do to make her return to the community more smooth, we would be happy to do.

C.C.'s painted lips drew back, standard Cheshire cat style. "How refreshing. A human being."

Before I could retract the offer, the clap of thunder boomed out, "Mrs. Crosswell! Well, the fun never ends! S'damn glad t'see you again! Where's your BMW?"

C.C. took one look at Screamin' Larry, blanched, and hauled Marlene back outside.

Due to public drunkenness, Larry had somehow missed seeing C.C. and Leonard at the big McKnight party, though thanks to Ivory he'd heard of their reentry into our high society. So this amounted to his first glimpse of her in months, ever since he blew her out of town so-to-speak. He yowled, eyes wild, and sang loud enough for her to hear through the walls of the Bistro, " 'Never treats me sweet and gentle, the way she should, I got it baaad, and that ain't gooood,' " to a roar of approval. Larry did have a good voice; you had to give him that.

C.C.'s eyes threw darts straight through the window glass. She pivoted on her high heels and click-clacked away to a generous round of applause.

I turned to Ivory. "Thanks a lot. You have no idea what you just started."

Ivory mimicked C.C.'s feline smirk. "No, child." She threw a dart Larry's way. "*He* has no idea what *he* just started."

CHAPTER 22

❋

I NEVER THOUGHT of music as a battleground, but
Ivory and Screamin' Larry made song their jugger-
naut. That Friday at the Bistro, the war commenced.
Larry seemed perfectly delighted to have another woman
to taunt besides C.C., and wasted no time in weaponiz-
ing the airwaves to full effect. Both C.C. ("the red-
lipped babe with the stinkin' BMW") and Ivory ("she
who was Maid in Hell") got an equal share of ugly dedications. Ivory responded in kind. Over the weekend,
she called every oldies radio program in the state and
had them dedicate the worst possible songs to Larry,
stuff like "Build Me Up Buttercup" and "Ooh-Wakka-
Doo-Wakka-Day," promising donations if they'd keep it
up for a month.

Come Sunday, the town had something to talk about
other than the stalker and the dog auction.

Tom bagged the Methodists for a day and joined the Frozen Chosen for services. We invited Charlie and Stewart, too, but by the end of the sermon, they were a no-show. When we stepped outside to partake of the usual summer fare, pink lemonade and ginger cookies, we'd barely taken a sip from our paper cups when Charlie's car pulled up with a screech.

He flung the door open, spotted Tom, and waved him over, eyes turbulent, jaw clenched.

Tom set his cup down and murmured, "You know what this means." He hurried to his brother.

The two of them conferred in low, serious voices no one could hear, even though you could have heard a feather drop, the church crowd gravely quiet. At the end of their discussion, though, both men's voices rose between gritted teeth. Then came the rustle of whispers. "The stalker." "Must be the stalker." "Oh, no, the stalker."

Moments later, Charlie angrily sped away, and Tom walked slowly back to the crowd. I could see in his eyes he didn't want to upset the women, but immediately fell under a barrage of questions.

"What's wrong?"

"Is it the stalker?"

"What is it, Tom? Is everything all right?" Garland clung tight to Hilda's arm.

"Is Stewart OK?" I asked.

We all held our breath, expecting the worse.

"Stewart's in the hospital in Frederick."

Before he could say another word, women started squealing and gulping for air.

"No, no," Tom raised his arms, palms down, trying to calm the rising hysteria, "she's all right. She's just there for observation. She'll be fine. That's all I can tell you right now."

As he spoke, he cupped a hand around my elbow and led me toward his car, the mumbling crowd behind us growing louder and louder, the questions popping off like corks. Everybody wanted to rush home and lock their doors.

Once inside the car, I blurted, "What really happened?"

Tom started the car, rolled up the windows, and turned on the air. "She was attacked."

"What!"

"Stewart called Charlie a little while ago. I don't know every detail, but Charlie said she invited him out to dinner last night. She convinced Jackson to take his scheduled time off even though Conrad was delayed at a meeting. She promised to stay at the Bistro, where he dropped her off, until Conrad called. A nice, safe public place. Apparently, this temporary trip out of the goldfish bowl went to her head and she called Charlie for a dinner date."

"Thrilled to do something normal, right?"

"I guess so. When Conrad called her cell, she failed to mention her location or her companion. Just said, 'See you at home,' and asked Charlie to drop her off right away. Which is precisely what he did. Dropped her off and left, stupidly assuming Conrad had called from home and held down the fort. Anyway, Suggs, Neighbor of the Year, 'happened to be walking by,' and Stewart chatted with him a few minutes then went inside. Suggs hung around a bit, keeping those eyes and ears open, you know. When Stewart entered the house, she started to flick a light on in the kitchen when a man grabbed her from behind. She said rough suede hit her face, like gardening or work gloves. He tried to hold a cloth over her nose and mouth that she said smelled like ether or chloroform, but she broke away and screamed for Suggs. The guy got away through the back door."

I blinked. "Suggs. Suggs 'happened to be walking by.' The faithful bulldog. Do you realize how many things have happened to Stewart while Suggs is in the vicinity? I think this stalker knows what a lamebrain he is."

"Give the guy a break, Flip. Suggs may have saved her life. Jackson didn't pull up until right after-the-fact, and Conrad's limo arrived even later."

"Honestly. Stewart knew she was walking into an empty house. She took a big risk."

"And the stalker took every advantage. Charlie never should have left her and driven off like that."

So that's why they argued. "How is she?"

"A strained neck, a little woozy, but she's all right, thank God. Her father and Charlie will bring her home in a couple of hours."

"You mean, if Conrad allows Charlie to get within ten feet of her. He can't be a happy camper about this one. Where's two-minutes-late Jackson now?"

"Conrad ordered him back to the house to search for evidence."

I looked ahead at the road. "Is that where we're going?"

Tom narrowed his dark, hawk eyes. "I want to have a talk with Jackson, see if he found anything. It is way past time to bring in the local authorities. Maybe Jackson will agree with me on that."

"Really. And it's not like Sidney doesn't already know. It's all anybody around here ever talks about besides getting a dog."

When we pulled up to the sidewalk in front of Stewart's house, Jackson's white Chevy sedan sat in the driveway next to Stewart's vintage Mercedes. He must have seen us coming because he instantly appeared on the front porch, face as grim and dour as always.

Tom spoke first. "Jackson, you find anything?"

He showed no expression when he said, "I report straight to Mr. Larkin."

Tom, never put off that easily, replied with force. "As you well know, Jackson, Mr. Larkin and Stewart sought my legal advice on this and other matters. I represent their interests. If I don't have complete information, I cannot serve them adequately nor do what is in their best interests. Flip can stand outside. She understands confidentiality. So why don't you show me what you found?"

Jackson's two steely eyes seemed to measure the weight on each scale. He nodded, motioning Tom to follow him into the house.

I meandered around the front yard and into the back, checking out the new plantings, adding Stewart's landscaping ideas to the list for our new house. My mind wandered farther afield as I took in the white daisies and red geraniums alongside the new rhododendron. Abner and Lindbergh drifted through my mind, and Horace and Leonard. I puzzled over how the stalker got inside Stewart's home, especially with new locks and bolts. Then I remembered what he called himself. The Locksmith.

In the heat of the June sun, I shivered. Stewart would have to immediately change the locks again and add an alarm system.

"Flip." Tom poked his head out the back door. "Why

don't you go on home and start lunch. Take the car.
I can walk over in a bit."

"OK. You sure? I can wait. I don't mind." Maybe
they'd invite me in and I could do a little snoopy scouring.

"No, you go on. I won't be long."

I'd heard that before. He tossed the car keys and disappeared into the house. I scowled and climbed into the
car, grumbling.

This day felt like a tall Bloody Mary. I headed home.

The Bloody Mary hit the spot and so did the chicken
salad I whipped up. When Tom hadn't walked through
the door two and a half hours later, I got behind the
wheel of his car and headed back to Stewart's, punching
on the radio. Screamin' Larry spun yet another tune
dedicated to the Maid in Hell, George Benson's "Willing to Fight."

A black limousine disappeared around the corner as
I pulled to the curb five minutes later. Charlie's rented
SUV had joined the Mercedes and Jackson's car. As
soon as I stepped in the yard, I heard yelling through the
open windows, five voices at once. No big shock, emotions ran high.

I reached the porch and hesitated. Nobody needed a
sixth voice screeching—none of my business, really. So
I plopped into the porch swing and eavesdropped like
any decent cleaning lady would, one eye wandering
through the window.

"All right! One at a time!" Tom demanded. "We're
not getting anywhere barking all at once."

"Well, I think I have the most at stake here." Stewart fought to control her jitters.

A general mumbling quickly subsided. She continued, voice shaky. "I was the one attacked. I'm the one he wants to . . . to put in a cage. And yes, maybe if Jackson had been here instead of Suggs, Jackson would have caught him, but that's water under the bridge. As far as I'm concerned, Suggs saved my life, and I'm thankful he's been in the right place at the right time. So Tom and Jackson, back off about him." She drew a breath. "And as scary as this experience was for me, I have to agree with Daddy. As long as someone is with me or within earshot at all times, I'm safe. This is just one man. He did not have a weapon. Nobody got shot or stabbed. I don't think that's where he's coming from."

Charlie jumped in to argue. "But you don't know . . ."

"*I* know," Conrad snapped. "And let me tell you another thing I know, mister. I know I never would have consented to Stewart going out alone with you."

"Daddy, we were hardly 'alone,' and that was my—"

He cut her off, the charm and wit replaced by a tough business stance, distinguishing a genuine risk from a harmless probability. "Your decision, I know. An extremely poor one. You bear a share of responsibility, but so does Jackson and so does this man." He turned on Charlie. "*You* didn't even have the common sense and decency to walk my daughter into the house and make sure of her safety. You drove off and left her with a man no one but Stewart seems to trust! Where did you go then, Charlie? Home? Or through the back door?"

Through the window, I saw Charlie's eyes flash, his fists clench. But Stewart redirected the focus. "You're being unreasonable, Daddy, but you're right about one thing. This man is coming out. He's exposing himself. *He* took the big risk last night, not us. He'll do it again, and I'm prepared now. Tom, I am. Don't look at me that way. So that's why I think we should simply go on as before. No policemen running my life and sending this man back into hiding. I'm surrounded by people looking out for me, and watching out for the stalker at the same time. This whole town has embraced me."

I winced. Unbeknownst to Stewart, with each new incident people grew more leery of befriending her. At least the women did. Lee hadn't helped, either. She heaped a coal or two onto the flames whenever she could, no matter how hard I preached, and no matter how hard Stewart tried to make amends for old hurts.

"If I hadn't gotten behind a traffic accident," Jackson growled, "we'd be celebrating right now and that scum would be in jail."

"And if you'd followed the advice I gave weeks ago," Tom said flatly, "a police stakeout would have accomplished the same thing without putting anyone's life at risk."

"Jackson," drawled Conrad, in full control now, the charm and good humor resurfacing, "a man needs a respite now and then to keep his senses sharp. Once a week has been my standing order since we came here. You know that. Thank God Suggs came through, and if Stewart is comfortable with his extra pair of eyes on her, and with our plan to draw this man out into the open, that's enough for me. You are a brave woman, darling."

"Brave or not, Stewart should be with you, sir, during Jackson's respites," Charlie said evenly. "Better yet, I'd be happy to sleep on the couch any time."

Conrad balked at the suggestion, offering a sharp rebuke. "Trust *you*? That won't be necessary."

Tom gave it another shot. "You know, we don't have to call the FBI to get results. And as much as I think a dozen policemen should have been swarming all over this house before Jackson's investigation, at least listen to this one suggestion."

"What is it?" Conrad's tone betrayed his impatience, despite the friendly smile.

"We have one town cop. When he's not in Frederick, he's keeping an eye out around here. He's a good man."

"You mean Sidney?" Stewart asked.

"Yes, Officer Garrett. He knows as well as anybody what's been going on here. Folks are angry with the two of you for bringing this kind of frightening scenario to a town where the most crime we get is bathroom graffiti at the high school. More than one person has approached Sidney and asked him to keep a watchful eye. He respects that you have Jackson on the job and are conferring with the L.A.P.D. He doesn't want to encroach on your private decision-making. But like the rest of us, he's concerned that you're in over your heads and somebody's going to get hurt. I suggest we ask him to step in, in an official capacity."

"Tom," Charlie piped up, "I talked to Sidney about what he's capable of doing to help. He said he doesn't have the expertise to trap a stalker, but the department . . ."

"Forget it," Conrad filleted the sentence. "We have been there, done that, with some of the nation's finest, and it still wasn't good enough. Involving the police only drags out the inevitable or makes it impossible. We need a confrontation with this man. *We've* accomplished that and more in the last four weeks. The L.A.P.D. wasted my time and Stewart's for six months."

Charlie asked the question I wanted to. "Speaking of which, did you find anything, Jackson? Is there any further evidence?"

"You're certainly curious about the evidence we've collected," Conrad answered for his P.I. "Evidence we are not at liberty to show you."

"And why not?"

"Because," Conrad spoke as he would to a caddie or a slow waiter, "it has already been forwarded, express mail, to L.A. Jackson discovered a note in the kitchen after the stalker fled."

"Tom," Charlie, amazingly cool, asked, "did you know about this? Did you get a chance to see the note?"

"Yes, Jackson showed it to me. It's a ransom note, designed to be read after a successful kidnapping."

Charlie turned on Conrad. "A ransom? That doesn't sound like a jilted lover to me. That sounds like somebody who has it in for *you*."

Conrad ignored him, but Stewart's eyes locked onto Tom's.

Charlie immediately picked up on it. "There's something else going on here. What is it?"

Stewart blurted, "Someone's been blackmailing my father over an illegal transaction he made about a year ago."

"Stewart!" Conrad boomed.

"Oh, Daddy! Why not lay it all out on the table? Charlie isn't going to turn you in!"

Everyone in the room seemed to know this information, anyway, but Charlie.

Conrad glowered, boring down. "I told you I don't trust this man."

"And I told you I do."

"You've made more than one poor decision lately."

"Nothing like the one you made a year ago."

Charlie pressed Conrad. "Are the stalker and the blackmailer one and the same?"

"Are you asking me, or telling me?" Conrad spat.

Tom stepped in. "Yes, it's the same person. A steady flow of funds is riskier than one big kill, so he switched tactics and began threatening Stewart. He's anxious to grab a huge purse and disappear."

"Either way," Conrad fumed, "I'll be bankrupt unless we take care of this man."

Stewart broke in. "We never told the police about the blackmail. It's too sensitive. Public knowledge could send our stocks reeling. Privately," her eyes on the floor, ashamed, "we've done all we can to rectify my father's mistake. But when the stalking began, we did ask the police for help, for all the good it did. When we realized the blackmailer and the stalker were one and the same, which didn't take long, we knew we had to trap him on our own. Then I ran into you again, Charlie, and with all our talk about the past, well, suddenly I knew—Solace Glen—the perfect place to spring our trap."

"I see," Charlie said quietly. He shoved both hands in his pockets. "So what's this guy want for a ransom?"

Jackson rattled the note off verbatim. "It said, 'To Whom it May Concern: Fifty million will get her back alive. Wait for instructions, The Locksmith.' That's all. Same magazine-type letters, same kind of paper."

"Fifty million." Charlie spoke in a lifeless tone. "This

Blonde Stranger everybody's been loony about really has it in for you, Mr. Larkin. A dangerously vengeful man who hates your guts. Hates you enough to go after your only flesh and blood."

"Charlie, listen to me. Listen." Stewart crossed over to him. "I don't want to spend my life running away. I want to live my life. I want to settle down, have children of my own, and not be afraid. The only way to rid myself of this fear is to face it. To kidnap me, this man will have to get close. Now we know what he wants. Now things can go in *our* direction. *We'll* be in control, not him. Now we know what to expect."

"No," Charlie's lips tilted up in a strange smile, "no, you don't. You haven't got a clue." He turned away from her, from all of them. "It's your funeral."

The front door banged open and Charlie passed hurriedly by, not noticing me on the porch.

For a few moments, no one spoke, then Tom said slowly and firmly, "I want all of you to give this matter your most serious consideration. We need to be on the same page, for Stewart's sake. Think about what I said. Think how you could use the services of a very fine police officer to add to your level of protection. Don't try to handle this stalker, this *kidnapper*, alone. It's not working."

I heard his steps on the floor of the hallway. I watched his hand push open the front door. I saw his eyes when he turned toward me. Tragic, sad, incredulous eyes. The eyes of one witnessing a suicide, unable to reach the hand with the gun in time.

•

CHAPTER 23

❊

IVORY AND I started off the holiday week by cleaning Lindbergh's house. The moment he opened the door and I looked into those twinkly little eyes, I knew he had something to tell me. Ivory bustled upstairs, plugged into her oldies station, hooting every time she heard a song go out for Screamin' Larry.

I immediately hopped to it. "Well? Did you find out anything?"

Lindbergh beamed. "Persuasion is my middle name, biography my only game."

"A poet, too. Don't keep me in suspense." I started in on the dusting, all ears.

Lindbergh picked up his notebook from the desk and flipped it open with a flourish. "Now, all this information comes from personal interviews (men do like talking about their service days), supplemented by quick, although I believe meticulous, research of my own."

"Gotcha. He wouldn't unfold every layer of his life and you scrambled to fill in some missing pieces."

"Precisely. But enough scrambling to yield unexpected results." Then he proceeded to astound me. "Abner Diggs, born April 17, 1941, Tulsa, Oklahoma, into a family of farmers. Poultry and grain, to be exact. Graduated high school, one year trade school. Various construction jobs, entered army, 1961, superb guerrilla training, Vietnam combat officer, 1965, prisoner of war for six months, managed to escape and free fifteen other men. Numerous medals, including a Purple Heart."

"Wow."

"Wow, indeed. While in army, married Annette Turner, 1964, one son, Steve, born 1966, during time Abner was a POW. Divorced, 1970, ex-wife died of cancer, 1988, in Portland, Oregon. Moved to Los Angeles same year to be near son in college. Started a construction company, did booming business. Son graduated from college, received MBA, 1990, at Stanford. Even before degree awarded, son becomes fast-rising young executive at L.C.S.—drum roll, please—a subsidiary of Larkin Industries."

"I knew it! That's how Abner knows the Larkins. His son works for them."

"Not quite. He *worked*. From what I can gather, and I really have much more research to do on this issue, there was some sort of scandal and Steve lost his fast-rising career as a result. He may have spent time in prison, too."

Miss Fizzi's words echoed, . . . *something scandalous happened, and Stewart was very upset . . . ,* and the story Lee told of the young executive, Stewart's lover, *crushed like a bug.*

My jaw dropped and I sank into the nearest chair. This explained a lot. "No wonder Abner hates the Larkins so much. He blames them for his son's downfall. Ohhh, myyyy. Lindbergh, you must find out more. We need to know where the son is now."

"I'm afraid I've only scratched the surface. I will delve further into this Steve Diggs. Perhaps I can come up with some pictures, too. A front view and profile . . . with numbers on the bottom?"

"Ohhh, myyyyy!"

Lindbergh rested a palm against a fluffy sideburn. "So you said."

LEE FLOPPED INTO the empty chair between Ivory and me. "What's on the menu today? Cabbages and kings?"

Ivory unplugged one ear. "Wings? You want good wings, you gotta go to Frederick."

She replugged, and I said rather drolly, casting an eye toward the Eggheads, "Fresh out of kings, too."

Lee followed my eyes and plucked a napkin into her lap. "Jesters-R-Us. So how's tricks? I heard about all the excitement yesterday. Tom confided to Sam, and everybody else gabbed to me, about Stewart's attack. I think she made it up to get attention."

"You're incorrigible."

She smiled brightly and checked herself out in a wall mirror. "So I am."

"She ended up in the hospital, you know."

"So? Nobody heard what she told the doctor. She probably went in the exam room and whined about cramps."

I let out a groan, causing the Eggheads to drop their forks and look concerned. "You are harsh."

"Ha! What did I tell you from the beginning? Stay away from that fakey feline. She's nothing but trouble."

"As you've been telling anybody with ears."

Lee looked down her nose at me. "Don't blame me if Stewart's popularity has dipped off the chart. Nobody with any sense wants to cozy up to a target of crime."

"But you just said she made it all up."

She gave a little squeak, waving a hand in the air. "True, false, reality, lies. I don't care if any of it's true or not. I don't want anything to do with the golden girl of the west."

I leaned into her, glancing around the room. "While we're on the subject, you won't be-*lieve* what I found out. That young executive fiancé Conrad threw into prison was Abner Diggs's son!"

Lee's hazel eyes widened and her head snapped up. "No, the name wasn't Diggs. I don't remember what it was, but not Diggs. Who told you that?"

I was about to divulge my secret source when Leonard entered stage left. Horace, sunglasses stylishly atop his head, sashayed close behind, Leonard's closest chum these days.

Slinking by, Leonard caught sight of Lee. He raked his black fox eyes across her like she was a mouth-watering fillet. "Lovely to see you again, Miss Jenner."

"It's *Mrs.* Gibbon now. And the pleasure's all yours." She swiveled around, showing him her stiff back.

The two made their way to a table, setting briefcases on the floor. *What devious plan lay hidden up their expensive shirtsleeves?* I wondered. *Which one had the most to gain from using the other?*

Just then, Sally swept by with a sandwich box and a

bag of chips. She spotted the three of us and skipped over.

"Hey, honey-bunnies!" She slid into the fourth chair at the table, chattering like an excited squirrel the whole time. "I was about to starve! I swear, I'm never gonna lose this baby weight. Look, my tush is as big as Tina's! Ooo, guess who blew into the salon this morning, kicking Miss Fizzi to the end of the line, and demanding a style-to-go on the spot, like I'm some kinda do-you-want-some-fries-with-that McHair?"

"I can only imagine one woman rude enough to behave so coarsely," Lee sniffed, barely getting the words out before Sally zoomed off again.

"You betcha, sweet potato. C.C., who else?"

I gulped a piece of ice and said, "I thought she only haunted the Red Doors."

Sally smacked her ever-present Wrigley's. "Oh, normally that's the case. It's first-class cutters, colorists, and stylists all the way. But today she got caught in that little rain burst we had around ten—hair emergency, call the fire department. She had an appointment with her decorator, which she 'had to look perfect for,' so she was forced to grace my humble hair choppery."

"Awww," Lee pouted her lips, "did she live?"

Sally puffed up. "Not only did she live, honeydew, she actually left my hair shack with a smile on her lips and gave me a twenty-dollar tip!"

"C.C. does have a way with money," I quipped. "What else?"

"Well! You know us hairdressers, how we get to talkin', and get our customers to talkin', and pretty soon there's so much talkin' that something in-ter-est-ing trots right out. Well! Ms. C.C. got goin' and she went on a regular roll. Truly. There is nothin' that woman didn't tell us about . . ." She bent down and Lee and I followed. "Mar-lene and Hor-ace."

Lee's shoulders jiggled in anticipation.

I must admit, I felt jiggly myself.

"Well!" In a whisper now, eyes darting toward the subject matter. "Horace completely fooled Marlene into thinking he loved her because he had heard Marlene's momma was rollin' in it and Marlene had blank check access. The 'marriage' lasted about sixty-four hours, as long as it took for him to figure out the only thing blank about Marlene lay between her eyes. Couldn't hide his true nature to save his life. Lord, I never thought I'd feel sorry for Marlene, but what he put her through got my attention, sugar cubes." Sally shivered head to toe. "It's a wonder she's not on the top floor of a psycho ward."

We all stared at the table top, afraid our noses would rotate toward Horace's table and give us away.

Sally's face flushed redder than her nail polish. "I can't even repeat what all she said, it was so traumatizing. I thought Miss Fizzi would pass out."

Lee grimaced. "Miss Fizzi heard this disgusting story? Probably aged her another decade or two. Who else heard this misery?"

Sally reflected a second or two. "Let's see. Tina had stopped by to drop me some nail polish she'd borrowed. The whole thing made her late getting back to Tom's office. Then Hilda poked her head in for a quick shaping."

"Oh, Lord." I could only imagine her naïve, teenage shock and the bizarre sprinkles and nuts she'd pile onto this sundae. "Anybody else?"

"Stewart. But as soon as C.C. got into the cruel details, she leaped up and sprinted outside to Jackson like a deer."

I groaned again, loud and long. An Egghead responded, using his best professional tone. "Flip, you need the Heimlich? Or a Tums?"

Hilda stood by their table, looking sheepish. She'd already started piling it up, no doubt. Suddenly, like Sally, I felt terribly sorry for Marlene. When Horace motioned Hilda to come give them a little service, Hilda balked and shot a look at the Eggheads that said it all. The Eggheads stared at Horace with bewildered faces, as though Scottie had beamed them onto the wrong planet.

Before Hilda could shuffle to the table where Horace and Leonard impatiently tapped their feet, wondering what her problem was, the door burst open and Melody shouted, "I think I just saw him! The blonde guy! The stalker! In a car! Where's Sidney?!"

Everybody but Leonard, Horace, and Ivory (still plugged in) leaped up and ran to a window or through the door to see.

"Are you sure?" Garland jumped in front of me, eyes zipping around the room to see where Hilda stood, breathing a sigh of relief to spot her at the window.

Hilda craned her neck to see farther down the street. "Sidney's in Frederick today!"

The Eggheads ran into the middle of Center Street, twisting this way and that. "What kind of car was it, Melody?"

Melody stood glued to the top step of the Bistro's entryway, afraid to even venture onto the sidewalk. "Gray. A smallish kind of sedan, gray, not silver. I know silver; this was gray."

Since I'd never told anyone but Tom and Sidney my suspicions about the gray car, this grabbed my attention.

"Well, it's gone now." The Eggheads strained their eyes in each direction. "Are you sure it was the stalker and not just some tourist passing through?"

"Melody?" As the only one who'd seen the Blonde Stranger, I waited for a description.

"I'm pretty sure it was him." She patted her chest, breathing hard. "I was walking down the street toward the Bistro, and something caught my eye. That's when I saw a man in a gray car rattling a newspaper, parked to the side, but the car was running, which I thought strange. Right when I drew parallel to the front end of the car, the paper dropped, and I saw a very blonde, very pale-skinned man with sort of narrow, thin features, but these real intense eyes that jumped out at me. I screamed, and just like that," she snapped her fingers, "he was gone."

Everyone turned to me with question marks in their eyes.

I nodded somberly. "Yes. That certainly sounds like the man I saw at the party."

MY FEARS WERE confirmed later that night when Tom stopped by for supper.

He tossed a legal file on the kitchen table, kissed my cheek, and held me tight. I could feel the tension in his neck and arms.

"Tom?"

A pause, then he murmured, "Stewart received another note from the stalker this afternoon." He pulled away from me, looking utterly defeated. "It's not good."

CHAPTER 24

✳

Stewart,
Sorry we missed a sweet reunion and sweeter
reward. Someone must pay. If not you, someone.
Remember, you always hurt the ones you love.

The Locksmith

This time, Tom held a Xeroxed copy of the note, a mild concession from Conrad before he mailed off the latest evidence to his great, impotent experts in L.A. who hadn't come up with anything useful—no fingerprints, no DNA, nothing. Even now, he would not compromise on his stand against the local police. Instead, Tom said Conrad reacted as though this latest note equaled a winning lotto ticket, thrilled that the gambling game he played had brought him so close to ensnaring the prey. Only when Jackson had the man at gunpoint, Conrad told Tom, would he call on Officer Garrett. Worse, Conrad showed absolutely no concern that now someone, anyone, could be at risk. He simply brushed aside the threat as a desperate ploy to drive away Stewart's friends and protectors. Stewart remained the true target, he argued, the gold at the core of the maze, and no one should lose any sleep over the stalker veering off in a different direction. As long as this criminal zeroed in on his daughter, *he'd* call the shots. He'd design the maze to entrap the stalker. End of game plan.

For once, Tom gave me wide latitude to open my big mouth and get the word out about the latest note, especially after he heard Melody spotted the Blonde Stranger in a gray car. As he put it, this now became the community's problem, not just one woman's. Maybe Conrad, with his love of games and sport, could brush away the stalker's threats, but the rest of us weren't about to.

BECAUSE OF THE short, holiday workweek, with the Fourth of July picnic nearing, Ivory and I scrubbed and mopped our fingers to the bone, cramming in houses so nobody would miss a cleaning. At each house we entered, the talk revolved around a central theme: The dogless residents of Solace Glen worked themselves into a frenzy.

Sam and Lee, dissatisfied with the amount of protection Jeb offered, discussed the upcoming dog auction ad infinitum. They finally decided to bid on the Irish setter because Lee liked the hair color. Not a sound reason in my book, but that's how Lee's brain worked.

"They're not a very protective breed from what I've read," she explained, pointing to a stack of dog books, "but they like to bark, which is all we need. Jeb, as you may have noticed, hates to bark. Shedding is his only weapon."

"And since we don't own a gun, because we're so politically correct, *and* Lee might accidentally shoot me," Sam confessed, "our only means of defense besides cat hair are some very dangerous garden tools." He raised one finger with a Band-Aid on it, expecting sympathy.

A lot of people worshipped at the Giant Schnauzer shrine, much to Ivory's dismay. At the Bistro, we picked up more tidbits of information. Pal's glee knew no end when he heard that the Puli breed had once appeared in beer commercials, which led to a big fight between him and the Eggheads on the virtues of bottles versus cans, and the recitation of twenty thousand brands of brew. The two Eggheads hoped to share the Chihuahua, but every old lady in town coveted something that small and barky. Margaret bristled when she heard the men discussing ownership of the dogs. She moralized on the spot, finger wagging in their faces, using her strictest teacher's tone, saying they ought to show some chivalry and step aside for the poor, defenseless women. The three of them slunk down in their chairs like they were back in tenth grade, but the moment Margaret turned her back, I could see in their eyes they'd do what they damn well pleased.

Finally, the big day arrived, a gloriously sunny, steamy, fragrant fourth. The grounds of the fire pond overflowed from four o'clock on. Picnic sheets and bedspreads blanketed the grassy fields, hemmed in by the massive evergreens. Portable grills sent the aroma of roast chicken and hot dogs into the air, along with the sweet sizzle of peppers and Vidalia onions. Children ran riot, throwing off their sneakers and sandals, playing tag and hide-and-seek in the rim of the trees. Their laughter and squeals punctured the heavy July air, lifting all our spirits and relieving our minds of recent worries and burdens. A portion of the high school band played popular tunes and patriotic songs, with a little jazz thrown in so Larry wouldn't make trouble. He lay alone on a Syracuse Big Orange sheet near the musicians, a beer bottle in one fist, the other hand draped inside familiar territory—a large bucket of KFC. His beloved Syracuse University baseball hat covered his face, if not his crumb-filled beard, and his tangerine shirt, completely unbuttoned, exposed the enormous belly to an unsuspecting public.

Unlike Thanksgiving, where huge tables groaned with the weight of game meats and chocolate cakes, people preferred to bring their own picnics in baskets and coolers. That way, no food spoiled in the summer sun. The fire pond served as a watery racetrack for everything from radio-operated boats to homemade skiffs to animal-driven rafts. The year Lee won first place in the animal-driven category with a water snake prompted the Picnic Council to post a new rule: mammals only. Otherwise, Lee said, she would have liked to try a baby shark or a piranha sometime.

"Boy, it's hot." She slapped a cold, wet paper towel around her neck and sipped beer from a plastic cup. "There must be over five hundred people here this year."

"Yeah, there are a lot of people I've never seen before." Scanning the faces in the crowd, I still couldn't help searching out the Blonde Stranger. "Oh, Lee, look at that. Sidney just put his arm around Hilda's waist! He's slow as a slug, but he is making steady progress. Who are those two guys?"

"Probably friends of Sidney's, off-duty cops. Which reminds me, who told you Abner's son went to prison for something to do with the Larkins?" A little burp popped out of her mouth. "S'cuse me. Ooo, lookie over there. Margaret and Lindbergh are making time."

"Speak of the devil, Lindbergh told me. He's doing some research." I gazed on the older couple. "They make a good match. I wonder where Miss Fizzi will send them on their honeymoon. Williamsburg or Cape May?"

While we laughed and clucked away about other possible matches in town, Sam and Tom finished unloading the big cooler we brought. Tom poured himself a glass of cold white wine and rubbed his back. "You work me too hard, woman. The engagement's off."

"You just keep drinking that wine; it'll be on again. How about a cup for me?" I whispered to Lee, "He better quit joking about that. I just ordered the dress and I'm not sending it back."

By this time, poor old Eli finally caught up with his master and collapsed on the quilt, long pink tongue dangling to the side as if he'd just run the Iditarod. Tom poured some spring water into a bowl and placed it beside his faithful companion.

"Hey, Lee," Sam popped open a can of low carb beer, already complaining about the effects of his bride's good cooking, "they've got the dogs over there in the shade for people to see. Wanna go check out our setter? The auction starts in an hour."

A large crowd had gathered around the four dogs.

People took a number printed on a small, white flag and signed up to bid. Rescue representatives accompanied all four animals to check out the background of the high bidder, visit the new home of the dog, and lend advice and literature before signing on the dotted line. Reverend G.G. made her way through the crowd like a regular politician, shaking hands and encouraging folks to help out the youth group, give a fine animal a good home, and give themselves the gift of companionship and protection. Everyone came out a winner.

Lee and Sam wandered toward their coveted setter, while Tom and I rested quietly on the quilt, watching our friends and neighbors. Presently, I fell into a pleasant trance, warmed by the waning afternoon sun on my skin and the tranquilizing effects of the wine.

"Don't you just love Thanksgiving and the Fourth of July?" I sighed after a few minutes.

"Yes, I do." Tom stretched his legs out and leaned back on his elbows. "And not only because we come to this wonderful spot, which always makes me want to spout poetry." He lightly kissed the underside of my hand and recited,

> *"Stop this day and night with me and you shall*
> *possess the origin of all poems,*
> *You shall possess the good of the earth and sun,*
> *(there are millions of suns left,) . . ."*

Then he picked up where he'd left off, as if he hadn't made my heart stop. "I love Thanksgiving and the Fourth of July because there are no presents to buy, no cards to mail, no long church services to sit through, and no tree you have to saw up when it's over."

"And no candy left in the bowl for weeks with your name on it."

"And no decorations to put up and take down."

"And no long credit card bills to pay afterward."

We could have droned on, but Abner Diggs moved into view. He stood apart from the throng, near the edge of the evergreens and the parking area. His eyes shifted almost rhythmically between the picnic crowd below him and the new arrivals hauling food and barbecue equipment from their cars.

"Tom," I bumped his elbow, "look at Abner. Don't you think he looks suspicious?"

Tom sat up and shaded a palm over his hawk eyes. "I see what you mean. Mmmm. Is that a 9mm Uzi in his back pocket, or is he just happy you think he's a criminal?"

"You think you're so funny."

"You think you clean for the FBI."

"But what about what I told you about Abner?"

"Oh, yeah. What Abner didn't tell Lindbergh, what Lindbergh told you, what you told me, and now what I'm telling you, which is—so what?"

I sat up straight as a board. "So *what?* So *what?* He has a motive! He hates the Larkins. So must his son."

As we watched Abner from a distance, his face lit up a tad, never excited, and a couple of men he worked with sauntered toward him with their families in tow.

"Yep," Tom yawned, slapping my hip, "he looks downright fiendish today. Who else out there grabs your investigative attention, Agent Paxton? Can you spot Miss Fizzi with her laser gun? Are the Eggheads wearing their Neo-Nazi battle fatigues? How about C.C. and Leonard? Did they bring their Nation of Islam bodyguards?"

I tried to look superior. "Go on. Have your pathetic little joke at my expense. You won't think it's so funny when I help catch the stalker, thanks to my brilliant observation and deductive qualities. I'll be the big heroine, and you, you will laughingly be referred to as Mr. Not-So-Smartie Pants."

"Ow," he rolled onto his side, "a stinging rebuke. Pass the bottle, please, my heroine. If you're not too busy staking out the stalker."

I smiled sweet as cupcake frosting and graciously waited on him (no sense exposing my vengeful side before the wedding). That good deed done, I immediately got back to scanning the picnic faces while Tom alternately sipped and snoozed.

Marlene zigzagged about, on the prowl for somebody, the syrup of a cherry snow cone dripping down one arm. She almost had a head-on collision with Horace, making tracks toward Leonard. He graced her with a long, creepy leer before cackling in her face and rushing off. Marlene clutched her stomach. She looked like she might keel over, but fortunately an Egghead tripped by and noticed her stricken state. Rather than have him touch her, she recovered.

Dressed in long shorts and boat shoes, as if he'd just stepped off the yacht from Bermuda, Leonard stood alone by a beer vendor. He swirled the liquid in a plastic cup, examining the beer like it was a ninety-year-old scotch in fine crystal. I watched as Horace approached and drew an envelope from his pants pocket. He handed it to Leonard with raised eyebrows and a knowing smirk. Leonard nodded, tight lips dipping downward. He slid the envelope into a pocket and waited while Horace bought himself a drink.

Melody and Michael strolled alongside Tina and Sally, who pushed the twins in a stroller. They all waved. Tina and Melody struggled with mouthfuls of cotton candy, but Sally yelled, "You and Tom gonna bid on a dog? Looks like you could use a new model."

Eli took no offense, since he'd lost most of his hearing.

"No, we have enough to deal with! New house, wedding, jobs. How about you all?"

The four nodded excitedly and headed for the dogs. A little ahead of them Charlie and Stewart walked side by side. Jackson flanked them; Suggs flanked Jackson.

"He is obsessed with her," I said out loud.

"What?" Tom spoke with closed eyes, trying to relax.

"Suggs. Obsessed with Stewart. I wonder if he could have staged that kidnapping. What do you think?"

Tom's chest heaved. "You'll have to do better than that to earn your badge at the academy."

"Well, at any rate, I've rested a lot easier since Stewart said she'd change the locks on the house—again. Jackson nixed the idea of an alarm system, though. Doesn't want bells and whistles scaring his prey away."

In an instant, the high-pitched screech of a microphone pierced the heavy July air. Mayor Cumming, a shy public servant (a rarity), welcomed everyone to the annual picnic and immediately introduced Reverend G.G. While he bowed out of the limelight, the Reverend bounced up on the platform like Tigger, rattling off a little background on the idea for the auction and what worthwhile projects the proceeds would benefit. Each Rescue club would receive twenty-five percent of the take, with the remaining seventy-five percent going to the Presbyterian youth for a summer trip to Montreat, North Carolina. At that beautiful mountain retreat, she burbled, they would hike, swim, square dance, and love the Lord to death. Without any further ado, she called a professional auctioneer to the microphone. He appeared along with the Rescue handler who held the leash to the first dog offered for bid, the Irish setter.

Tom and I made our way to the edge of the crowd, feeling the fun and excitement even though we weren't bidding. The auctioneer, a stout, bald-headed man with a straw hat he occasionally took off and waved to incite the crowd, had done his homework. He knew the story behind every dog, the sad circumstances that led to a rescued condition, the brilliant characteristics of each breed. He highlighted the particular dog's personality, and by the end of his introductory speech, even if you owned thirty Irish setters, you would have bid any amount of money to take this one home.

Lee looked like a dam about to burst. Even Sam, usually so cool and laid back, chewed his lip and pawed the earth with his sneakers, a bull eager to charge.

The bidding commenced and Lee's hand shot up.

"May I remind you, ladies and gentlemen," the auctioneer's voice boomed across the fire pond, "that you must raise your number flags to bid. You must raise your flags for your bid to count. Now, do I hear twenty? We will start the bidding at the ridiculously low price of twenty dollars for this magnificent canine. Feast your eyes on the color of this shiny coat! This is a high-class bitch, ladies and gentlemen!" He cupped a hand around his mouth, pretending to tell a secret. "Don't ya just love using that word in public without fear of arrest?"

Everyone laughed and within seconds, the bid jumped to two hundred dollars and climbing. Lee never put her flag down. That determined Jenner jaw I'd known most of my life jutted out ahead of the crowd. She would claim that bitch for sure.

When the bidding reached four hundred, flags started to drop and fall away. But not Lee's. And not Roland's.

"Look at that." I poked Tom in the ribs. "That SOB is bidding for the setter just because Lee wants her."

Roland Bell, nursing his supersized grudge, slid Lee the evil eye every time he raised his flag. He'd never forgive her for inheriting most of his sister's estate, especially the beautiful antebellum mansion where she and Sam now lived a happily married life.

Tom crossed his arms and scornfully remarked, "Roland hates dogs. He tried to kick Eli in the ribs one time when he thought I wasn't looking."

I stared at the graceful Irish setter, horrified at the thought of her living in Roland's backyard, chained to a stake in the ground.

When the bidding hit four hundred and sixty, Lee glared at Roland and jutted her jaw even harder. He shrugged and sneered right back.

The whole thing gave me a nervous stomach.

The auctioneer, the crowd, and of course, Reverend G.G., responded to the battle with wild enthusiasm. Besides Tom and me, Garland and Hilda wore worried faces. Garland's worry, however, turned to anger and she wormed her way over to Roland, making comments whenever he raised his flag. I don't know what she said, but Roland's cheeks started to blaze and he lost focus.

The auctioneer called, "Going once!"

Roland snapped back into battle mode and up flew the flag.

"Five hundred and twenty! Do I hear . . . yes, ma'am, five-forty!"

All eyes swung to Roland, but Garland wove her spell. Roland started chewing her out, fists clenched. Hilda shoved Sidney in Garland's direction.

The auctioneer boomed, "Five-forty! Five-forty! Going once, going twice . . ."

Roland's flag shot up.

"Five-sixty! Do I hear . . . yes, ma'am, five-eighty!"

Garland drew close enough to Roland so that no one else could hear. But whatever she said, the bidding stopped at five hundred and eighty dollars, and Lee had her sweet Irish setter.

She yipped like a coyote and leaped off the ground into Sam's arms. The two of them rushed up to the platform where the handler greeted them and the Setter looked like she could jump over the moon. Lee melted into tears—her first baby.

While they made their exit to fill out forms and arrange for a home visit, the second dog took his place on center stage. A stunned silence, than the whooping and hollering began.

CHAPTER 25

✳

"WHAT THE HELL is *that*?"
"It's the Puli! That's what they look like!"
"Who'd want it? Looks like a walking mop!"

And, for sure, it did. According to the auctioneer, the Puli, about a foot and a half tall, weighed in at thirty-three pounds. He looked hot under the black mop of tendrils, but happy. The flashing pink tongue accentuated the round, shiny nose, and he boinged around the stage as if he wore springs on all paws. The crowd fell in love, and once the auctioneer explained what a smart, tough, protective, alert dog this was, flags unfurled in a fury.

I heard Sally say to Wilber, "But all that hair! I'd be working on him so much, I wouldn't have time for my regulars!"

Pal, slightly out of character, dauntlessly faced the

prospect of intensive grooming. He grinned wide as a tire iron and waved his flag over and over. The Eggheads, one on either side, shivered with excitement and cheered him on.

"You could use him in your advertising, Pal!"

"Yeah, just like in the beer commercial! You could wear him on your head and ask people to buy your gas! I bet you'd make a million dollars!"

Once again, when the number hit four hundred, hands dropped and the few serious bidders dug in. Pal kept bidding, Lindbergh (to everyone's shock), Garland (feeling her oats after knocking Roland in his place), and C.C. (although nobody wanted her to win, of course).

Reverend G.G. glowed, delirious over the mounting success of her auction. The Rescue reps wore huge smiles, and the dogs lapped up all the attention, sensing their importance. People chanted the names of their favorite bidders, adding to the hoopla. When the number reached five hundred dollars, Garland shook her head and bowed out. When it hit five-forty, Lindbergh called it a day.

Now at five-sixty, the auctioneer geared up to top the number brought by the Irish Setter. He egged Pal on. C.C., vexed that the bidding dragged on this long, would most certainly not accept defeat from the man who pumped her gas. She powdered her nose, waiting for Pal to make up his mind to venture into a financial stratosphere where she knew he couldn't breathe.

"Going once! Going twice! The gentleman wants five-eighty! Five-eighty for this charming, loyal companion with championship lines! AKC registered, folks! Ready to enter the show ring and strut his stuff with the best of them! Only two years old! Yes, ma'am, six hundred! I have six on the table, sir. What will you bid?"

C.C. tried to appear disconnected, but I could tell this whole business brought out the raving lunatic in her, competitive to the hilt. Back at the vendor's stand, Leonard swilled more cheap beer and watched C.C. spend his money. He looked downright morose.

Poor Pal wavered, already having offered twice what he would have to buy a dog, even a champ. The crowd rose to the occasion. "Pal! Pal! Pal!"

Pal haltingly raised his flag as if he suffered from a broken arm, his face pale and drained.

"Six-twenty! I have six-twenty for the Puli!"

C.C. yawned and primly patted her red mouth. She stuck her flag up.

Pal went weak at the knees. He looked longingly at the black Puli, who seemed, under all that hair, to telegraph a yearning right back.

I bit my lip and hugged Tom's arm. How would it end?

That's when Garland stepped up to the plate again. She slid behind Pal and whispered in his ear. His face lit up and the flag did, too.

"Six-sixty, ladies and gentlemen! That's the spirit! Look how excited this little fellow is!"

We knew he meant the dog, but all eyes fastened on Pal—trembling and giddy enough to shoot off like a rocket. Garland beamed, a guardian angel at his elbow.

Tom hugged me into his side and laughed. "She's going in with him! I bet she's matching him dollar for dollar. Good for Garland!"

Meanwhile, C.C. took on her more normal Cruella De Vil qualities. Her bottled-black hair spiked out and her penciled eyebrows formed two high arches. She hoisted her flag and scowled at Pal.

"Six-eighty! We have six-eighty for this brave young Puli—a loyal family pet, a possible show ring contender, a marvel to behold! Seven hundred from the gentleman!"

C.C. reared backward in a fury and almost fell off her high heels. (Leave it to her to wear spikes to a picnic.) Marlene, standing close by, grabbed C.C.'s skinny arm and pulled her straight.

"Going once!"

C.C. waved her flag like she worked at Daytona.

"Seven-twenty! . . . Seven-forty . . . Seven-sixty! . . . Seven-eighty!"

The crowd screamed in delight and the auctioneer whipped off his straw hat, fanning the flames.

Just as C.C. attempted to stick her arm up for the umpteenth time, Leonard clasped her wrist and brought the flag waving to a dead halt. "Over my dead body," he growled. "This is absurd."

C.C. squawked. I thought she might spit in his eye, but instead, she gave a little squeak of indignation and huffed away, Marlene at her heels. She knew who buttered her bread.

So much for that. The auctioneer congratulated Pal for contributing seven hundred and eighty dollars to the Rescue Club and youth group, two worthy causes, and Pal and Garland slowly worked their way to the platform, hands slapping and patting their backs the whole way. They presented themselves as dual owners and plunked down three hundred and ninety dollars each. Hilda yee-hawed and sprang into Sidney's flabbergasted arms while the Puli sprang around, top dog at Westminster.

The applause continued for a good five minutes before the third dog made her entry.

"Our third dog, ladies and gentlemen, is another bitch." The snickering rose and fell. "This is Impy, an adorable black Chihuahua. She's a little on the old side compared to the others, about seven, but there's still fire in her belly."

Most of the old ladies in the audience began to twitter. They couldn't wait to use their flags. Margaret's eyes brightened and Miss Fizzi kept asking Melody, "Now? Do I do it now?"

Tom screwed his nose up. "That is one ugly dog. Whoo, I'd be embarrassed to call myself a dog if I looked like that."

"You better hush. You know one of your clients is going to get it. Then you'll have to *ooo* and *ahh* over the thing every time you see it."

The bidding commenced and flags flew up like a flock of sparrows. The price quickly rose to four hundred, the usual point where the serious contenders weeded out the noncommittals.

Margaret raised her flag with a shocked expression, one hand over her heart, expecting it to give out any second. Lindbergh encouraged her on, and I wouldn't have been surprised if he'd made the same generous offer Garland offered Pal. Miss Fizzy stood sandwiched between Michael and Melody, gaily hoisting the flag skyward each time they told her to. But when the bidding reached four-sixty, they told Miss Fizzi she could rest now.

Stewart bid for awhile, but just for fun. She stopped a few dollars short of Miss Fizzi, leaving only Margaret and the Eggheads in the running. Margaret's spine turned to starch. She frowned at the two of them, no doubt recalling the haughty sermon she'd delivered that obviously didn't sink in.

Now that their buddy Pal claimed half ownership in a beer commercial dog, the Eggheads turned into Pigheads, stubbornly bent on sharing ownership in the taco commercial dog.

"Itn't he cute? He'll be our very own little, black doggie friend."

"He's a she, dummy. Raise the flag, you almost missed that one!"

"She sure is cute. Won't she look nice sitting up on the dashboard of the ambulance?"

When the number hit five hundred, Margaret turned ten shades of purple and Lindbergh had to prop her up. "Oh, no. Oh, Lord. I can't stand it another minute. Please, help me, Lord!" She raised the flag, eyes crunched.

"Get it up there, stupid! She's trying to get our little dog!"

The auctioneer revved the motor. "I have five-twenty for the Chihuahua! Madam, it's up to you!"

Margaret's knees buckled. "Oh, Lord. Oh, no. I need a respirator." Her flag went up.

"Damn! She did it again! Put the flag up!"

"Are you sure? How much did he say? Have we got that kinda money?"

The straw hat fanned the fire of the crowd. "I have five-twenty! Going once!"

"I said raise it, dummy!" The flag flew high.

"Do I hear five-sixty? Five-sixty! Going once! Going twice!"

Margaret collapsed into Lindbergh's arms. "Save me, sweet Jesus! I can't go on!"

"Sold to the two gentlemen on my right! Congratulations and thank you!"

The two "gentlemen" took turns knuckling each other's bristly scalps and pounded each other on the back before galloping to the stage to collect their little doggie friend who scowled and yipped at their approach, surly-faced at the news of her pending ownership. When an Egghead stooped to pet her, she pulled tiny lips back and snapped at his fingers. The handler looked notably concerned and all three hustled off-stage to discuss the situation.

Now at last, the apple of Ivory's eye took center stage. The Giant Schnauzer made an impressive entrance, and at once the crowd moaned at her dark beauty and stature. And stared in sorrow at her haunches. She was missing her right hind leg.

"Oh, no!" I heard someone lament. "That poor thing's handicapped. Who would want her?"

"Look at the tripod," guffawed some ignoramus. "I guess this one's the blue light special."

Ivory sidled up beside Tom and me. "Look at her! Isn't she fine! Look at her ears, so alert, and her head, my, my, my!"

"She is a beautiful girl," Tom said in all sincerity. "What's her story?"

Before Ivory could open her mouth, the auctioneer launched into the tale, with all of us listening in rapt attention. Born with an impeccable German pedigree, the Giant had found a good home at the beginning of her four years with a kind, elderly couple whose health soon failed. When one died and the other entered a nursing home, the young Giant ended up in a shelter, quickly adopted by a man who thought she'd make a superb attack dog in his hardware store at night. She spent her days in a crate, ignored, and her nights alone in an empty store. Ill-fed, ill-treated, her coat disintegrated into mange, her ribs showed through the unkempt fur. Finally, a rare cancer caused her leg to shake uncontrollably, and the man abandoned her to a vet who actually wanted more than five dollars to treat her. That's when the vet called the Rescue Club. He treated the cancer, but was forced to remove her leg. With the aid of the vet, the Club saw to it that her coat regained its gloss and her ribs filled out with a healthy diet. The kindness of strangers restored the Giant's pride and boundless spirit. Now all she needed for a happy ending was a good home. Half the audience had broken into tears by the time the bidding began.

"Ladies and gentlemen, the lack of a leg does not mean the lack of a heart. And this beautiful animal is all heart. The lack of a leg doesn't hold her back one iota. You can see that for yourself, the way she leaped up on this stage. This lady has been through hell. So how about a little heaven for a member of a breed that is known for its fierce loyalty and hard-working temperament? Protector, clown, and queen, this girl has it all. What is my first bid?"

Due to the size of the Giant, many bidders hesitated; the missing leg disappointed more than a few. But Ivory and about a dozen others raised their numbers.

The Giant held her head as high as the flags, taking an immense interest in the proceeding that would seal her fate.

Once again, bidders dropped away one by one until only two were left standing at the price of four hundred and twenty dollars. I figured Ivory would be in it for the long haul; I didn't figure on her competition.

"Yo, babe! Maid in Hell! Beat this!" Screamin' Larry drunkenly waved his flag at Ivory as if tossing about an obscene gesture.

Ivory's round eyes popped and flashed, but she called upon her Christian upbringing, turned her head, and raised the flag without comment.

As the crowd saw it, this represented a pretty clear choice between good and evil. As much as we loved Larry's taste in music and his obscure talent for driving away untouchables like C.C. and Leonard, Ivory garnered the popular vote. A groundswell of support washed through the crowd like a rising tide.

"Ivory. Ivory! I-vor-y!"

"Do I hear four-sixty for this very special girl? Four-sixty! Yes, sir! The man with the big beard goes four-sixty for the big dog!"

Ivory confidently upped the ante.

"Thank you, ma'am! The tall lady says not today, mister! What's your answer, sir?"

Larry would have unloaded a ton of foul words, but Sidney and his two off-duty buddies stood close enough to cuff him. Larry opened his mouth, thought better of it, and simply raised his flag, all charm.

"Do you want this gorgeous girl, ma'am? You can have her now for five-twenty!"

Ivory didn't flinch. She met the bid to the delight of the audience.

"Ivory," I tugged on her fire-red blouse, the chanting loud and raucous now, "do you have that much money?"

"I didn't eat bag lunches for twelve years for nothing,

honey. Anyway, even if Larry wins, he's so disgustin' no self-respectin' Rescue Club's gonna hand over a precious dog like that to somebody like him."

She did have a point.

With popular opinion against him, and the dizzying effects of a double six-pack sinking in, Larry hesitated a second too long. The auctioneer shouted, "Going twice!"

Ivory captured Larry's glazed eyes long enough to punch her flag in the air like a sword of justice, a defiant glow lighting her up, a red-bloused Statue of Liberty. "Come on! You drunk or somethin'? How un-usual! You heard the man, 'goin' twice!' Whatchoo gonna do, you Screamin' Heathen?"

We were wondering, too. The crowd's roar fell to a hush, waiting on Larry's next move.

Larry blinked and tilted. Lights out, game over. Onlookers scrambled out of the way as he crash-landed, baseball cap folding neatly across his face, fists still holding the flag above his bare, massive chest as if the marines had finally taken this hill.

"Sold to the tall lady in the red blouse for five hundred and twenty dollars! Thank you, ma'am, and this auction is at an end. You have all done the community, the Rescue world, and the youth a wonderful service today! I'm here to remind you, too, to stick around for the fireworks in one hour. Enjoy the band, play some games, buy some food and drink from the various charities you see working the concessions today. Thank you! Happy Fourth of July!"

And so it was that a select few from Solace Glen purchased peace of mind and protection. Or so we thought.

PART FOUR

❊

Leashes and Locks

Chapter 26

※

After the auction, Tom and I, high rollers, played a couple of games like balloon darts and bottle rings, but didn't win a darn thing, not even a plastic key chain. We strolled back to our picnic spot to start the feast, admiring cakes and pies on sale, homemade quilts and sweaters, and all manner of canned goods.

Margaret swept by, on cloud nine with Lindbergh at her side, and a grinning little doggie friend cradled in her arms. "Look, Flip! The Rescue lady said the Eggheads weren't fit owners for Impy. Poor, scared thing was very vicious with them. So Lindbergh and I are going to share her! Isn't that wonderful?"

Tom smiled rather sickly at the panting, bug-eyed canine, and complimented Margaret on her beautiful new pet. "She's certainly an eyeful," he said diplomatically.

Margaret and Lindbergh chuckled together and

suddenly looked very much alike. I knew in an instant, we could have a real December wedding in Solace Glen.

By the time Lee and Sam made their way through the throng to our picnic spot, ecstatic Irish setter in tow, night had fallen and the sky held "the millions of suns" in Tom's poem.

"These will be the first fireworks of our engagement." Sometimes nostalgia filled me to the brim and I spouted such nonsense.

Tom frowned. "Is this like one of those times you've said, 'Oh, our first April Fool's day engaged,' or 'It's our first Daylight Savings Time engaged?' "

"You get the picture."

Sam and Lee descended on us, Lee squeaking and squealing, high as the fireworks about to go off.

"Isn't she goooor-geous! Have you ever seen such a pretty color coat?"

Sam admired his bride, a toddler playing with her first rocking horse. "Yeah, if it doesn't work out, we can always skin her and have a red rug in front of the fire."

"Sam, stop it. You already love her as much as I do. Here's Eli, Katie!" The baby talk commenced. "Kaaatie, here's Ewiii."

"Is that her name?" I watched Eli drag his old bones up to present himself to the lady. The two sniffed away, wacky grins, tails wagging at a lethal speed.

"Watch the wine!" Tom shoved Eli off the quilt. "Why must you always attack the wine?"

"No," Lee answered my question, "she had so many different names before arriving at the Rescue Club, we got to choose one. Katie is my favorite Irish name."

"I wanted to name her Geraldo," Sam groused. "Hey,

it's almost time for the fireworks. Lee, you want me to run up to the car and get that new collar and leash we bought?"

"No." Lee hopped up. "I'll get it. I left my lipgloss in the glove compartment, and you can't find anything, even when I tell you where it is."

"Fine." The insult trickled down his back. "Miss Katie and I will lounge around here and gun a few beers till you return."

We spread out the food and launched into some serious picnicking. Sam produced a rawhide bone for Katie, and Tom threw Eli a scrap now and then. The fireworks began and everyone's eyes lifted skyward to the sight of red, white, and blue sizzles and fizzles and zooms and pows.

At every explosion, when the sky illuminated the grounds of the fire pond, I still searched the multitude for that one pale face of the Blonde Stranger. But I never saw him.

Ten minutes into the fireworks, Sam began to turn his head toward the parking area. "Wonder what's keeping Lee?"

Four minutes later. "Where did Lee get to?"

Three minutes later. "What *is* she doing?"

One minute later. "Tom, watch Katie for me, please. I'm going to check on Lee."

The fireworks ended with spectacular booms and zooms, and the entire fire pond seemed lit by "the million suns." As soon as the show ended, families started collecting children and calling for help to carry baskets and coolers back to the car. The mass exodus began. I heard Sidney recite a traffic safety plan to his two buddies, directing this lane to go out first, etc., etc. It sounded like the three would have the lot cleared in a jiffy.

Still no Sam and no Lee. Tom and I stayed put, petting the dogs and savoring the wine. Ivory shouted goodnight from a distance, the noble Giant trotting beside her in a surprisingly graceful gait. Pal, Garland, and Hilda stumbled up the hill to their cars, fussing over which one would keep the Puli for the first night.

"I guess the new dog owners can expect a home visit tomorrow from the Rescue reps," I said to make conversation, a bit perturbed with Lee for abandoning us. Probably ran into Sally and the twins and lost track of time.

Tom moved his lower jaw back and forth, sharp dark eyes sweeping the faces in the exodus. "Yeah, it's sort of like social services or the foster care system."

Within fifteen minutes or so, Tom and I realized we were the only ones left on the ground. More than half the cars had departed the parking area. Sidney and his two buddies, whistles in their mouths, quickly saw to it that the rest of the cars made headway.

"I can't find her anywhere!" Sam came running up, breathing hard. "I've asked everyone we know and then some. She's disappeared!"

Tom and I jumped up.

"Did you see Sally?" I asked. "Melody? Miss Fizzi? Roland?" Maybe he'd dragged her into the woods for a shouting match over estate furniture and china doodads.

"Nobody. Nobody's seen her. The car still has the leash and collar inside."

Tom wasted no time. "Flip, stay here with the dogs. Sam, let's get Sidney. He has two officers with him tonight. We can fan out. If she's anywhere around here, we'll find her."

How long I sat on that quilt, surrounded by a half-eaten picnic and two sleepy dogs, I do not know. I turned on a flashlight and busied myself packing up food and plates.

Tom rushed by once to grab two other flashlights, then raced toward the other men. Some people stopped their cars to ask what was wrong. Many of them pulled over and joined in the search for Lee. They divided into three groups, a cop at the head of each, and spread out, covering the fields, the pond area, and the tree line. I watched as flashlight beams flickered in the woods and around the pond, large fireflies, eerie and bizarre. Terse, muffled conversations on cell phones filled the muggy night as the searchers called everyone they knew, inquiring about Lee. Her name punctured the air, shouted over and over again.

By the time Tom and Sam trudged back to me, I shivered, in tears. Tom offered to take Katie with us for the night. Sam, exhausted, nodded and left to join Sidney.

"Come on." Tom took me in his arms, holding on tight. "Let's go to your place. I'll grab a little sleep there, then catch up with Sam and Sidney in three or four hours. He contacted the county police and the state troopers, but you know how that goes. They don't pull out all the stops until the first twenty-four hours is up." He drew back, clasping both my shoulders. "We're going to do everything humanly possible to find her, you hear?"

I heard, but couldn't respond except to cry and shake.

He had her. The man with the cage and the handcuffs had my best friend.

CHAPTER 27

❈

NOT THAT ANYBODY slept that night. Even the two dogs roamed restlessly through the Historical Society as if searching for Lee. I told Tom to go upstairs and try to sleep; I was too wired up. I brewed a pot of tea and pulled an afghan around my shoulders, curling into a fetal position on the sofa to watch the late evening news. Two hours later, I half-expected the movie I pretended to watch to be interrupted with a special announcement, and Lee's face would cover the screen. Tears flowed and Katie, more than once, stuck her nose on my lap in comfort.

At some point, I finally drifted off to sleep. When I awoke, a note from Tom lay on the coffee table, urging me to stay put, he'd be in touch.

The morning dragged, interrupted only by the ring of the phone. Every time it jangled, I jumped, nerves shot. By nine o'clock, all of Solace Glen had heard the awful news of Lee's disappearance and friends called wanting the latest report, but I had nothing to tell. Instead, I fired off questions: Did you see Lee? What time? Did you see anyone who fit the Blonde Stranger's description? Did you notice any gray cars?

No one had seen anything but the fireworks.

When Tom finally called, he tried to sound positive. An impossible task. Sidney and his two buddies, now fully on duty with the go-ahead to investigate Lee's disappearance, had been busy. They'd interviewed dozens of people, focusing on possible sightings of the Blonde Stranger and the gray car. But they also zeroed in on specific targets of interest, a list Tom and Sam drew up. Roland proved uncooperative, big shock, and told Sidney he wouldn't put it past Lee to have kidnapped herself, just to get him in trouble. He said he'd gone straight home after the dog auction, and didn't have any blonde friends. (No brunettes or redheads, either.) Leonard expressed outrage at the questioning and threatened to sue. C.C. cackled in his defense, claiming he'd been too drunk to kidnap a woman, though she did let slip they'd become separated and he hadn't come home till the wee hours. Horace treated the whole event like a tantalizing cat-and-mouse game. He had the pleasure, he insisted, of carousing with Leonard half the night in Frederick, but couldn't recall the names of any of the places they'd frequented. Abner couldn't be found for questioning, but Tom was sure he'd turn up. He refused to believe that Abner could orchestrate a stalking.

Lots of concerned souls volunteered to expand the search and drove around the outskirts of Solace Glen poking their noses under bridges, in old barns, in wooded areas, along the banks of the Monocacy. Meanwhile, the clock ticked slowly without any word. Nobody turned up a thing.

And then the dog handler stopped by.

A tall, graceful middle-aged woman with russet hair tied back in a ponytail, the Rescue Club handler bore a striking resemblance to the Irish setters she loved. She'd gotten wind of Sam's predicament and sought out Katie to make sure she'd landed in good hands. Garland, one of my morning callers, told her I had temporary custody. She smiled when both Katie and Eli greeted her at the door, tails wagging in unison.

"I feel better already," she declared, stepping into the Historical Society. "I heard about Mrs. Gibbon's disappearance. I am so sorry! Was she a friend of yours?"

Was. I burst into tears. Twenty minutes later, over coffee, I'd poured out Lee's life story and the tale of the stalker. In desperation, I asked the handler if she'd seen anything unusual, anything at all, and if she'd noticed a pale, blonde man with intense eyes.

"I don't think . . . ," she paused, reflecting. "Well, I left before the fireworks started. I walked to my car, parked near the woods, and just as I started to get in, I saw someone through the trees. It struck me as odd because he stood all alone and didn't look like he was doing anything other than looking down at the crowd. Then I thought, oh, maybe he didn't want to wait in line to use the facilities. I never saw his eyes, but he certainly was blonde."

Within seconds, I was on the phone to Tom and the dog handler was on her way to give Sidney a statement. Gratitude mixed with horror as our worst fears began to jell.

* * *

SAM NEARLY COLLAPSED late in the afternoon. Tom made him go home and rest, telling him to let the experts do their job; Lee would want him to take care of himself.

Not up to cooking, I called Tom and urged him to meet me at the Bistro. I knew how tired and hungry he must be. Still a little early for dinner, the restaurant wouldn't be crawling with customers and we could take it easy.

When he walked through the door, my heart wanted to break. He trudged to the table and fell into the chair.

Garland zipped over and set a beer in front of him. "On the house," she murmured. "Is there any news?"

He looked at me with vacant eyes. "Did you tell Garland what the dog handler saw?"

I nodded, beyond gloomy.

"Then you know everything there is to tell, Garland. Thanks for the beer. I can use it." But he only stared at the glass, the corners of his mouth deeply creased.

"It's almost been twenty-four hours." My voice quivered. "Will that make a difference in what the police do?"

"Yes. Sidney and the two officers helping him are about at the end of their ropes. Dead tired. They agreed, two more hours and they'll take off. A special unit is poised to take over then."

"Oh, when I think of poor Sam! Has he gotten any rest?" I could imagine every Circle Lady in town banging on his door with casseroles and hankies.

"I hope so. Stewart gave him one of her sleeping pills."

Stewart. It would make all the difference in the world if she got involved and opened up. "Is Stewart being co-operative with the police? Any information could prove so helpful."

Tom took a long drink from the beer glass. "Yes, she's been very helpful, much to Jackson's annoyance. The man wouldn't speak one word to Sidney. Stormed into the next room and sulked. And fortunately, Conrad wasn't there to influence her. He hopped on his private jet and made a quick one-day trip to L.A. to confer with a forensics expert who's been working on the evidence, and to take care of some 'urgent business.' He'll be back shortly."

I scoffed. "Urgent business. What's more urgent than what's going on right here?"

"I agree, but the man does have an industrial empire to run. Jackson's kept him informed on what's happening here."

"As if he'd care! He's probably dancing a jig Lee got kidnapped and not Stewart! If only he'd listened to you."

"Flip." The circles under Tom's eyes seemed to darken. "It wouldn't have mattered. This was a crime of opportunity. This guy was waiting in the woods for a straggler. Any straggler. It happened to be Lee. Nothing Conrad could have said or done would have mattered."

Just then, Lindbergh and Margaret entered the Bistro. They saw us and hurried over, slipping into the other two chairs at our table.

Margaret reached for my hand. "Oh, Flip, this has been the worst day of our lives! Is there any news, Tom?"

He told them all he knew.

Lindbergh rubbed his fluffy sideburns and tossed a knowing look my way. "Has Abner been questioned?"

"He hasn't been available," Tom answered, and added flatly, "But I'm sure he'll be fully cooperative when found. He probably went fishing or something."

While Margaret drenched Tom with more questions, I sent Lindbergh an inquisitive glance, to which he quietly replied, "I really must get back to my research soon."

We ordered our dinners, and tried to talk about something else, but the conversation couldn't be steered in any other direction. Our voices almost echoed, the Bistro unusually empty and quiet. Margaret speculated that, under the circumstances, people preferred to stay locked up at home.

"I know." I picked at a salad. "Going out to enjoy a good dinner doesn't seem right when Lee . . ."

I collapsed into tears for the hundredth time just as the door to the Bistro burst open and Stewart raced in, out of breath, Jackson close behind.

"They found her!" she exploded. "We were on our way here to grab some take-out when we saw Sidney. He just got word from one of his buddies! He blazed off with the lights flashing!"

We all leaped to our feet with the same questions. "Where? Where did they find her? Who found her? Is she all right? Where is she now?"

Garland and Hilda came tearing out of the kitchen. Stewart and Jackson spilled what little information they had.

"The covered bridge at Loy's Station, in that little park."

"Suggs, if you can believe it."

"We don't know her condition."

"She's at Frederick Memorial."

Margaret and I asked in unison, "Does Sam know?"

"Yes," Stewart placed a hand over her heart as if it might jump out, "Suggs called him first, then phoned the police station."

"Hey!" The Eggheads entered the picture. "What's goin' on? Something happen? We just saw Pal driving Sam out of town like a bat outta hell!"

"Oh, the sleeping pill," Stewart explained. "Sam must have taken it right before he got the call and grabbed Pal for a ride."

"What call?" The Eggheads had to know everything. "Did they find Lee?"

"Yes! Yes!" we all crowed.

"Did they get the stalker?"

"No, no stalker." A sobering thought in our celebration.

"Flip." Margaret sank into the closest chair. "Lord, I have to sit back down before I keel over from excitement. Flip, you and Tom go on to the hospital. Lindbergh and I will take care of the bill. Go on, now, scoot."

"We'll be over later," Stewart said, "after we pick my father up at the airport. Oh, has anybody seen Charlie? I've been looking for him."

We all shook our heads as Margaret waved Tom and me out of the Bistro; it didn't take much encouragement. We flew to Tom's car and headed for Frederick, nervous, gritting our teeth, barely speaking the entire drive, both of us thinking the same thoughts: *What happened to Lee the past twenty-four hours? Why did the stalker let her go? And what did he plan to do next?*

CHAPTER 28

✳

WHEN WE ARRIVED at the hospital, we learned that Lee had already gone through the emergency room and had assigned quarters for the night. In a sitting area near her room, we found Pal and Suggs, studying their feet.

I rushed up to Suggs. "How is she?"

"OK," he mumbled.

This would be like pulling teeth, but I launched ahead. "How did you find her? How was she when you first saw her?"

Suggs's bulldog features darkened and he grimaced. "I already told the police this stuff. Ask them. They're in her room right now."

"I'm asking you, Suggs. The police are busy. *Please*."

"Come on, Suggs," Pal prodded, dying to hear. "I'll give ya another day off."

Suggs's dark cloud lifted. He nodded and gulped, gearing up to say more at one time than he ever had in his life. "Well, Aunt Fizzi said she'd lend me her car for the day if I'd help a little with the search. So I drove north, taking the back roads, figuring I could do some fishing while I was at it. When I got to Loy's Station . . ."

"Loy's Station?" I interrupted. C.C. and Leonard's new neighborhood. In the excitement at the Bistro, that fact had bounced over my head. "Sorry. Go on."

"When I got to Loy's Station, I saw something on the ground under one of the picnic tables. At first I thought somebody had dumped a bag of trash, but then it moved. I pulled over and stopped the car to check. That's when I saw it was a woman. She kind of groaned and I saw it was Lee. She wouldn't wake up. Drugs or something. And . . . and she was handcuffed."

I slapped a hand over my mouth in horror. Pal sat speechless.

"My God." Tom shuddered. "What she must have been through."

"I picked her up and put her in the back of the car. That's when I noticed the note."

"A note?" Tom shifted into lawyer mode. "What kind of note?"

"In an envelope, like the others Miss Larkin got. Pinned to the front of her shirt."

"Did you read it?"

"No. I did what Jackson taught me to do. Let it alone. The first cop to arrive at the hospital took it from the emergency nurse."

I pressed further. "Did Lee regain consciousness?"

"Yeah. She came to after she got here, about the time Sam arrived with Pal."

"My goodness!" Pal wrung his hands, eyes wide as wheel covers. "Didja see anything else at the bridge? Didja see any blonde guys lurkin' around?"

"Oh, sure. Like he'd be sitting there waiting for me and the cops to show up."

Suggs had had enough. He lumbered off to the water fountain.

"My goodness!" Pal said again. "Listen, I gotta get back to town. Wouldja mind seein' about Sam?"

He probably couldn't wait to skid into Solace Glen and spill the tale to the Eggheads and anybody else within earshot. We assured him Sam would be fine; he'd no doubt want to stay the night with Lee. Suggs apparently had to stick around in case the police had more questions after talking to Lee.

Tom and I settled down to wait, the disturbing image of Lee, drugged and in handcuffs, unshakable.

After a few long minutes of sitting, watching Suggs pace around with a paper cup, I thought the least I could do was compliment him.

"Suggs, thank you for finding Lee and getting her to the hospital. God knows how long she might have been out there if you hadn't come along. When I think of her waking up on the cold ground in the dark, realizing that she had those *things* on her hands."

Tom wrapped an arm around my shoulders. "She's fine, she's fine. Don't think like that." Still in lawyer mode, he gently pumped Suggs for more facts. "Did you see anything unusual at the picnic yesterday? Any recollection of someone who might fit the description of the man Flip and Melody saw?"

Suggs scratched an ear and glared into space. "I

dunno. I was pretty much focused on Miss Larkin." He grunted. "Nope. Can't think of a thing."

"Did you see Abner?" I asked, pursuing a theory despite Tom's smirk.

"Yeah. Saw him before the fireworks."

"Did you see Leonard and Horace?" Another theory, more far-fetched.

"Yeah. Saw them before the fireworks, too. Two peas in a pod."

A third theory, even stranger. "How about Roland?" After all, he could have used the panic over the stalker to take his own revenge against Lee. But could he have faked the note?

"During the auction I saw him. Not after that."

Tom tacked on another question, barely audible. "And Charlie?"

Suggs heaved his shoulders. "Saw him with Miss Larkin for awhile."

Sam stepped out into the hallway, eyes red and glazed, a two-day stubble decorating his drawn face. "Suggs, I . . . oh, Tom, Flip. I didn't know you were here. Thanks for coming."

I went straight into his arms and gave him a bear hug. "How is she? How are *you*?"

"Fine. I'm fine, I'm good. As long as Lee is OK, I'm good." He stepped away from me a moment and clasped Suggs's hand, shaking the daylights out of it, his voice raw emotion. "Suggs. I don't know how to thank you. She could have been lying out there for hours, all night, before somebody spotted her. I'm glad it was you."

Who'd have pegged Suggs for a hero? Miss Fizzi

would be beside herself. She and the Circle Ladies would be baking him cakes and pies for weeks.

"The police are finishing up now. They said you could go, Suggs. If they have any more questions, they know how to reach you."

Suggs, either red from embarrassment or having his hand pumped dry of blood, crumpled a water cup and galumphed away without looking anybody in the eye.

Tom watched him go and smiled wanly. "Will wonders never cease?"

"Sam, when can we see Lee? What could she tell the police?"

"Oh, you can see her as soon as they're through." He ran his long fingers through his reddish hair, suddenly more gray. "She wasn't able to tell them much. Right when she got to the car, somebody grabbed her from behind and covered her face with a cloth soaked in something that knocked her out. Next thing she knows, she's here, looking up at a doctor and me. The blood test showed she'd been injected with some drug with a long chemical name that's basically a sleeping agent. She won't suffer any ill effects, thank God. All she lost was a gold bracelet I gave her as a wedding present."

"Things can be replaced. Sit down. You look ready to drop." Tom pushed him into a chair. "How about the note pinned on her?" We all knew its importance.

Sam hesitated. "This one's typewritten. I guess because he had a lot more to say. It's addressed to Stewart and her father."

"To Conrad, too?"

"Yeah. This guy is taunting them both, bragging about how easily he grabbed Lee, and how he'll do the same to Stewart unless Conrad pays big bucks."

"Fifty million?" The figure named in the last note.

"No," Sam huffed. "One hundred. The price doubled because he's been 'forced' to waste his time driving home a point with Lee."

"How's that much money supposed to be delivered?" I jumped in. Surely, the police could nab him.

"Oh, he came up with a real doozy. All this sophisticated computer transfer stuff that the techno-expert cop said would be virtually untraceable, or at least would take forever to unravel. Says this guy obviously knows something about computers."

"What if Conrad refuses to pay?" A certainty.

"Then he'll go after Stewart. The note got pretty graphic." Sam paused, cleared his throat, ashen. I knew what gripped his mind—Lee could have suffered the same fate. "He said no amount of security could keep Stewart safe."

Tom drew a deep breath. "It could be a bluff. I don't think this guy's so smart. He's been seen at least three times."

"But," I interjected, "we don't know if he's acting alone."

Just as the investigators filed out of Lee's room, we heard Stewart and Charlie quick-stepping up the hall with Conrad and Jackson in tow. Sam directed them to our group and returned to his bride. Sidney mumbled hello and good-bye, dead on his feet. He stumbled, heading home like the two buddies who'd helped him all night and all day. They'd wanted to make sure of Lee's health and safety before leaving. He briefly introduced us to the new team of two officers and a detective named Fisher before trudging away.

Conrad didn't give the cops any time to ask questions.

He fired first. "I understand this young woman's had a rough twenty-four hours. We ran into Suggs Magill on his way out of the hospital. I'm heartened to hear she's going to be fine, thanks largely to him, it appears. Now, Detective, may I see the note addressed to me and my daughter?"

"Certainly, sir," he replied, "but I'm going to ask that you not take it out of the plastic covering."

Conrad tensed; his jaw hardened. "I don't believe you have the right to tell me what to do with something that's addressed to me."

Detective Fisher, a gruff young guy with a jaw as hard as Conrad's, responded, "We are not the U.S. Postal Service, sir, nor was this piece of evidence conveyed through the mail system to you. This is a criminal investigation of a Maryland kidnapping. This letter was pinned on a woman who ended up dumped in a county park, unconscious. We're going to have to run some tests on this letter—paper, ink type, that sort of thing. I'm sure you understand. We want to find the person responsible."

Conrad reacted as though morally insulted. "Don't you think I want that? I've got the best forensics team in Los Angeles working on this evidence! After all, it's *my* daughter who's the primary target! We were beginning to make good progress here!"

The young detective, who could easily have been intimidated by the missiles Conrad hurled, never flinched. "I'm glad the boys in L.A. are in on this, and now we are, too. The more resources, the faster we'll have this case solved."

"That has not been my experience," Conrad remarked dryly.

"Right, so I've heard. Your *experience* has been to avoid and distrust local police involvement. Your *experience* has led to putting a young woman's life at risk and has landed her in the hospital. Now, because of your *experience,* sir, we *are* involved."

Conrad bristled. "Show me the letter."

Detective Fisher pulled the letter, encased in plastic, from a leather portfolio. He handed it to Conrad while Jackson and Stewart peered over his shoulder. Charlie kept his distance. After a few seconds, Stewart's mouth slowly dropped open and her sapphire eyes watered. Even Conrad appeared shaken. He handed the letter back to the officer with trembling hands. "I would like a copy of this letter immediately, before we leave the hospital. Perhaps one of your men could run a copy now."

Stewart stumbled toward Charlie and into his arms. He hesitated, eyes shifting to Conrad, then enveloped her.

The detective silently passed the letter to a cop and pointed at an office down the hall.

"Now," he began, whipping out a notepad, "I'd like some information from you and your—"

"Detective," Conrad raised the bridge to the fortress, "I'm not here tonight to spend hours giving you information. I merely accompanied my daughter here to check on the well-being of Mrs. Gibbon. Now that we know she's recovering from this harrowing experience, we will take our leave. I've hardly slept the past two days and just this hour returned from L.A. Perhaps later." He turned abruptly on his heel. "Jackson, get the copy from the officer and meet us at the car. Stewart, come darling. You could use a good night's sleep, too."

"Sir! That's not going to cut it! This is a criminal investigation and your cooperation is vital! Your daughter's life is at risk!"

"As I'm well aware. Tom," Conrad put a hand on Tom's shoulder, "take care of this for me. Give Detective Fisher our number and address. I'll be in touch."

"You'd be doing yourself and Stewart a favor if you'd—"

But Conrad cut him off. "Take care of it, Tom." He peeled Stewart away from Charlie and hustled her down the hall. Charlie ground his teeth and followed.

The great tycoon would not cooperate with the inferior Maryland police. Not tonight. Maybe not ever.

"Detective," Tom turned to the irate cop, "you know you can't hold him here. Come on, now. It's late. Let the man get some sleep. We can start fresh tomorrow."

Detective Fisher threw up his hands. "Does he have any idea what a dangerous game he's playing?"

Good choice of words, I thought, and left Tom trying to explain the situation, and his client's psyche, to the angry detective. I knocked lightly on Lee's door and stepped into the room. All quiet, but for the sound of gentle breathing.

In the soft light of a bedside lamp, Sam, asleep at last, lay on the bed with his slumbering wife, arms wrapped around her body, the two entwined like a single cord that defied severing.

CHAPTER 29

✳

AT THE PRESBYTERIAN Church on Sunday, the sign out front trumpeted Reverend G.G.'s sermon for the day: "Man's Best Friend?" Thanking Heaven above for Lee's safe return, Reverend G.G. admonished us that dogs, guns, locks, and fences may offer a small degree of security, but true security, she preached fervently, could only be found in our faith in the Son of Man, Man's Best Friend.

Ivory leaned over and whispered, "But having a Giant don't hurt. My girl's got a protective streak nine miles wide."

Her chest swelled with pride at the lemonade table as she bragged about the intelligence of her new best friend, Ebony. The announcement of the dog's name naturally led her into an oldie's song. "E-bo-ney and I-vo-ry," she belted out, swaying her hips. "We're to-ge-ther in ca-nine har-mo-ny."

Garland and Hilda laughed and started telling tales of the Puli. The two of them and Pal couldn't agree on what to call him so for the time being the dog answered to Nameless.

The mood of the church crowd soared. Every time somebody mentioned Lee, "Thank God's" and "Praise the Lord's" rang out. Sooner or later, though, the talk did get around to the dire question, *What next?* Those who didn't yet have a dog or a burglar alarm claimed they'd get both. Members peppered me with questions about the investigation and the stalker's latest note, hardly relieved that his threats refocused on Stewart and not the community at large, rankled that the stalker remained a fugitive.

"What do you think, Flip?" a Circle Lady asked. "Do you think Mr. Larkin and Stewart will cave in and let the police take over?"

"I don't see how they can avoid it," I reasoned. "Lee's kidnapper *is* Stewart's stalker. Since Conrad wouldn't expose himself to questioning last night, the detective grilled Tom and me. Tom had to be a little careful, you know, about what he could say. Attorney–client privilege and all that. But you know me, once I get started, you can't turn off the faucet. Between Sam and Lee, and Tom and me, and Sidney and Suggs, that detective has a lot to go on even without Conrad."

"I saw a police car outside Stewart's house this morning," a lady volunteered, "but he knocked and knocked. Nobody came to the door."

"Nobody wanted to. Stewart might have popped over to Wilmington or some place with her father," I happily volunteered in return, Miss Know-Everything-About-Everybody. "Oh, and did I tell you the stalker took a gold bracelet Lee got from Sam as a wedding gift?"

"Flip," Reverend G.G. slipped up behind me, "do you know what room Lee is in at the hospital? I know she's not a member here, but we're such a small town, that doesn't matter. I thought I'd pop in for a visit."

Reverend G.G. had already won the hearts and souls of her new congregation; why not branch out? "She'll be home this afternoon, but she and Sam want a little time to themselves. Sam asked that we spread the word to wait and call tomorrow."

"Spreading the word"—never a problem.

People drifted away, heading home to cook Sunday dinner or find a picnic spot. A dose of relaxation after a wrenching week. I looked forward to meeting Tom at the Historical Society, and spending the whole day with him. We would weed the garden, slap something on the grill, drink gin and tonics, and later, run out and look at our new home and our beautiful new trees. Charlie and Stewart were expected for supper.

Church members strolled along the sidewalks, the sun caressing smiling faces. The constraining guard we'd erected among ourselves seemed to drop a little, with Lee safe and sound and the police taking on a major role. The report of the police car at Stewart's house that morning buoyed our spirits even higher. The crime spree finally reached an end.

Little did we know.

CHAPTER 30

✻

STEWART GLOWED. A good night's sleep and the new safety net of police involvement seemed to erase every worry line. Her mood sparked a change in Charlie, too, who clowned around like a sophomore, the Charlie of old, trying to draw Tom into a sword fight with barbecue tools. Stewart held her stomach and howled at his antics while the stone-faced older brother rolled indulgent eyes, poking Charlie with a two-pronged fork every chance he got. Maybe the two brothers could be brotherly, after all. I watched the two of them—so alike, so different—and now and again, I'd spy Stewart gazing dreamily at Charlie, her deep blue eyes soft and glazy. The horror of the stalker's last message seemed to melt away as if it never existed, although the contents had obviously wrought a change in Stewart's attitude. She admitted relief in finally having the local authorities in on the case, lifting the burden she'd been forced to share with her father and Jackson (who lurked, as usual, near the house, in shadow). Stewart even managed to talk Conrad into meeting with Detective Fisher, who'd been calling tenaciously, before he whisked off in a chauffeured car for an overnight trip to Washington. An appointment was set for the next afternoon, Conrad refusing "to have his Sunday ruined by the ineptitude of uniformed idiots."

When the laughing couple departed after supper, nary a care in the world, we had every expectation that soon our lives and theirs would return to normal.

And then the phone rang.

A LITTLE AFTER six in the morning, Tom's cell phone blared like an alarm, the tinny ring extraordinarily loud for such a small instrument. When he finally reached it, after groping through his shirt, his pants, groggy, he croaked, "Yeah, hello."

I raised up on two elbows, content to flop back down again, or rouse and make coffee.

"What? . . . When? . . . I'll be there in ten minutes." The hand gripping the cell phone dropped against his side. "Stewart's been kidnapped."

I shot up. "What?! When?! How did this happen? Who was that on the phone?"

"Suggs." He answered the one question, jumped into pants, threw on a shirt, headed for the bathroom, dialed into the cell phone.

"Are you calling Charlie?"

"Good God, no! He'll be in the thick of it soon enough."

I threw off the sheets and grabbed my clothes, methodically laid out for a normal workday of cleaning the houses of Solace Glen.

This would be no normal workday.

BY THE TIME we arrived at Stewart's house, Sidney's police car sat parked in the driveway. Another police car pulled in directly behind his and we saw Detective Fisher and two officers leap out and hurry into the house.

When Tom and I entered, we could see Sidney through the doorway, pointing out to the two cops evidence on the floor of the kitchen. Detective Fisher crouched over Suggs, who lay stretched out on the couch in the living room, an arm flung across his eyes as if they hurt, a bag of ice on his head.

The house, the only home I'd ever known, felt suddenly strange and unfamiliar.

"Wait here," said Tom, "and don't touch anything."

He approached Detective Fisher who immediately bawled at him that this was a crime scene, for God's sake. His forehead wrinkled deeper when he saw me lingering in the hallway. "Jeez. Who else did you invite, counselor?"

He didn't have to wait long for an answer because the Eggheads screeched to a halt in front of the house and raced in toting their medical bags.

Egghead One brushed past me and called, "Suggs? You still breathin'?"

The second one trotted right behind. "Tom said it was a head clobbering, not a heart attack, stupid."

They set to work examining Suggs's head, heart, and

blood pressure while the detective ran through questions. Unbeknownst to Fisher, the Eggheads would be blabbing about this for weeks, discoloring every word he uttered.

Suggs described to Fisher the gist of what happened. Around two in the morning, he "happened to be in the neighborhood" (a regular "happening"), when he thought he saw a figure sliding through the trees in the backyard. When he went to investigate, somebody knocked him over the head with a heavy object. The first thing he saw when he came to was the back door to Stewart's home, wide open. He searched the house, calling out for her, heard a groan and found Jackson in the same sorry state, a bump on his head the size of the Blue Ridge. He phoned Sidney right away and Tom, too, since he figured Mr. Larkin might want his lawyer present. The unpleasant duty of phoning Conrad with the news of Stewart's disappearance fell to Jackson who lay upstairs in bed, no doubt dreading the imminent arrival of his boss.

The Eggheads worked less and less feverishly now, hanging on every word, reluctant to leave Suggs and attend to patient number two.

Sidney passed by with barely a nod, toting two plastic bags, a wrench, and a rag. The cops in the kitchen, their hands gloved, began dusting for prints on the doors and windows.

In answer to Fisher's question, Suggs denied touching anything but the telephone. The detective turned and listened to Sidney.

"The rag smells like ether. From the looks of things, the guy could have come through the front or back, but definitely exited through the kitchen. No signs he broke in. Before entry, he conks Suggs on the head with this wrench, then slides upstairs and gives Jackson the same treatment. He slithers into the bedroom where Miss Larkin's sleeping, places the rag over her face, no struggle, she falls into a deeper sleep. He picks her up and carries her out through the back door in the kitchen. Probably parked beyond those trees. And he takes off, a clean getaway."

The stairs creaked and I looked up to see Jackson clutching an ice pack to his head, making his way down. He eased to the bottom step and sat, listening.

"Let me see that wrench." The detective examined the tool through the plastic bag. "Black and Decker . . . serial number . . . and letters in magic marker . . . D.C.C. That mean anything to anyone here?"

"Abner." I stared at Tom, wide-eyed. "Diggs Construction Company."

Tom blew a breath out. "Detective, that wrench could have come from a local construction company run by a man named Abner Diggs." He hesitated, but knew he had to disclose the facts. "Apparently, Abner's only son, Steve, used to work for Larkin Industries about thirteen years ago. Conrad Larkin brought criminal charges against him and the son ended up in prison. I know this sounds bad for Abner. . . ."

"You damn tootin' it does!"

"Detective, I've known this man for a number of years. I'd bet money he has nothing to do with any of this."

"You might lose your bet, too, counselor." He turned to Sidney. "Find out if Steve Diggs is still in prison. California, right? Start with the L.A.P.D. You know where this Abner lives or works?"

"Yes, sir. I tried to reach him over the weekend for questioning when Mrs. Gibbon went missing. We never could locate him."

"OK. Let's make another attempt to track him down. If he's still a no-show, I want a warrant out for his arrest today."

Tom clamped his lips tight and rubbed a hand across his forehead.

A car pulled up outside. Pal's Chevy. He hit the ground running, almost bowling me over when he galloped into the house, blasting out, "I saw it! I saw it! The gray car! The blonde guy! Well . . . come on!"

"Holy smokes!" an Egghead croaked, bouncing up, ready to lead the charge.

Jackson rose, reeling. "I knew it! I told her all along! I'm coming with you, I can identify this creep!"

I jumped to the side at the sound of trampling feet.

"Come on, boys!" Detective Fisher, on the run but officious, made a quick call for backup. "We're going hunting."

CHAPTER 31

✵

"GREAT BALLS OF FIRE, Suggs!" an Egghead whooped. "This is like a James Bond movie!"

Suggs groaned and sank back into the couch. An Egghead reached down and picked up the ice pack, throwing it on Suggs's square head like a lopsided beret. "Yeah, *Live and Let Die!*"

"No, no. *The Spy Who Loved Me*."

"Naw. *You Only Live Twice*."

"Would you two cut it out!" They gave me such a headache, I almost grabbed Suggs's ice pack.

Suggs grunted and rolled over, turning his back to us.

I walked over to Tom and wrapped my arms around his waist, head against his chest. "I feel so bad for Charlie. I hope Stewart's all right."

"I was just thinking of Charlie," Tom said grimly. No answer came when he phoned.

* * *

LESS THAN FIFTEEN minutes later, Conrad entered, breathless. I could see his chauffeur through the window, just reaching the door Conrad had flung open.

"What's happening? Where's the detective? Where's Jackson?"

Tom addressed each question one by one, calmly, somberly, filling Conrad in on the details. "So that's where they've gone."

"I can't believe it." His voice edged higher, dazed and in shock. "I can't believe he could reach Stewart. Not with Jackson here. She even slept with a gun under her pillow!"

A lot of good that does when you're drugged. I'd never seen Conrad Larkin, suave industrialist, so torn apart. His clothes, disheveled and unkempt, his face unshaven. The smooth, platinum hair stuck up, frazzled, almost electrified from the energy within. He jerked a piece of paper from his back pocket and unfolded it—his copy of the Locksmith's latest letter from Lee's kidnapping.

"He says I—I have twelve hours." His voice trembled; the two hands shook. "He says I have twelve hours to make the financial transfer or he'll kill her in a horrible death. But if I pay, she'll live. She'll live. I'll have her back the morning after the transfer. I'll have her back." He completely dissolved. "How could I have let this happen! Why did I follow my foolish pride and not good sense! Why didn't I listen to good advice—your advice, Tom—and stay in L.A.? No. I had to create my own maze. Now I'm the one lost in it. I'm the one trapped. Oh, my daughter, my only child . . ."

Tom placed a hand on his shoulder. "Don't give up hope. Let's wait and see what the police find."

"Mr. Larkin." Suggs slowly sat up, holding the bag to his head, eyes bloodshot and watery. "I'm so sorry. I let you down. I let Stewart down."

I felt pity for Suggs, the antisocial bull who, before Stewart came to Solace Glen, had rarely spoken except to say something ugly.

I expected the famous tycoon to blow up, but he displayed a surprising strength of character. "No, son. It's not your fault. I am entirely to blame. I'm reaping what I sowed."

Nobody said anything. Tom patted Conrad's shoulder. I stared at the floor. The Eggheads still attended to Suggs in slow motion, dying for something to happen before they finally had to drive off in the ambulance, their patient safely on a stretcher, looking forward to a good head x-ray.

The minutes ticked by at glacial speed. One Egghead tinkered with the stretcher as if it had a screw loose. Conrad paced, occasionally picking up a framed photograph, crumpling at the sight of the beautiful face.

A little after eight, Tom's cell phone rang. We all jumped in our skins.

"Sidney!" Tom shouted. "What's going on? Mr. Larkin's here with me."

When he got off the phone, Tom's face turned an odd color gray.

"What about my daughter? Does he know anything?"

"In a manner of speaking. They lost the car briefly, but somehow, and I don't fully understand this part, Jackson pointed the way to a house he knew about. They found the car parked at a place at Loy's Station. They were able to enter and search the premises. They did not find the blonde guy or Stewart. But they did find Lee's bracelet, among other things."

"Oh!" This was one time I had little to say.

"They're sweeping the place now." Tom drew Conrad away from Egghead ears. "They found the bracelet in a locked room in the basement where Lee had obviously been held, along with papers, cut-up magazines, and the kinds of restraints he's mentioned in his notes. They've got search dogs out. Trust me, if he decides to return to the scene of the crime, somebody will be there to greet him."

"Noooo." Conrad sank down on the couch, head in his hands. "No! I can't wait! I can't sit here and do nothing! I'm going to do what he says. I'm going to get my daughter back!"

He ripped out his cell phone and the Locksmith's letter, dialing furiously.

"Conrad, wait for the police! Let them tell you what to do."

"No! I put Stewart in this position; I'll be the one to get her out! This maniac's run off with her. He's got her hidden somewhere, some sleazy motel room, probably drugged." He exploded. "I've got to do something!"

With that, he pushed Tom out of the way and raced from the room, giving the Eggheads icing on the cake. The chauffeur saw Conrad coming, snapped to attention, and, in a flash, opened the door and Conrad dove in. The door slammed shut, and in another flash, they were gone.

"There's nothing more we can do here," Tom said wearily. "I better go find Charlie."

"Do you want me to come with you?"

"No. If I do find him, more than one of us would look like an audience to him. I'll take you home so you can get some work done. As if any of us can get any work done today."

No. This would not be a normal workday at all.

WE GOT OFF to a late start, but before Ivory and I scrubbed down anybody's house, we dropped by to check on Lee's progress, and reunite the newlyweds with Katie. The setter bid Eli adieu with a good licking and cheerfully trotted after us.

I knew, thanks to the Eggheads, and the sight of several police cars, word of the kidnapping and Suggs's clunk on the head had seeped Lee's way by now. Sure enough, when we arrived at the Bell family mansion, several cars sat parked in the circular drive, a bevy of Circle Ladies, no doubt, among them Margaret, Garland, Melody, and Tina.

In the front parlor, Lee lay on a Victorian divan, dressed in a slinky, yellow satin nightgown and robe, looking all the world like the queen bee. A large coffee urn in the dining room sent out a wonderful aroma, and plates of baked goods complemented the welcoming scent. Sam stood in the doorway to the kitchen, enjoying the companionship of the only other male in the room, Lindbergh Kohl. They waved at us, and Lindbergh called, "I think I'll have something to talk to you about tonight. Would that be all right?"

Such a polite man. I nodded with the barest hint of enthusiasm. Whatever he might find out about Abner wouldn't matter now. The real deal was the Blonde Stranger.

"Katie!" Lee leaped off the divan while the Circle Ladies screeched at her to get back in a horizontal posture. To no avail. The Irish setter and her new lady fair flew into each other's paws and arms, together at last.

Usually, a good amount of time would have been spent talking about the dog, complimenting her coat, asking the usual doggie questions. But not today. The women skimmed right over that mild subject and got down to brass tacks.

"Oh, Flip, we heard about Stewart!"

The Egghead Broadcasting Network, what else?

Melody tottered on tippy-toe in her excitement. "I heard the stalker almost killed Suggs! Hilda drove Miss Fizzi to the hospital to see him. They're there now."

"He got a good bang on the noggin, but he'll live. Suggs does deserve a lot of credit. The way this guy operated, even Jackson couldn't compete."

Margaret set down her coffee cup and trilled, "We heard about all the police! How did fifty-five men fit into your old house?"

Definite signs of Egghead. "They wouldn't have. But four got along fine."

"Did they find Stewart at Roy's Hatian house?"

"Loy's Station." I spoke slowly so they'd get it and keep it. "No. But they found . . . they found . . ." I couldn't bring myself to say the things the police had discovered in the locked room in the basement, not in front of Lee and Sam. At least the Eggheads hadn't heard that part. "They found your bracelet, Lee."

That news alone caused her to go weak in the knees.

She flopped down on the divan. "Then I was in that house. I was alone in that house with *him*."

The Circle Ladies did what they do best. They encircled Lee with love and support, with words of inspiration and encouragement. Sam stood back and let them work their wonders, knowing he had his own role to fill in helping Lee through such an experience. She'd missed out on twenty-four hours of her life. Twenty-four hours she couldn't remember—not with horror, not with sadness, not with joy. Twenty-four hours of empty space, where the only thing she knew for sure was that she kept breathing.

After enjoying a cup of badly needed coffee, I opened my mouth to tell Ivory we'd better get going, when the doorbell rang. Sam opened the door and Sidney walked in.

"Excuse me, everyone. Mrs. Gibbon, I need you to identify something for us."

He waded through the Circle Ladies, who parted on either side like the Red Sea. We craned our necks to see what Sidney held in his hand inside a zipped plastic bag.

"My bracelet," Lee said weakly. "Yes, that's mine. I can make out the inscription from Sam to me on our wedding day."

"Thank you," said Sidney, courteous and professional. "We're going to have to keep it, I'm afraid. It's your bracelet, but it's also evidence."

Lee bobbed her head up and down, clearly rattled. Sam stepped in and snaked a long arm around her shoulders. The ladies signaled their approval. Such a good choice Lee made.

"Any news, Sidney?"

"Have they found her, Sidney?"

"Please tell us the police have captured that horrible man!"

Sidney retained a professional demeanor. "I can tell you we have a suspect under arrest, yes, ma'am."

Bursts of joy! Mountains of adulation! The room erupted. Then the inevitable interrogation commenced.

"You *have* to tell us all about it, Sidney! Sit down!"

"Somebody get him a doughnut and a cup of coffee!"

"Come on, Sidney. You know you're dying to tell us!"

Ivory and I didn't need to ask the other. We hunkered down in the nearest chairs, pulling close to Sidney.

To his credit, Sidney began with a caveat. "Now, this is an ongoing investigation. I may not be able to tell you everything."

Little did he know what a lamb he looked in that den of cotton and lace wolves. "Oh, don't you worry about that, honey. We don't need to know *every* little thing."

"Well." Sidney cleared his throat and thanked the lady who slid a plate into his hand and plunked a cup of coffee by his side. "We were sweeping the house, you know, collecting evidence—can't say what we found"—I already knew, anyhow, privy to Sidney's call to Tom—"when a blonde man steps out of the woods looking kind of puzzled."

"Gah! He simply walked up, right into your web?!" Garland clapped a hand across her breast.

"Yeah." Sidney laughed a little. "Not too smart, huh? He approaches one of the guys in my unit and says, basically . . . well, I don't think I should say what he said to us. . . ."

"Oh, just give us an outline, Sidney. We can fill in the blanks."

Sidney's brows met, but he continued. "Anyway, basically, he'd gone for a walk."

"So early in the morning?" Melody asked skeptically. "A likely story."

"Anyway, we cuff him and read him his rights, but he's like a crazy man, especially after he finds out he's being arrested for kidnapping Mrs. Gibbon and Miss Larkin. The guy goes bonkers!"

"Did you have to club him with your baton?"

"Did you have to slam his head against the car?"

Sidney's eyebrows remained joined. "Noooo, but we sure got an earful, even after the detective repeated his rights, in case he hadn't heard the first time."

"Well, then, Sidney," Margaret reared up imperiously, showing off her best TV courtroom drama skills, "everything he said can be used against him. It's not protected speech. You can tell *us*."

The textbooks from the police academy, stored neatly inside Sidney's brain, got chucked out through his ears. "I–I guess so. So this guy, Doug Host is his name, claims he's innocent and somebody has set him up big time. When confronted with the physical evidence, he says that this was a rented house, and he didn't even have a key to the room in the basement. Didn't know what was in there, and didn't care."

Tina, who should have been at work for Tom by this hour, scoffed. "Another likely story!"

"He claims Miss Larkin begged him to come to Maryland to help protect her from the true stalker."

"Uhh! This is the classic stalker mentality. He's delusional!"

"By Doug Host's account, when Stewart and her

father left L.A., they practically put an ad in the paper, to guarantee the stalker would follow. Said Stewart wanted his extra eyes because she didn't feel Jackson offered enough protection. Plus, Host claimed her old man is being blackmailed and he himself is investigating for the California attorney general."

"Lordy! What a load of fertilizer!"

"He claims Stewart sent him messages through Jackson, like to go to the party for the McKnights, so Host could watch her without anybody knowing. He had no idea people started connecting him to the stalker and freaked out at the sight of him. He couldn't understand why that lady screamed when she saw him in town. Thought maybe her nerves were shot from the tension, so any stranger would provoke a strong reaction. He was just trying to lie low, you know. Kind of zipping around on the outskirts, like when he stayed hidden in the trees at the picnic."

"He admitted attending the picnic? Skulking around in the trees?" Melody panted. She couldn't believe her ears.

Margaret for the prosecution. "That coupled with the bracelet is enough to hang him. What happened next, Sidney?"

"OK. So Jackson walks out of the house, and yells, 'I knew it! I knew you weren't investigating anything! What have you done with Stewart?!'"

"And Doug Host starts screaming at him to tell the cops the truth, that Stewart feared for her life and knew Jackson would screw up, that Conrad had gone overboard, playing a game way over his head in order to trap his blackmailer. Then he started blaming everybody in the world for setting him up. He wouldn't harm a hair on Stewart's beautiful head, he said. That's when Jackson hauled off and punched him."

"Wow!"

"Good! He had it coming!"

"What about Stewart, Sidney?"

Sidney downed a doughnut hole and stood up. "I'm sorry. Nothing to report. Host has been hauled to the station to answer more questions. Since he's got such a bad case of diarrhea of the mouth—oops, sorry ladies—I mean, since he's so willing to talk, maybe he'll crack. Maybe we'll have Miss Larkin back before you know it."

While the brood surrounded Sidney, clucking praise and thanks, Ivory and I slipped away, work to be done. The faster we swept, the faster the end of the day would fall. And the closer we'd come to having more answers.

CHAPTER 32

✷

I COULD HARDLY wait to get to the Bistro. In an excru-
ciatingly brief call, Tom told me to meet him and
Charlie there. And to be *very* cautious with his brother.
Whatever that meant.

When I walked through the door, exactly on time, the
place bubbled over with customers, everyone eager to
escape the self-imposed confinement brought on by fear
of the stalker. Now that the police had the proverbial
bird in hand, tension subsided. Solace Glen was ready
to party.

Hilda pointed out Tom and Charlie, adding, "Thought
you'd like to know Suggs is back home with Miss Fizzi.
She's so proud of him getting conked on the head, she's
gonna buy him a used car he's been hankering for."

"Oh, yeah? Maybe the knock on the head shook out
some of the mean and nasty."

Hope springs eternal, as we like to say. I didn't have such high hopes for Charlie, a face chiseled out of stone, eyes cold and hard.

I pecked Tom on the cheek and gave Charlie a quick hug. "Don't worry. I'm sure the police will find her."

"Yeah. Dead or alive."

"Charlie," Tom chided him gently, "don't do this. Stewart's life is on the line right now."

"You're right." He studied his beer. "She turns some normal guy she dated into a psycho and I'm weeping into my glass about such a trivial thing as love lost and lives ruined. So sue me."

Whoa. I remembered how Lee described Charlie after his breakup with Stewart years before. Not knowing what else to say, I prodded, "Have the police talked to you?"

"Oh, yeah. Today I spent several memorable hours feeling like a criminal. Thank you, Stewart."

Tom threw his napkin down. "Oh, Charlie, stop it! You, you, you. Grow up."

So much for being *very* cautious with Charlie.

Charlie drained his beer and stood up, tossing a few dollars on the table. "Since nobody wants my charming company, I shall gladly vamoose. I hear Borneo calling."

As he walked away, Tom, nostrils flaring, called, "Borneo, my foot! You know you can't go anywhere until Stewart's found! You're in enough trouble!" But Charlie kept walking.

A couple of tables away, C.C. and Marlene leaned into each other, yakking away, probably comparing poison recipes. Screamin' Larry sat close by, chomping down his normal three meals a day in one sitting, gleefully bearing down on C.C. with an industrial-strength leer until she squirmed and made Marlene trade seats with her. Oddly, Leonard sat across the room from his wife, engaged in discussions with Horace. Horace appeared utterly engaged, but every so often lifted his lizard eyes to gaze at the ex. Marlene did a bit of squirming herself.

"What do you think those two are up to?" I quizzed Tom.

He barely glanced up, still fuming over Charlie. "None of *my* business. Though I did overhear Leonard congratulate Horace on a successful conclusion to the venture, whatever that means. I think they're making vacation plans."

"Together? How modern. Maybe C.C. and Marlene will follow suit."

Tom choked on his beer. "Let's talk about something else, shall we? How's Lee?"

I filled him in, tacking on everything I'd learned from Sidney, all of which Tom already knew. "As a matter of fact," he said, "I'm going to have to make this a quick dinner. Detective Fisher wants to meet tonight with both Jackson and Conrad, who's been somewhat evasive all day—not unusual for Conrad. Apparently, he's received another set of threatening instructions. Of course, Doug Host could have sent them before his capture. Or he's working with someone."

I couldn't help but point out, "You know, I've said that all along."

Tom ignored my brilliance. "Anyway, Conrad wants me to review this new note with Fisher, and try to convince the detective he did the right thing in transferring the money. He's absolutely positive Host has an accomplice and Stewart will be dropped off in the wee hours of the morning at a public park somewhere in Frederick County, just like Lee."

"But you don't think so, do you?"

Tom shut his eyes and leaned back in his chair. "I pray so. But I'm afraid . . ."

He didn't finish. He didn't have to.

TOM LEFT FOR Frederick before nine o'clock, expecting to camp out all night with Conrad and Jackson at the police station, playing the waiting game. I ended up partying with the revelers. When Sidney walked in, the conquering hero, Pal and the Eggheads drilled him for well over an hour on forensics, which he knew little about, but which they claimed a certain expertise in based on television. We heard endless blathering about how they could have guided the police on collecting evidence at Stewart's house and operated on Suggs's brain tumor at the same time. When Sam and Lee popped in, the real celebration began. Thankfully, Sam made an immediate, heartfelt request that people not drill Lee about what happened, that our job was to see she had some fun. A job we took very seriously when you count the number of drinks we bought her.

By the time I got home to the Historical Society, tired and sleepy, the hands on the clock almost touched midnight. The light on my answering machine blinked incessantly.

All six messages came from Lindbergh, each time his voice more anxious. I noted the time of the last call—11:47. I rang him up.

"Lindbergh, what in the world is it?"

"Oh, Flip! Thank you for calling me back! I've come across the most extraordinary thing!"

The sleepiness evaporated. "What is it?"

"I've been researching Larkin Industries and Steve Diggs, as I said I would."

"Yes?" He had my full attention.

"First of all, Abner's son is not Steve Diggs; he's Steve *Turner*. After Abner and his wife divorced, she had the son's name legally changed."

So that's why Lee never made the connection. She said the young computer whiz had a different name. "OK, and . . . ?"

"And Steve Turner got out of prison several years ago. He drifted awhile, but recently worked for a retailer in Los Angeles. A job he quit two months ago. That's where the trail goes cold."

"Oh, my."

"That's not all. The chief witness for the prosecution at Turner's trial, the man who proved crucial in the jury's guilty verdict, was none other than Jackson Parker."

"What? Are you sure?"

"I'm positive. The caption reads, 'Security guard, Jackson Parker,' et cetera, et cetera. What do you think this means?"

"I'm not sure, but I'm going to find out." I thanked him, and we hung up.

Now the questions stampeded through my head like a team of horses: Did Doug Host act alone? Was he set up, double-crossed by his accomplice? Was the accomplice Steve Turner? Stewart kidnapped, Conrad threatened—would Jackson be next on the list?

Tom's cell phone lay on top of my dresser. He was

probably in the middle of deep discussions with Detective Fisher, Conrad, and Jackson, all safe and sound at the police station, awaiting word of Stewart. I paced the kitchen, biting a fingernail, mulling over facts and more questions. No evidence that the kidnapper broke into the house. Someone Stewart knew? A lover? Doug Host? Steve Turner? Charlie? Did she give him a key? Did Stewart change the locks a second time? Something pecked at me. . . .

I couldn't stand it another second. I had to find out for myself. Grabbing a flashlight and a ring of keys, I ran down the street.

A BLOCK BEFORE I reached my old house, Ivory surprised me, coming around the corner with Ebony on a leash. The giant jerked her head high and sent out a hefty bark, positioning herself between her mistress and me.

"Goooood girl!" Ivory shortened the leash and hissed, "That's my boss. Don't bite her."

"Ivory!" I screeched to a halt, breathless. "It's you!"

"Yeah, my pretty girl needed a walk. You mighty jumpy. Whatcha jumpy about, honey? Why you runnin' around town alone in the middle of the night?"

Ebony relaxed the serious stance. Friend instead of foe.

"Something's come up and I have to . . . well, I have to see if I can get into my old house."

"You breakin' in? Girrrrllll!"

"It won't really be breaking in if the key fits. Will it?"

"You don't have permission to do that 'cept Wednesday mornin's, and you know it."

We stared at each other a few seconds.

"Are you gonna help me or not?"

"Count Ivory in, girl. Ebony, too. We'll be your back-up."

We edged our way toward my old home, Ebony moving on all three legs at an equal pace, as quickly, as slowly. We slipped through the brace of trees screening the house. No sign of a car in the driveway or on the street, Conrad and Jackson safely in Frederick. Everything dark. The only sound an occasional cricket.

"I have to check something inside the house," I whispered furtively, the night taking on a damp chill. "If I can get in. If I can, we'll sneak in the front door. These trees will block us from view."

Ivory nodded. Ebony, too.

If the house key I had still fit, despite my warnings to Stewart to change the locks, that raised questions. But something else needled me. Did Stewart run off with a lover her father never would have approved of? Did she and Steve Turner fool everyone? If the ring her mother gave her was missing, that raised an alarm. She would never willingly leave behind the ring hidden in the staircase.

I crept like a cat burglar toward the front door, crouching lower as I neared the porch. I signaled to Ivory with a wave of my hand, and she and Ebony loped forward, at my heels. We crept up the steps on to the porch. I drew in a breath, slid the key into the lock, and turned.

The key fit perfectly and we slunk into the house.

Inside, I eased the door shut and gently placed the key ring in a pocket, imagination racing at the unchanged locks. We stood like museum statues, listening for any hint of life, but the only sound came from an antique clock on the mantle. Tick. Tick. Tick.

Taking no chances, I whispered, and Ivory bent low to hear. "Stay here by the door. I'll be back in two minutes."

She nodded, both hands keeping a tight grip on the Giant's leash. But Ebony seemed to sense what was required. She stood still and silent, a natural accomplice.

I clicked the button of the small flashlight, the beam set on low. Although I knew the house from top to bottom, Stewart had made changes. I didn't want to trip over a chair and crack some irreplaceable Chinese urn. Slowly, steadily, I made my way to the staircase. Creeping up each step, one by one, I breathed easier, but still strained my ears for the sound of a car pulling into the driveway.

Halfway up the stairs, I shined the light on the bookcase built into the wall. Almost exactly as Stewart had left it, the dappled glass egg on a wire stand covered the secret plank. "Almost" because the egg seemed slightly off kilter, and the plank stuck up about a quarter inch, as if someone had been in a hurry. I gently slid the egg to one side and lifted the plank. The light shined into the square space.

The platinum and diamond ring caught the light and sparkled. A certainty, then. Stewart had been kidnapped. She'd never leave this precious ring behind. I reached in and clasped the chain between my fingers.

"I'll take the ring, if you don't mind." A bright, blinding light. A voice—low, firm, commanding.

"Mr. Larkin?" I whispered, still in sneak mode. *Conrad? What was he doing here? He should be with Jackson in Frederick meeting with Tom and Detective Fisher.*

"I don't have all night, young woman."

I threw a fist over my eyes, the ring clutched tight in my palm. "Could you turn off your flashlight, please, sir?"

"I don't think so. Then you'd see the gun in my hand. It might frighten you."

"Gun? Oh, you don't think . . . you can't think I was stealing Stewart's property?"

"What else am I to think? You come like a thief in the night."

"I know it looks bad, but . . ."

"Give me the ring. Now."

A tiny thought reverberated like thunder. *My hand still dipped inside the square space when Conrad said, "I'll take the ring."*

I gripped the chain in my sweaty palm, Stewart's own words flaring up. *Some things should only be shared between two people. This will be what we share.*

"How do you know I'm holding a ring? You can't see what's in my hand."

I'll never tell a soul. I promise.

"Give me the ring!"

The light dawned brighter than the light blinding my eyes. A broken promise. The fake interest in Charlie. The setup of Doug Host, investigating "blackmail" and a stalker. A stolen wrench. The house keys that still opened the door, the locks never changed. Jackson, the loyal "bodyguard."

I took a step backward. "She sent you here to get it, didn't she? She left in such a hurry, she forgot it."

I eased down another step, but Conrad eased with me. "Hand it over, and I won't hurt you."

Fat chance. "Where is she now? Out of the country? Collecting the one hundred million you stole from your stockholders?"

A pause, then a low chuckling. "Oh, ho. It was much more than that."

The gun clicked.

I screamed, and took a flying leap down the last few stairs. An explosion, and light flared; something stung my leg. I collapsed in a heap on the floor.

Another scream, another flash of gunfire. Splintered wood hit my face, the smell of smoke and gunpowder pierced my nostrils. A large black form collided, then bounded over my body. Loud, guttural sounds of attack mixed with the thud of falling objects, streaking lights, another explosion. Smoke. A man screamed. A cry outside the house.

I dragged my body toward the door, toward the streetlight, pain shooting through one leg into my hip, praying this nightmare would end, hardly moving a yard or two, my face soaked, my whole body a dead weight. The open door so far away. The man with the gun so close.

So close.

Then all the lights, the sounds, the smells—ended.

CHAPTER 33

�֎

"FLIP. OH, GOD, Flip. Can you hear me, sweetheart. Oh, God."

My eyes flickered open, just a moment or two. A car? A truck?

Tom. Tom, holding my hand. My love, my life. My Tom.

The clink of glass. The sway of plastic. A high-pitched siren. The rhythm of speed. Such a strange light, like an incubator.

Stop this day and night with me . . .

THE SUN SHONE through the hospital room window, bright and welcoming. Welcoming me back.

Tom's head, nestled close to my breast—the slight gray in the thick, black hair—rose and fell with my breathing, he'd fallen asleep so connected to my heart.

I nudged him from slumber. "Miss me?"

The dark eyes bored deep. "You're awake. You're here."

"I'm here."

He wrapped his hand around mine, intertwining our ten fingers. "I thought I'd lost you." He kissed my every finger. "Oh, my God, I thought I'd lost you."

"You didn't," I said weakly. But not too weak to add, "*Now* will you set a wedding date?"

A hesitation. Another kiss.

"As soon as you can walk down the aisle, dear."

THE CIRCLE LADIES encircled me. The loving, familiar, motherly faces of my whole life, enveloping, caressing, warm, and sincere.

"Ivory, tell the part about Ebony again!" Melody hugged herself, so engaged in the saga.

"Well, naturally, it does bear repeatin'."

The hospital room buzzed. My day nurse paused in her duties.

Ivory hoisted herself onto the foot of the bed, careful not to disturb my bandaged, plaster-encased leg. "That girl behaved like a trained police dog. Stealthy. Quiet. Waitin' for the order to attack. You've never seen the like. There she was, standin' beside me by the front door, ears up like posts, tense, at attention. And there I was, shakin' like a tree of leaves in October, wondering what the hell Flip was up to. Didn't take long to find out. Next thing I know, Ebony and I hear a man's voice, low at first, but gettin' louder. Heard every word. Ebony starts to get a rumble in her throat. I'm thinkin', Jesus

Lord! Don't let this dog start barkin' and expose Ivory and get my boss killed! But she holds it in. Not a second later, I'm thinkin', oh, good, she's gonna keep quiet, a blast goes off—*BANG!*—and Ebony lunges away from me! And the screamin' and the guns and the lights and the chaos commences! I flip out like a crazy woman, throw open the door, run into the street screamin' for help! People walkin' home from the Bistro hike up their skirts and trousers and fly in from all corners! Sidney gallops in with his gun drawn, me yellin', 'Don't shoot my dog! Don't shoot Ebony!' He finds Ebony; she's got Conrad pinned down like a pro wrestler. The Eggheads do their business, Tom pulls up, jumps in the ambulance with Flip, Conrad gets hauled to the clinic then jail, with Sidney as his personal tour guide, thanks to what Ivory overheard, and my Ebony—she gets a Milk Bone and a citation from the governor! End of story! Slam, bam, thank you, ma'am!"

The audience burst into applause. Lemonade, compliments of the Presbyterian contingent, passed cup by cup among the saints, a substitute communion. Not long afterward, the nurse herded everyone out, and Detective Fisher and Sidney entered the room.

"You've had a busy day, even for a cleaning lady," said Fisher dryly. "I'd lecture you into the ground about the risk you took last night, but we wouldn't have solved this case so soon, and an innocent man may have spent time in prison but for you."

My chest swelled for a moment, but contrition sunk in. "I know it was a stupid thing to do. I know how lucky I am things turned out the way they did."

Fisher's hard jaw softened. "Yeah, well, thought you'd like to hear the whole story. Have the gaps filled in."

"Oh, yeah, thanks. You're very kind."

"You figured it out yourself," he began, pulling up a chair, "which is why you wound up here. Larkin and his daughter had a major scam going. They were gonna bilk all his companies out of millions, flee the country, and set up digs in South America. Their own little father–daughter Shangri-La. They'd been planning and siphoning off funds for months, looting the empire and duping investors. But one investor grew suspicious— Horace Worthington. He tips off the attorney general's office with a skeleton of facts, and they agree to plant an inside man from the securities division, a computer expert, Doug Host."

"So Host told the truth all along."

"Yeah. He checked out. Anyway, he starts working for Larkin, but Stewart and her old man are no easy target. They see through the ploy and decide to turn the tables. Play the game their way. They know they can't make a big killing and a quick getaway now. As soon as they hop on a plane, Host would be at their heels lickety-split, connecting all the dots. So Stewart does what she does best. She seduces the poor guy and convinces him the money draining out of the big empire has been going to a blackmailer turned stalker."

"She and Conrad—father–daughter victims."

"You got it, and so did Host. He falls hook, line, and sinker. The moment she waves a pinky, he's on a plane to Maryland. Partly out of love, partly to investigate and get to the bottom of the blackmailer–stalker threat."

"But why not stay in L.A.?" And save *us* the trouble.

Detective Fisher snorted. "No way they could get away with this in L.A. But in a gullible, podunk, one-cop town like Solace Glen, familiar to Stewart, they might succeed. Running into Charlie Scott cemented the idea. They enlisted the help of one Jackson Parker, an unemployed, down-on-his-luck actor and sometime security guard. He'd been useful to Larkin before."

"The Turner trial."

"The Turner kangaroo trial. Another victim of the siren. Steve Turner caught on to Stewart's games early in their relationship and dropped her like a hot grenade. Problem was, she exploded. She and Conrad ruined him for sport."

"Using Jackson, huh? So he played the Dick Tracy of Solace Glen, pretending to protect Stewart from a stalker who didn't exist, running around planting the notes and other evidence—Abner's wrench, Lee's bracelet, the handcuffs, and cut-up magazines—setting up Doug Host."

"Precisely. From the beginning, Conrad told Jackson that Host formed the linchpin in a big bucks project. If Jackson played his part well, setting up Host, he'd make a million bucks and could leave the country right after fingering Host. After delivering a damning statement at the station last night, he left with Conrad, who pretended to be ill and exhausted from worry. We grabbed Jackson at Dulles this morning, boarding a plane for Zurich."

"So Jackson Parker did all the dirty work." And I worried he'd be the next victim!

"Yeah," the detective smirked, "he even managed to get Mrs. Gibbon into that basement room before Host returned from the picnic. The next day, he drops by playing his go-between role, sends Host on a fool's errand, and transports her out again. This morning, to fill in another piece of the puzzle, I had a little visit from

Leonard Crosswell and Horace Worthington. Apparently, word of Conrad's arrest had spread."

What a shock. The Egghead Express.

"Crosswell and Worthington told me the two of them had been separately tracking Larkin's financial shenanigans for months, gathering evidence, hoping to make millions on a gargantuan investors' lawsuit. When they discovered their mutual concerns, they hooked up, vowing to bring the big man to his knees."

"And he almost beat them to the punch."

"Right. In the guise of a 'ransom.' The complicated computer transfer trail in the 'Locksmith's' letter—a total fabrication—would have kept the boys in tech up to their elbows for days. Larkin figured he could stall long enough for Stewart to set things up, then he could disappear, the victim of another 'kidnapping,' and all eyes would focus on Doug Host and his 'accomplice,' Steve Turner, out for revenge. They conjured up enough fake evidence to throw him back in jail, too. Planted by Jackson, of course."

"Jackson. What's going to happen to him?"

"Jackson gets to play the real role of star witness. He came clean pretty fast. As soon as he heard we'd nabbed Stewart in Miami and had Conrad locked behind bars, he could see the writing on the wall. He spilled the beans on both of them. Also said Solace Glen made the perfect stage. The police would run around like headless chickens flapping their wings at Charlie and Abner Diggs. Made their whole story more plausible."

"And Tom?"

"Using Tom to do a few simple legal maneuvers and advise them on the 'stalker' problem lent legitimacy to the scheme. A well-respected local attorney. But because the Larkins adamantly refused to go to the police, his hands were effectively tied most of the time."

My poor pawn. "But Lee figured into the picture. Why was she kidnapped?"

"Two reasons. First, to heighten the fear factor. People would be searching out the Blonde Stranger under every twig. Lee's disappearance hit the gut and made the whole scenario look real. Second, to settle an old score. The cat's claws couldn't resist a nasty scratch. And Lee was bad-mouthing Stewart all over town."

"Wow. All this intrigue, right in Solace Glen."

"True. Well!" He slapped his hands on his knees and stood up. "Time for you to get some rest. You've been an amazing help, Ms. Paxton, even if you did almost get yourself killed. Hope that leg heals up quick."

"Me, too. There's a church aisle with my name on it."

I HAD A couple of other visitors that day. Margaret returned with Lindbergh. She brought yellow-and-white roses, and fussed over me to no end. She used the words *darling* and *sweetheart* so much, you'd have thought we were an item.

I watched the two of them together, laughing at each other's jokes, patting each other on the hand, sparking like a couple of teenagers. They made me feel eighteen again, back home in my old house, with two lively, living parents who doted on each other and me. At the same time, I looked into their loving faces and saw mirrored in them Tom and me, years from now. Our lives sweetly meshed in all the right places. All the poems in the world written in our hearts.

All the good of the earth. All the good of the sun. We would have our millions of suns.

POSTSCRIPT

※

THE FIREFLIES DEPART in the fall, the soft flickering clicks off in the cooler air so as not to distract from a season of new colors. The fireflies know their business. You can trust them to do the right thing.

Trust returned to all of Solace Glen. Margaret suggested we put up a sign at the town limit: WELCOME TO SOLACE GLEN, HOME OF THE HAPPY HOODWINKED. She and Lindbergh made it official in early September, with a march down the aisle promised before the close of autumn. They would have said, "I do," right away on account of age, Margaret confided, but it does take time to plan a *good* party, and Solace Glen so loves a good one.

Miss Fizzi and Suggs have discovered mutual ground, his hero status effectively elevating him to Jesus' right-hand man in her eyes. She actually brags about him now, which has had some measure of import. He seems to have a better opinion of himself and will speak when spoken to, like a good boy. He dresses better, too.

Pal and the Eggheads—well, what can I say? Some things never change. Their latest battle has revolved around dog food brands, the ones they can pronounce, and the Puli, still Nameless, suffers from their experiments despite Garland's and Hilda's warnings to lay off. Their favorite joke is to make Pal wear the Puli on his head so he looks Jamaican, like the old beer commercial. But the Puli's gotten so fat, he rolls off before Pal can recite from the script they wrote.

Garland finally got her divorce from Roland. He tries to spread rumors now and again about typhoid and salmonella at the Bistro, but not even his regulars buy it. They check out *his* bacon and eggs pretty closely, though. Meanwhile, Garland's business is booming and she looks fabulous. "On the prowl for a pair o' pants with a brain," according to Sally. Sally and Tina couldn't stand it anymore and finally tied Hilda down to the makeup chair for a lesson. If Sidney considered her pretty before, now he's really got something to drool over.

Michael and Melody closed up shop for a month and took a dream cruise vacation. Miss Fizzi told them where they should go. Now she's planning Margaret's honeymoon, and I fear she's had a hand in mine as well.

Marlene still pals around with C.C., who threatens to open a ladies-only exercise studio in the empty space above Marlene's Gift and Flower Shoppe. Loud and nonstop at the Bistro, she sets herself up as quite the yoga expert and talks about yoga this and yoga that so much, Leonard has to leave the table. He usually ends up at the bar arguing beer brands with the Eggheads. Shave his head and burn the silk ties, he could be a triplet.

Screamin' Larry heard C.C. bragging about her yoga one day, and thought she said Yoda. So now he screams out, "Yoda! May the Force be with you!" whenever she struts by, and bows down on his knees, the most exercise he ever gets. She doesn't like the song dedications to "my red-lipped Yoda Babe," either. Give Larry credit, though, he did tip his hat to Ivory after the big gunfight at my old corral. On at least two occasions he dedicated a song to her, "Ebony and Ivory," but complained he had to have a barf bag on hand to get through it.

Sam and Lee are still trying to start a family, but lo and behold, they got more than they bargained for with Katie. She beat Lee to the finish line and threw off a litter of eight little redheads in September. Pal claims his Puli's responsible and he should get half the litter for free. He's already promised two to the Eggheads and one to Suggs.

Charlie scooted off to Borneo, as promised, but relented to my begging and returned home to stand up as Tom's best man. Lee served as my matron of honor, of course, but refused to let anybody call her a matron. "Sounds like I run a prison," she grumbled, and Sam reported that she did, slamming his fishing pole into a locked closet until the leaves get raked up every Saturday.

The leaves were spectacular this year, the red and gold colors blowing through the air like Valentine messages from heaven. They greeted Tom and me as we left the church, and swirled around our shoulders and feet in place of rice. I got tons of compliments on my gown of raw silk, and Lindbergh, who'd proudly walked me down the aisle, said he'd never seen a prettier bride. Abner said the same and, as a wedding gift, presented us with a fine toolbox to keep Tom out of the office and at home.

Home. Our new home, surrounded by trees that will flower, grow green, turn color, and endure winter, is everything I ever dreamed. The interior holds things collected and treasured over the years, a perfect mesh of both our lives. Tom's books of law and poetry, my histories and romances. Tom's English mahogany, my collection of old American quilts. Two roots, intertwined, now planted in the same ground, ready to break through this earth and grow tall. Ready to face the rain, the wind, and the cold. Ready to take possession of all poems, the good of the earth and sun.

There are millions of suns left. . . .

Don't miss the first book in this series

THE BELLES OF
SOLACE GLEN

"A moving, charm-filled novel of lost loves, mysterious old letters and small-town friendships."

—EARLENE FOWLER

by
SUSAN S. JAMES

Flip Paxton is forty-two, single and the town maid in quaint Solace Glen. With no husband, children or relatives of her own, she's always taking care of everyone around her. But now she's involved in a mess that's going to be hard to clean up—a murder.

0-425-19713-1

Available wherever books are sold or at
www.penguin.com

*Librarian Megan Clark
and her reading group
solve mysteries by the book.*

This series by
D.R. Meredith
"is a mystery lover's delight."
—Carolyn Hart

Don't miss a single volume!

Murder in Volume
0-425-17309-7

By Hook or by Book
0-425-17465-4

Murder Past Due
0-425-17800-5

Available wherever books are sold or at
www.penguin.com